A LIFE OF SHAKESPEARE

'You are a genuine soaker in Shakespeare, and have not read him as a task. You have him by heart.' Bernard Shaw wrote in a letter to Hesketh Pearson.

Before he became a well-known biographer, Hesketh Pearson was an actor and this is reflected in this reissued Life. Few facts are known about Shakespeare, but with an actor's eye and a supreme self-confidence Pearson has drawn a recognisable portrait of Shakespeare the man – even telling us the colour of his hair and of his predilection for black-haired women. The plays and poems are assessed in the search to discover and build up a picture of Shakespeare's character. Pearson has included an anthology of his favourite lines and passages.

This edition includes a new introduction by Anthony Burgess.

A
LIFE OF SHAKESPEARE

by
HESKETH PEARSON

With
An Anthology of Shakespeare's Poetry

Introduction by Anthony Burgess

A HAMISH HAMILTON PAPERBACK
London

First published in Great Britain in 1942
by Penguin Books Ltd
Revised edition published 1949
by Carroll and Nicholson
First published in this edition 1987
by Hamish Hamilton Ltd
27 Wrights Lane London W8 5TZ

ISBN 0241 12006 3

Printed and bound in Finland
by Werner Söderström Oy

To
HUGH KINGSMILL

'The stream of time, which is continually washing the dissoluble fabricks of other poets, passes without injury by the adamant of Shakespeare.'

Samuel Johnson.

'The striking peculiarity of Shakespeare's mind was its generic quality, its power of communication with all other minds . . . He was just like any other man, but that he was like all other men. . . . He not only had in himself the germs of every faculty and feeling, but he could follow them by anticipation, intuitively, into all their conceivable ramifications, through every change of fortune or conflict of passion or turn of thought. He had "a mind reflecting ages past," and present:—all the people that ever lived are there.'

William Hazlitt.

'At every new accession of information, after every successful exercise of meditation, and every fresh presentation of experience, I have unfailingly discovered a proportionate increase of wisdom and intuition in Shakespeare.'

S. T. Coleridge.

'With the single exception of Homer, there is no eminent writer, not even Sir Walter Scott, whom I can despise so entirely as I despise Shakespeare when I measure my mind against his. The intensity of my impatience with him occasionally reaches such a pitch, that it would positively be a relief to me to dig him up and throw stones at him, knowing as I do how incapable he and his worshippers are of understanding any less obvious form of indignity.'

Bernard Shaw.

'What did Shakespeare do? What did he add to the world's totality? . . . If he had never lived, things would be very much as they are. . . . He added no idea, he altered no idea, in the growing understanding of mankind.'

H. G. Wells.

CONTENTS

INTRODUCTION

BY

ANTHONY BURGESS

Hesketh Pearson died in April 1964, when the world was celebrating the quatercentenary of Shakespeare's birth. My contribution to the occasion was a novel on Shakespeare called *Nothing Like the Sun*. Pearson had been given the work to read in proof, and he seemed to like it. Almost his last public act was to write a few words of praise, and these duly appeared on the dust-jacket. I was, of course, well aware of his own biography of Shakespeare, written during the first years of the Second World War, but it was one of the books I did not consult while I was doing research for my novel. This was not because I disapproved of it but rather because I admired it so much. It was a book I even feared to re-read in my long period of research, since it had, despite the immense scholarship behind it, so many of the qualities of a novel – readability, a narrative drive, humour, daring, fancy, the idiosyncratic flavour of a highly creative mind. Pearson had presented Shakespeare so well that to re-read him would have been to be discouraged. I had discouragement enough without having to seek it in Hesketh Pearson.

I have read all his biographies and love them all, though I recognise their limitations. The term 'biography' connotes for many of us a kind of life-story that Pearson would not have much relished having to write: I mean the huge professorial job, crammed with footnotes, many-paged and very expensive. We need such biographies, and I have many, which are often too heavy to lift, on my shelves. They are necessary works in that they represent final factual authority, but they do not have to be readable. You consult them, but you do not take them to bed. What Hesketh Pearson wished to do, and succeeded in doing, was to produce racy lives of the length of a novel, unencumbered by a professorial apparatus and yet evidently accurate, their scholarship a property that the reader could be seduced into taking on trust. Pearson's biographies are charming and, indeed, heavily seductive. There is a smile in them, but it is not a meretricious smile.

One of the virtues of the charming biography you hold in your hands, and over whose reissue I am delighted to preside, is its boldness, a quality which professorial biographers are not encouraged to profess. Pearson has decided that Shakespeare did not like Queen Elizabeth I very much, and he adduces textual evidence to the effect that when Shakespeare was stabbing at the cruelty and insolence of power he had in mind the most immediate embodiment of tyranny, namely Gloriana. This insistence on Shakespeare's loathing of autocracy was highly relevant to the national atmosphere in which the book was written. Britain was at war against cruelty and insolence, and Shakespeare was, as he still is, the voice of the British people. Pearson's analysis of *Julius Caesar* demonstrates that its author was prophetically aware of the lengths to which tyranny could go and knew, moreover, with a twentieth-century intimacy, the loathsome categories into which political power-seekers can be divided.

Pearson is also bold in maintaining convictions which, at best, can be based only on guesswork. Possessing so little firm knowledge of Shakespeare's life and character, the academic biographer has to be tentative, approximate and apologetic for suggesting that this or the other thing might conceivably have been so but also conceivably not so. Pearson's affirmations about the colour of Shakespeare's hair, the roles he played in the theatre, and his attitude towards Jews may, if we wish, be taken as a kind of shorthand for the possible or the hypothetical, in which case none may reprove him for lack of a scholarly attitude. But his main and surely justifiable aim is to give us a recognisable portrait. This Shakespeare lives. He plays Richard II as well as the Ghost in *Hamlet* (we cannot prove that he took either role, but we cannot disprove it either). He has a nose for money. He has a phase of extreme misanthropy and also a period of illness (in my novel I suggested syphilis). He has a taste for black-haired women which is sustained from *Love's Labour's Lost* up to *Antony and Cleopatra*. He is too open, too ready to pour out his heart. He is a born sufferer, but a winner too. The portrait is convincing, it chimes with the plays and the poems. If this was not Shakespeare it was some other playwright with the same name.

Pearson is witty and a good epigrammist. 'To leave the theatre of Shakespeare for, say, the world of Charles Dickens, is sometimes like leaving the real world for the theatre.' He has a fine cadenza about James I's delight in sycophancy:

'Undoubtedly your Majesty speaks by the special assistance of God's Spirit', said Archbishop Whitgift. 'I protest my heart melteth for joy that Almighty God, of His singular mercy, hath given us such a King as since Christ's time hath not been', said Bishop Bancroft, who naturally succeeded Whitgift as Archbishop of Canterbury. 'There hath not been since Christ's time any king or temporal monarch which hath been so learned in all literature and erudition, divine and human', said Francis Bacon, who naturally became Lord Chancellor.

As for Shakespeare, 'he did not record his judgment of James, which was sensible of him, because the King promptly became the patron of his company'. If we can guess Shakespeare's response to any new contingency, clearly we know Shakespeare. Or rather, through the Pearson magic, we are seduced into believing that we know him.

I think that the plays are soundly judged (the poems less so), and that there are some neat and original assessments which make sense in the context of Pearson's main aim, which is the building of a character. Thus, the old bitch Elizabeth commands the reluctant poet to make Falstaff caper in a farce about lechery, but the Elizabethaphobe Elizabethan refuses to prostitute his greatest creation to the unclean pleasure of a tittering court. He confects a buffoon to whom he attaches the arbitrary label Falstaff. If we attempt to analyse this wretched pantaloon in terms of the real Falstaff, we shall come to grief, which was Shakespeare's intention. That old harridan up there is not going to get away with the debasement of high art. Pearson is perhaps as unkind to *Love's Labour's Lost* as he is to the sonnets, but his enlargement on the onomastic background of the comedy is masterly. He tells us where in England Shakespeare found Sicilian Dogberry. He is full of information. Where there are surprising lacunae, these are probably volitional. There is not much Marlowe and there is practically no Philip Henslowe. Any contemporary of Shakespeare's who bids to upstage the Bard is ruthlessly sent off. There is only one hero. As for comic relief, Pearson can supply most of that himself.

It is important to remember that Pearson was an actor, and that he took up the trade out of a love for Shakespeare learned in extreme adversity and danger, when *Henry IV* was therapy more efficacious than any doctor's drug. He first met Shakespeare in the classroom and promptly rejected him. He met him again in the hard business of war and saw what he was really about. He became a member of Beerbohm Tree's company but never had the chance to grow into a modern Burbage (whom, with total justice, he acclaims as the greatest actor who ever lived: *it must have been so*). He ended up in horrors like *The Blue Lagoon*, but Shakespeare must have supped full, as a professional player, of comparable horrors. The point is that Pearson is able to bring an actor's eye to the texts, and the eye of a man who played in *The Blue Lagoon* is of more value than the aesthetic yardsticks of professors when it comes to asking questions like 'Why did Shakespeare commit this ghastly error of taste, why this total irrelevance, why this speech at this point and not that?' An actor has to go off, snatch a quick beer backstage, then mount the tarras for his next scene. He needs a brief flourish of lines from someone to cover the transition. That scene is there because this quarrelsome *jeune premier* threatened to walk out without it. Will the obliging, the accommodating, a man who followed Hesketh Pearson's trade.

Hesketh Pearson gave up that trade to practise one which, though we call it the writing of biography, requires a more exact denomination. His books form a pattern which, if we examine it closely (and it seems as though the reissue of his oeuvre may enable a whole new generation to do so), resolves into a kind of lateral history of Great Britain. We do not confront British history head on, encountering a foreground of dynasties or armies; we enter from the side, seeing Britain through its rebels or eccentrics or merely men of talent. The conspectus provides a totally original series of insights into the makeup of British society, or the British temperament, if such a thing exists. With this portrait of the greatest British writer the conspectus is complete. A television series based on it and entitled something eye-catching like *Hesketh's Pearsonalities* would add up to a British epic stirring, amusing, deeply informative. But it is better to have the books, and it is very good to have this particular book in one's hands again.

CHAPTER I

LIKE so many youths of my time I made the acquaintance of William Shakespeare in a most disagreeable manner. At the age of fourteen or thereabouts I was told to stand up in class and recite the speech in *Macbeth* which begins:

> 'If it were done when 'tis done, then 'twere well
> It were done quickly.'

Having learnt it by heart I gabbled it off as fast as I could, safely reached the line 'And falls on the other,' and fell back on my seat with a sigh of satisfaction and relief. But the master was neither satisfied nor relieved.

'Stand up, Pearson.'

I stood up.

'I should be interested to know whether you understood a line of what you have just uttered?'

'Not a word, sir.'

'I thought so. Then your understanding is about to be quickened. You will write out that speech fifty times, and at the conclusion of the exercise you may have a dim idea of what it is about.'

Schoolmasters are lucky people. Their feeblest jokes arouse hearty laughter. This one went with a bang. I did not mind that, but I strongly objected to being kept away from cricket for two or three afternoons, and I registered a large black mark against Shakespeare for turning out such incomprehensible stuff. Why couldn't the fellow write as clearly as Stanley Weyman or Conan Doyle? I silently vowed never to read his wretched plays unless forced to do so.

It was my first conscious vow, and it was broken. Another master made me laugh when he read the part of Fluellen in *Henry V* ('God pless you, Aunchient Pistol! you scurvy, lousy knave, God pless you!'); and when Frank Benson brought his company to Bedford I actually enjoyed *The Merchant of Venice*

9

and two or three other plays. But I still refused to read Shakespeare for profit and pleasure, and it was not until I was nineteen that accident undid what magisterial folly had done. I was staying in a country-house where every day was spent in hunting or shooting and every evening in discussing the day's sport. It was not a promising atmosphere for the discovery of a literary genius; yet in such circumstances was Shakespeare revealed to me. One day it rained so hard that sport had to be abandoned. I searched the downstairs rooms for reading matter. The illustrated weeklies were all I could find. They depressed me as usual and in despair I roamed the house, at length finding a Bible and a one-volume Shakespeare in the attic. Having had far too much of the Bible as a child, it was Shakespeare or nothing. I went to my bedroom and began *Hamlet*, which thrilled me so much that I read it again that afternoon. Although in the ensuing days I continued to 'chase little beasts and shoot little birds,' I found myself returning to the house a good deal earlier than the rest of the party in order to put in an hour or two with Shakespeare before the tedium of dinner and sport-talk set in. Once I tried to switch the conversation over from the day's run to something more interesting. I chose the moment with care, breaking into a discussion of ''the pack'' with 'I should like to know Shakespeare's opinion on the breeding of these hounds.'

'Shakespeare's?'

'Yes. This is what Theseus says in *A Midsummer Night's Dream*:

'My hounds are bred out of the Spartan kind,
So flew'd, so sanded; and their heads are hung
With ears that sweep away the morning dew;
Crook-kneed, and dew-lapp'd like Thessalian bulls;
Slow in pursuit, but match'd in mouth like bells,
Each under each.'

Following a short silence, embarrassing for me, a complete blank for the rest of the company, someone said, 'Rum way to write about doggies,' someone else explained, 'Poet, y' know,' and the conversation resumed its course. I did not try again.

From that time Shakespeare became my constant companion. I read all his plays and went to see most of them acted as often as I could raise the necessary money, many times going without my midday meals when working in the City, starving my body in order to feed my soul, and standing for hours in pit and gallery queues. My business career was wholly uncongenial both to myself and to my employers. Shakespeare filled my world, and several fellow-clerks caught my enthusiasm. We saw almost every production or revival of the plays and talked about them in office hours when our minds should have been otherwise employed. Beerbohm Tree's annual Shakespeare Festivals at His Majesty's Theatre were a terrible strain on my resources: I used to beg, borrow, steal, starve, pawn my clothes, and would quite willingly have sold my soul to the devil for two front-row seats in the centre of the upper circle (my favourite spot when funds permitted) to see *Hamlet* or *Julius Cæsar* or *Twelfth Night* or *The Merry Wives of Windsor* for the tenth or twentieth time. I cannot remember how often I have seen *Hamlet*, nor all the names of the actors who played the part,[1] but I know that I saw Johnston Forbes-Robertson in it at least a dozen times, in the West End, in the suburbs, at Edinburgh and at Birmingham. I can still vividly recall many of his gestures and intonations, and this performance of a great Shakespearean part was the finest within my experience as playgoer and actor. Next to it, and only next because the parts did not give equal scope, I should place Ellen Terry as Mistress Page and Hermione. Add Lewis Waller as Henry V and Hotspur, Godfrey Tearle as Antony and Geneviève Ward as Volumnia and Queen Margaret, and my list of perfect Shakespearean performances is exhausted, although I have seen nearly every London production of the plays in thirty years and a few exquisite bits of acting in secondary parts, such as Lyn Harding's Enobarbus, linger in the memory.

My love of Shakespeare took me on to the stage and I joined Tree's company, having already played Cassius, Master Ford and Duke Frederick in amateur companies. But I only appeared in two or three very minor parts at His Majesty's, and, such is

[1] In order of merit E. H. Sothern, Henry Ainley, John Barrymore, Martin Harvey, F. R Benson, Beerbohm Tree and H. B. Irving were a few of them.

the irony of life, the rest of my theatrical career was spent in modern plays, most of which I heartily despised. I also tried to join Benson's company, and I recall an uncomfortable episode in a small room near the entrance to the Bedford theatre, where I recited Henry V's speech before Harfleur to Benson, who was standing about a yard away from me gazing out of the window to spare my feelings while I shouted the lines in a place where a whisper would have seemed noisy. He offered to take me into his company; but as I would have had to keep myself until he could pay me a salary sufficient to live on, I was forced to decline the offer. In those days Benson had a number of young people with him playing small parts for nothing while they learned their business; in fact it was considered a compliment to be allowed to join his company without the payment of a premium.

Shakespeare made me become not only an actor but an organiser. From 1912 to 1914 I was secretary to The British Empire Shakespeare Society, and in 1916, while I was in the army, I helped George Alexander to arrange the Shakespeare Tercentenary Performance at Drury Lane Theatre. My secretarial experiences did not make me warm towards my fellow-Shakespeareans: but I doubt whether Shakespeare himself would have liked Shakespeareans any more than Christ would have liked Christians.

By 1912 I had read a large number of books on my favourite subject, but none of them had given me much pleasure, and I cannot now remember anything about them. It seemed to me that they had all been written by men whose experience of life had been confined to the class-room or the quadrangle. Shakespeare was to them a subject for criticism, not one who had experienced and expressed every sensation of which mortal man is capable: they had written books for students of literature, not for such as might find in Shakespeare the joys, sorrows, and perhaps the final consolation of their pilgrimage. After ploughing through these wearisome productions I came across Frank Harris's *The Man: Shakespeare*, which at least had the merit of being alive, Harris having put a lot of himself into it. Its defect, I now see, is that Harris had put far too much of himself into it, and there can seldom have been two such dissimilar creatures as Shakespeare and Harris. But it effectually blew away the cobwebs of scholarship and substituted a human being for a waxwork. Unfortunately the human being, compelled to look at the world through the eyes of Harris, had no sense of humour, and because Harris fancied himself in the part of a great lover Shakespeare also had to be the victim of a grand passion which turned him into a tragedian and wrecked his life.

Bernard Shaw, while over-praising Harris's work, was too much of a humourist to accept such a tragic figure as authentic, and claimed Shakespeare as a fellow-comedian. It is natural for a writer to identify himself with the Grand Master of his art, and the dons have never failed to make Shakespeare dull, but I cannot accept either Harris's tragedian or Shaw's comedian as anything more than aspects of Shakespeare, whose nature comprehended a great deal more than they could apprehend. Shaw also accused Shakespeare of being a pessimist, of discouraging people. I should like to meet someone who has been discouraged or depressed by Shakespeare, except of course at school. Speaking for myself, I can say that he has been the most stimulating and exalting influence in my life. However ill or unhappy I have been, the mere memory of Falstaff and company has been sufficient to heal me and cheer me up. Such a statement must be supported by examples.

My early lunchless days in the City, due as I have said to my greater· need of stage Shakespeare, brought on tuberculosis, and when I went to Mesopotamia during the 1914-18 war I was given less than a year to live by the doctors. Mesopotamia, where I served for three years, cured me; but it balanced matters by prostrating me with several other diseases, each of which nearly proved fatal. First I was afflicted with septic sores. For a month I lay in a tent where the temperature during the day varied from 120 to 130 degrees, my legs swathed in poultices, the renewal of which every night and morning was torture. At last the medical officer told me that the sores were getting worse and that I might have to lose one or both of my legs to prevent gangrene. Major operations in Mesopotamia during the summer of 1917 nearly always resulted in death, and I would certainly have died if something comic about the doctor had not reminded me of Falstaff's description of Shallow: 'A man made after supper of a cheese-paring; when a' was naked he was for all the world like a forked radish, with a head fantastically carved upon it with a knife.' That started it. As I lay there helpless I exercised my mind by remembering as much as I could of *Henry IV*. In those days I could have reeled off the whole of *Hamlet*, *Macbeth*, *Julius Cæsar* and *Henry V* from memory; but I had only recently, under pressure of the war, fully appreciated the glories of Falstaff and his crew, and I had not yet got them by heart. Temporarily separated from my volume of Shakespeare, I reconstructed as many as possible of the Falstaff scenes, and in doing so felt renewed and inspirited to such an extraordinary degree that I disobeyed the doctor's instruction to remain on my back and hobbled to and from the entrance of the tent every morning after his visit, clutching whatever could support me on the way and almost fainting with the pain. This exercise, I am convinced, saved my life, because the sores began to dry up almost at once and a fortnight after the Falstaff treatment I was convalescent.

Four months later I was down with a combined attack of dysentery and malaria. The first transformed me into a skeleton, the second induced moods of such black depression that no one who has been lucky enough to escape it can have the least conception of the mental abyss into which the sufferer is plunged. The first ray of light to penetrate my darkness came with an Everyman volume which the nurse had managed to pick up somewhere, I having asked her for anything by Shakespeare that she could lay her hands on. The volume contained the historical plays, and I feebly opened it at the first of the great Shallow scenes in *Henry IV*, Part 2. I began reading it but could not take it in; the words conveyed nothing to my mind. I got as far as 'old Double' before consciousness returned, when I must have emitted a ghastly sort of gurgle, perhaps in recognition of the fact that the Double passage had once amused me, because a fellow in the next bed asked me what was wrong. Double was the first ray of light. Next day I tackled the whole scene. The effort exhausted me but the ray was wider and brighter. On the third day I read all the Shallow scenes. And then a very curious thing happened. My depression completely lifted; and though still so weak that I could scarcely lift an arm without the exertion of will-power, I felt as if I had been released from some dreadful load. I wanted to express my sense of freedom with a shout. I wanted to dance round the ward. I wanted to dive into the Tigris, which I could see through the window, and revel in the water. In some inexplicable way Shakespeare had cleared my mind by clarifying the universe. I seemed to be standing on a mountain, surveying the world with wonder and delight, understanding it, and affectionately sympathising with its struggling inhabitants. For some days I must have been very trying to the other occupants of that hospital, because of my light-heartedness under affliction, my meddlesome solicitude and obtrusive toleration. Anyhow my health began to mend, and though I remained subject to both disorders for several years I attribute my recovery from their first virulence to Justice Shallow and his companions.

More remarkable still was the application of the Falstaff cure to my head-wound. This too was not quite finished with for some years, but the cause of my immediate restoration to health was surprising. Again I was in hospital, dangerously ill. After two days of intermittent delirium I returned to consciousness, feeling so weak that when I tried to ask a question of the nurse at my bedside I could not force a whisper. My head throbbing painfully I closed my eyes, and it may have been some minutes or some hours later that I heard the nurse say to the doctor, 'He's got honour on the brain.' That did not sound a bit like me and I mentally echoed the doctor's surprise. 'Something about honour setting legs and arms,' she went on. 'Hm! That's strange,' mused the doctor. 'And he talked about surgical skill too,' added the nurse. The words were wholly out of character, yet they were vaguely familiar. Suddenly it all became clear. In my delirium I had been quoting Falstaff's speech on Honour. The humour of the situation seized me, and in spite of the pain in my head, the top of which seemed to be opening and shutting, I was convulsed with silent, helpless laughter, in which condition I again passed out. The doctor told me later that my recovery had begun when for no apparent reason my body had been shaken by successive spasms, which were followed by several hours of peaceful sleep.

Again and again, in sickness or despair, Shakespeare has

come to my rescue; and as, with the years, my understanding of life has been deepened by the sorrow and heightened by the joy I have known, he has taken an ever-increasing share in my spiritual development. Other writers are for certain moods; he is for all moods. Other writers appeal to particular phases in one's growth; he is for all phases. Other writers rise or fall in one's estimation at different periods; he continually rises. Other writers are exhaustible; he is inexhaustible.

I can remember as if it happened yesterday the first time he was of practical help to me. At the age of twenty-one I was living at Brighton and passing through a restless phase of questioning the faith in which I had been brought up and wanting but failing to find something to take its place. I used to spend occasional evenings with the Rev. Felix Asher, a master at Lancing and vicar of Holy Trinity, Brighton, discussing my problems, and though he did his best to help me I became more and more uneasy. I now know of course that belief and scepticism are merely questions of individual temperament; that, for example, one believes in a future life because such a belief satisfies a personal need; but in those days I was searching for final truth, little realising that there are as many truths as there are believers. One fine afternoon I was wandering along the top of the Downs, and attracted by the appearance of the little village of Poynings at the foot of the Devil's Dyke, I descended to explore it. After visiting the church I spent some minutes strolling about the graveyard. Reading the inscriptions on the tombstones I was more than ever downcast by such lapidary sentiments as THY WILL BE DONE. The most doleful tune in the church hymnal, 'On the Resurrection morning,' haunted me, and I was filled with a sense of mortality and of the fear of the soul's futurity. To be at the mercy of Fate in this world was bad enough, I thought, but to be forever condemned to an inescapable subjection in the next was too horrible to contemplate. Full of foreboding and uncertainty, fearing yet doubtful, I turned a corner of the church and saw a tombstone with a poem on it. It marked the grave of a man who (I heard on inquiry) had been struck by lightning on the Downs, and the poem, the unquoted parts of which I could easily supply, was from Shakespeare's *Cymbeline*:

'Fear no more the heat o' the sun,
    Nor the furious winter's rages;
Thou thy worldly task hast done,
    Home art gone, and ta'en thy wages;
Golden lads and girls all must
As chimney-sweepers, come to dust.

Fear no more the frown o' the great,
    Thou art past the tyrant's stroke;
Care no more to clothe and eat,
    To thee the reed is as the oak:
The sceptre, learning, physic, must
All follow this, and come to dust.

Fear no more the lightning-flash,
    Nor the all-dreaded thunder-stone;
Fear not slander, censure rash,
    Thou hast finished joy and moan:
All lovers young, all lovers must
Consign to thee, and come to dust.'

Immediately, so it seemed, my anxieties and apprehensions vanished. The poem, which I had previously valued simply as the most perfect lyric in the language, came to me for the first time as a revelation. I instantly perceived that one's life could be a blessing or a curse without the least reference to what might or might not happen beyond the grave; that it was all-sufficient, an end in itself; that it would close either in the peace of cessation or in the peace beyond human understanding; and that it did not matter which, since both meant the annihilation of the human mind with its cares, the human body with its tribulations. A mood of extraordinary serenity followed my phase of difficulty and doubt, and I have never since worried about the mystery of the universe, the ultimate truth, the nature of God, or any other insoluble problem.

So much for what has been called the discouragement and pessimism of Shakespeare. For me his works alone would have made life worth living; so I am writing about something I love as much as life.

The biography that follows is as simple and straightforward

as I can make it. I have long been of opinion that the man in the street would like to know all the undoubted facts about Shakespeare, and all the reasonable inferences, without having to wade through the works of scholars who have nothing in common with the poet or the conjectural subtleties of critics who wish to prove that they have everything in common with him. Pedagogues and pederasts have been the curse of Shakespearean biography and criticism. Shakespeare himself was 'the man in the street,' gifted with such an uncanny knowledge of human beings, such a miraculous power of expressing their moods, that he might be called the superman in the street. This first chapter will explain why I have tried to supply the kind of book that may be required. Shakespeare helped me to survive one war; he is now helping me to endure another.

For the biographical part of my work I am chiefly indebted to *Shakespeare, Man and Artist*, by Edgar I. Fripp, two volumes, 1938. I have also drawn upon *William Shakespeare: A Study of Facts and Problems*, by E. K. Chambers, two volumes, 1930, which reprints all the contemporary documents. Two other books have been helpful: Leslie Hotson's *Shakespeare versus Shallow*, 1931, and *I, William Shakespeare, do appoint Thomas Russell Esquire*, 1937.

The best Shakespearean criticism within my knowledge may be found in Dr. Johnson's Preface and Notes, and in *The Return of William Shakespeare*, by Hugh Kingsmill.

(1940-1)

CHAPTER II

THE most notable event in the history of literature occurred at Stratford-on-Avon, in Warwickshire, on the 22nd or 23rd of April, 1564, when Mary Arden, wife of John Shakespeare, gave birth to a son who was christened William.

John Shakespeare was a glover by profession: he cured and dressed the skins of horses, deer, sheep, goats and dogs. William's knowledge of his father's business is sometimes displayed in his writings. John Shakespeare also dealt in barley and timber as a sideline. The early part of his life was successful; his wife inherited property at Wilmcote; and he was able to buy the premises adjoining his house in Henley Street. By 1576, when he applied for and was granted the coat-armour of gentlehood, he had become prominent in public office. Beginning as juror, constable and assessor of fines, he was next appointed chamberlain, then rose to the position of alderman, and finally in 1568 reached the summit of civic ambition as bailiff. Though proceeded against for debt in '73, a warrant for his arrest being issued when he failed to appear, his position as a magistrate was nevertheless sufficiently secure in '76 for him to apply for the coat-of-arms. But from that year, when his son William was aged twelve, he began to suffer in purse and prestige; for not only did he decline the grant of gentlehood at the last moment, but in January, '77, he withdrew from the magistrate's bench and took no further interest in municipal affairs.

The rest of his life was passed in financial or social embarrassment: his wife's inheritance and his own property were sold or mortgaged; he failed to pay levies; in 1580 he was marked down as 'malecontent,' bound over to keep the peace, and fined forty pounds for non-appearance at the Queen's Bench; in '86 a new alderman was appointed in his place 'for that Mr. Shaxspere dothe not come to the halles when they be warned nor hathe not done of longe tyme'; and in '92 his name appeared in a list of people who refused to attend service at the church.

Apart from these facts we learn from someone who met him towards the end of his life that John Shakespeare was a merry-cheeked old man who cracked jests with son William. We also know that he was a puritan and became a recusant, which partly explains his sudden decision to abandon civic duties and his social declension. On the whole he seems to have been a forceful character, humorous, obstinate, outspoken, respected by his townsfolk, good-natured but dogmatic.

Of Mary, his wife, who bore him a number of children, we know nothing except that she raised no objection to the disposal of her property and was therefore helpful and docile. Exceptional men never use their mothers as material for their art unless, like Dickens, they dislike them; so we may infer from the fact that William left no recognisable portrait of his that he was fond of her.

The rise and fall of John Shakespeare must have made a deep impression on William. An ambitious youth who has seen his father parading the streets in state and bowed to by leading citizens, and has then seen him peering furtively through windows and only venturing out of doors after sundown for fear of arrest, will quickly make up his mind to follow in the footsteps of the bailiff, not the debtor; and one of the things William determined to do was to get that coat-of-arms which his father had asked for in prosperity and refused in adversity. 'Let fame, that all hunt after in their lives,' is the opening line of one of his earliest plays, and we shall see that he sacrificed some self-respect in order to rise in the world.

He was educated at the King's Free School of Stratford, where he attacked the Bible (the Geneva version) and received a thorough grounding in Latin. Ben Jonson declared that he had 'small Latin and less Greek'; but Ben was an exceptional scholar, and neither of his statements is quite accurate. Shakespeare learnt a good deal more Latin than the average boy who attends a Public School to-day; whereas he knew no Greek at all, his knowledge of Homer's characters having been obtained from Ovid, and Chapman's translation of the *Iliad*. In later years he was to write 'No profit grows where is no pleasure ta'en,' and like all intelligent youths he must have disliked the usual method of teaching in school. In time he became fully conscious of the fact that, compared with the university men whose plays he eclipsed, he had no learning, and in one of his sonnets he referred to his 'rude ignorance.' But with the actor's aptitude for assimilation with which he was pre-eminently endowed, he could portray the scholarly type as well as any other, for which purpose he had absorbed as much of the classics as he required. Caesar, Livy, Horace, Virgil, Seneca and Plautus may be traced in his plays; but the only classical author he knew well in the original text was Ovid, parts of whose *Metamorphoses* he studied closely.[1]

Here, however, we must note a curious fact, highly characteristic of Shakespeare. Apart from Holinshed's *Chronicles*, North's translation of Plutarch's *Lives* and Florio's translation of Montaigne's *Essays*, each of which fascinated him at different periods of his life, the two works that chiefly influenced him were the Bible and Ovid's *Metamorphoses*. Had he been a real student of literature, a born scholar, we should have expected to find not only that he had read these volumes through from cover to cover with diligence but that their influence would have appeared as clearly in his late as in his early work. Instead, we notice that his knowledge of the Bible was mostly confined to the first book of the Old Testament and to the first book of the New Testament, and even to the first four chapters of Genesis and the first seven of St. Matthew. Further, that his familiarity with the fifteen books of Ovid's *Metamorphoses* did not extend beyond the first and second, and that he knew the first better than the second. When it is added that the Biblical and Ovidian references in his work appear far more frequently in the early plays than in the late ones, we recognise at once that Shakespeare's book-learning was the reverse of what we should expect from a scholar and exactly what we should expect from an artist: he took what came first to his hand, absorbed it thoroughly, used it up, and passed on to fresh forms of study.

Owing to his father's straitening circumstances, he was removed from school at about the age of twelve, and thereafter for some years, except for the circumstance of his marriage, he is lost to history but not to legend. The biographer can only express his own conviction of what happened to the lad, built

[1] His own copy is in the Bodleian.

up on whatever legend is supported by evidence from the plays. One legend is contradicted by everything we know of his character: namely, that he was 'bound apprentice to a butcher,' according to one account his father, and that 'when he killed a calf he would do it in a high style and make a speech.' Passing over the curious assumption that when a poet slays a calf he does it to the accompaniment of blank verse, we remark, firstly, that John Shakespeare was not a butcher, and secondly that no one in history would have been less likely to make a song or a speech over killing a calf than William, whose tenderness towards helpless animals appears throughout his work, from his first poem to one of his last plays.

In *Venus and Adonis* we are given a moving picture of the hunted hare:

> 'By this, poor Wat, far off upon a hill,
> Stands on his hinder legs with listening ear
> To hearken if his foes pursue him still:
> Anon their loud alarums he doth hear:
>   And now his grief may be compared well
>   To one sore sick that hears the passing bell.

> Then shalt thou see the dew-bedabbled wretch
> Turn, and return, indenting with the way;
> Each envious briar his weary legs doth scratch,
> Each shadow makes him stop, each murmur stay:
>   For misery is trodden on by many,
>   And being low never reliev'd by any.'

And when the Queen in *Cymbeline* tells the doctor that she will experiment with his drugs on animals:

> 'I will try the forces
> Of these thy compounds on such creatures as
> We count not worth the hanging, but none human,'

he replies:

> 'Your highness
> Shall from this practice but make hard your heart.'

One wonders what Shakespeare would have said about vivisectionists. Dr. Johnson wondered, too, for here is his comment on the above passage: 'The thought would probably

have been more amplified, had our author lived to be shocked
with such experiments as have been published in later times, by
a race of men that have practised tortures without pity, and
related them without shame, and are yet suffered to erect their
heads among human beings.'

Shakespeare, then, would have made the world's worst
butcher. Listen to him on the subject:

> 'And as the butcher takes away the calf,
> And binds the wretch, and beats it when it strays,
> Bearing it to the bloody slaughter-house . . .
> And as the dam runs lowing up and down,
> Looking the way her harmless young one went,
> And can do naught but wail her darling's loss . . .'

He probably helped his father for a time, learnt the craft of
dressing skins, did odd jobs, ran errands, sometimes worked
indoors when business was brisk, sometimes out of doors when
business was slack and his father found it inconvenient to stir
abroad before dark. In his spare time he must have explored the
countryside, his observant eye and sensitive mind noting and
memorising those intimate small things in nature which are
visible to the poet's perception, and those large effects of
nature which in the poet's imagination are related to the
human emotions.

At the age of eighteen he married Anne Hathaway. Few
actions in history have been the subject of so much or such wild
conjecture. Because she was eight years older than himself, and
because they co-habited before marriage, passages in the plays
illustrating the drawbacks of a senior wife and pre-nuptial
intercourse have been quoted to support the theory that their
marriage was a failure, regardless of the fact that the value of
each passage is purely dramatic and should be considered in
relation to the character of the speaker. Just as many sentiments
could be culled from the plays to prove that Shakespeare's
marriage was entirely successful. A man's nature is revealed in
his writings, and his personal opinions may be gathered from
the repetition of similar sentiments in the mouths of dissimilar
characters. Also, by the constant recurrence of a description or
an episode or a peculiar emotion, we may feel pretty certain

that the personal experiences of the writer are appearing in his work. But it is quite impossible to define the circumstances of his private life from the scattered dicta of his dramatic characters. All we know for certain is that on November 27th, 1582, Shakespeare went to Worcester, where he obtained from the episcopal registry a licence to marry 'with once asking of the bannes.' It is more than likely, no other locality having been traced, that the marriage took place at St. Martin's Church in the Corn Market, Worcester, because two leaves of the register there, covering the date of the ceremony, have been removed by some pious or impious collector.

Anne Shakespeare had a daughter, Susanna, the following May. In those days (and even, it is said, in more modern times) young couples in every class of society frequently co-habited between betrothal, which then legitimised the offspring, and marriage, which made good their claim to dowry; so there was nothing in the behaviour of the Shakespeares to excite indignant comment, though a few winks may have been exchanged between William's friends and a few whispers between Anne's. These would scarcely have disturbed Anne, who was of a religious and charitable disposition. She imparted a thorough knowledge of the Scriptures to her eldest child, and her father's old shepherd left her forty shillings in his Will to be distributed to the poor of Stratford. She had two more children by William, twins, a son Hamnet and a daughter Judith, born in January, 1585.

Shakespeare cannot have shared the religious convictions of his wife and father. Warwickshire in his time was full of sectarian factions. His mother had Roman Catholic connections, and one of her kinsmen, Edward Arden, was executed in 1583 for complicity in a Catholic plot to murder the Queen, his head being displayed on London Bridge. Shakespeare would have wished neither to murder the Queen nor to execute the man who wished to murder her. Indeed the silly and barbarous actions of plotters and counter-plotters, of Catholics and Protestants, of ritualists and recusants, must have jarred on his nerves. If this were Christianity, he was no Christian. As an artist, the pageantry and historical significance of the Roman Church would have appealed to him. As a man, he was an individualist, with an intensely personal view of the universe and its mystery, and in that sense a Protestant. The little bands of enthusiasts who hid their hatred and lust for power under the cloak of religion, whether of Rome or Reformation, can only have excited in him pity and contempt, not unmixed with fear. 'A plague o' both your houses!'

After his marriage Shakespeare had to adopt a profession and earn a living. The evidence to be found in his early plays, his father's career, an inclination common to many writers of genius: all these point to the fact that he took to law. The legal terms which occur again and again in his work, very often to the detriment of the poetry and to the impairment of character, suggest that the court phraseology and procedure he picked up from his father were reinforced by experience in an attorney's office. Again, however, we note the revealing fact that these terms are more frequent in his first plays than in his last, which shows that his interest in law, like his interest in Latin, diminished as his horizon widened.

There is a strong probability that he learnt whatever legal terminology his father had not taught him partly at Stratford and partly at Dursley in the western Cotswolds. During those years the threat of Spain, which culminated in the Armada of 1588, caused much ferment throughout the country, and at moments of panic the towns and hamlets had to furnish fighters. In *Henry IV*, Part 2, Shakespeare brings Falstaff into the Cotswold country, though it is a long distance out of his way to Yorkshire. Falstaff calls on Master Shallow, a Justice of the Peace, and we are treated to the eternal comedy of recruiting. Shakespeare liked using the names of Warwickshire people and places in his plays, and it is not surprising to find local colour in his most perfect picture of contemporary life, set in the neighbouring county of Gloucester. Shallow tells his servant Davy that the headland must be sown with red wheat, a peculiarity of the district; and when Davy says 'I beseech you, sir, to countenance William Visor of Woncot against Clement Perkes o' the hill,' we are definitely at Dursley, for "Woncot" is the local pronunciation of Woodmancote, the wolds thereabouts are known as "the hill," while in the poet's time a family named Vizard lived at Woodmancote and another named

Perkes lived at Stinchcombe Hill. In a previous play, *Richard II*, Bolingbroke and Northumberland find themselves on the Cotswolds. Bolingbroke asks 'How far is it, my lord, to Berkeley now?' Northumberland replies:

> 'I am a stranger here in Gloucestershire:
> These high wild hills and rough uneven ways
> Draw out our miles, and make them wearisome.'

Henry Percy enters and Northumberland asks him the same question. 'There stands the Castle, by yon tuft of trees,' Percy replies. Shakespeare knew that aspect of it well. Hidden by the trees of its park, Berkeley Castle is only visible to-day, looking eastwards, from the projection of the Cotswolds between Dursley and Wotton. Incidentally a family of Shakespeares lived in those parts while he was staying there, possibly relations, and the tradition of his residence is perpetuated by a 'Shakespeare's Walk' in the woods above Dursley.

But something that appealed to him far more intimately than law was engaging his attention and arousing his emotion all through these years of adolescence. Troupes of players, each under the patronage of some noble or the Queen, toured the provinces regularly. From 1573 to 1587 Shakespeare had the chance of seeing twenty-three visiting companies at Stratford. Their arrival was a public event in the place. They made a sort of triumphal procession through the streets. Their horses richly caparisoned, themselves decked out in silks, they paraded the town to the sound of trumpets, advertising by their appearance the performances they were about to give in the Bridge Street inn yards, following an official welcome and a preparatory exhibition at the Gild Hall. In 1587, five companies, an unprecedented number, played at Stratford, including the Queen's, the Earl of Essex's and the Earl of Leicester's, these containing all the best actors of the day.

Whether Shakespeare joined one of them locally in an inferior position, or left Stratford to try his luck with one of them in London, is not known; but that their performances excited him to emulation and suggested the medium for his dormant poetical genius, and that he was tired of uncongenial drudgery and longed to see the great world of men and affairs, there can be no doubt. In his youth the outward shows of life made a great impression on him: one can sense it in the splendour of his early rhetoric, where grandiloquence too often takes the place of poetry and feeling. And those early contacts with the cardboard and tinsel substitutes for royalty and nobility, a stage on which a man might feel and express power so much less harmfully and more satisfactorily than in the real world of warring creeds and legalised murders, thrilled him as nothing else could have done.

The legend that he left Stratford as a result of poaching Sir Thomas Lucy's park at Charlecote or Fulbrook, and of being prosecuted by that knight and punished for his ribald verses, must be dismissed as apocryphal, the variations of the legend making it appear too much like a tale by someone who had heard it from someone else who had sworn that it was true because the person he had heard it from knew the man to whom it had happened. There was no deer-park at Charlecote in Shakespeare's time, and Fulbrook, which had been disparked in 1557, was not then in Lucy's hands. That Shakespeare misbehaved himself in some way or other is very probable, because even the slenderest tradition usually has a grounding of fact to grow upon, and because passionate and ambitious youths, especially when fretted by unexpressed or unconscious genius, invariably do misbehave themselves. But though we shall never know the form his restlessness took, it is improbable that the man who was shortly to create Richard III would have released his checked energies into so commonplace a business as deer-stealing. It is to be hoped that he did something far more nefarious and reprehensible than that.

Whatever he did, he left Stratford; but the memory of the Warwickshire folk and the countryside he had known in his youth remained vividly with him while he was yet happy, until the shadows crept up and he beheld a world darkened by evil and suffering. There were Stephen Sly of Burton Heath, and Marian Hacket, 'the fat ale-wife of Wincot,' and George Curtis of Clifford Chambers, all of whom once lived and continue to live for us in *The Taming of the Shrew*. A Stratford puritan named William Fluellen made an appearance in *Henry V* that would have surprised him; and another, George

Bardolfe, would scarcely have relished his red-nosed namesake in four of the plays. The hamlets of Greete and Barcheston (locally pronounced Barson) held memories for Shakespeare, for they crop up in connection with men whose arrival at the local inn would have been hailed with delight by their fellow-yokels but who exist for us solely as names on the page of a comedy. The ancient family of Jaques was introduced by the poet to a world beyond Warwickshire; and he instinctively laid the scene of almost his last light-hearted romance in the Forest of Arden, where he had run wild as a boy, discovered beauty as a lover, and felt the first stirrings of poetry in early manhood.

CHAPTER III

FROM being a jack-of-all-trades in the theatre, Shakespeare quickly became a master of one. Sir William Davenant, whose parents were Shakespeare's intimate friends, said that his first job at the theatre was to hold the horses of the fashionable patrons and to look after them while the play was being performed. Something about him, a combination of deference and smartness, soon gained him the attention of the wealthy visitors, who called out for him on alighting and at first would not be fobbed off with a less efficient or less pleasing substitute. But business became so brisk that he could no longer attend to everyone; so he hired boys, and the moment a new arrival shouted for 'Will Shakespeare' one of them dashed forward and announced 'I am Shakespeare's boy, sir.' His popularity came to the notice of the leading actors, and in view of later events we can easily guess the name of the nobleman who spoke so highly of him to the management: Henry Wriothesley, third Earl of Southampton, who had left Cambridge and was studying law in 1589 at the age of sixteen. Shakespeare was taken into the theatre and rose rapidly from call-boy to actor, no doubt maintaining his business connection with the 'boys' he had left outside.

The drama was just emerging from its first groping attempts to fuse instruction with entertainment. It was already so popular that in 1576 two theatres had been built in Shoreditch known as the Theatre and the Curtain, where plays were performed during the summer months. The actors were now well provided: they had a theatre in the City for the winter, and the companies that were not so fortunate appeared, as of old, in the inn yards. Shakespare arrived in London a year or two after the resounding success of Marlowe's *Tamburlaine*. The theatres were coining money; the possibilities of coining more were considerable; and the puritans in the City were annoyed, ostensibly because of the non-didactic tendency of the entertainments and the rowdy audiences that enjoyed them, possibly because of the irritation engendered by the deflection of so much money from their own pockets.

The Theatre and the Curtain in Shoreditch were within a stone's throw of one another. Both were managed by James Burbage, who also owned the first. His son, Richard, later became the famous actor who played Shakespeare's great tragic roles. Both of them were sturdy, quick-tempered and independent. In the course of a fracas which terminated in a lawsuit, James spoke disrespectfully of the peerage and Richard beat someone about the legs with a broomstick. Also James did not become the leading theatre-manager of the day without the employment of methods which his opponents would have described as unscrupulous. Richard was nineteen years old in 1590, and a leading actor in Lord Strange's company, which Shakespeare had joined and which then played at the Cross Keys in Gracehurch Street during the winter, at the Curtain in Shoreditch during the summer. Will Kemp was its chief comedian.

At the commencement of his career Shakespeare lived in Shoreditch, then a rural district, much frequented by pleasure-seekers, who went in crowds to witness a public execution and often indulged in free fights before, during or following the presentation of a play. He could not have picked a better spot for the study of humanity in the raw. With the help of con-temporary references we can see him fairly well in those first London years; and it is necessary that we should do so because without some knowledge of his character we shall fail to understand either his personal popularity, which was immediate and lasting and forwarded his financial success, or that temperamental peculiarity which explains the nature but not the measure of his genius.

His physical appearance was in his favour: he was 'a handsome, well-shaped man.' We may give him what height and colouring we please; most of his admirers like to think he was of their own height and colouring. We are on firm ground when we leave his features for his manners, which were an index to his mind. He instantaneously struck people who met him as ingenuous, and this impression never wore off. Everyone remarked on his natural civility, his candour, his openness; the testimony is unanimous: he seemed to give the whole of himself, freely, in conversation. One got to know and like him well at a first meeting, and the liking soon developed into affection. There was nothing particularly striking about him. An acquaintance would not have said after leaving him 'I have just been talking to a most remarkable man'; he would have said 'I have just been talking to an exceptionally nice man.' He was less of an egotist than any famous man in history. He was friendly, gentle, obliging, kindly, unassuming, engaging, sweet-natured and good-mannered: such were the qualities that impressed his contemporaries and gained him their love, while his honesty and uprightness in dealing gained him their esteem. But a quality of a different sort captured their admiration: he was extremely witty. There was not a trace of malice in his wit, which was described as pleasant and smooth. It flowed spontaneously, was ready on all occasions, unstudied, artless, effortless. It made him very good company, and it was not the effect of high spirits artificially raised by liquor. Indeed he seems to have had a poor head for drinking and in his Shoreditch days often excused himself from what threatened to be a drunken debauch on the ground that he did not feel well.

Such was the man as he appeared to those who knew him personally. With his works to help us we know that his social attractiveness was primarily due to a sensitiveness that has no parallel in art. Most people who are personally sensitive are often insensitive to the feelings of others. Shakespeare was hypersensitive and his own feelings gave him the key to the feelings of others. The real poet, said Keats, 'has no identity,' is continually 'filling some other Body.' That is one way of putting it, but in Shakespeare's case it would be truer to say that he was so tremulously aware of his own identity that he endowed others with an equal consciousness and treated their feelings as if they were his own. This explains Timon's terrible bursts of rage, which could only have been written by a man who had bestowed every scrap of sympathy in a phenomenally sympathetic nature, and then, in the bitterness of physical breakdown and mental despair, believed that it had been wasted on beings wholly devoid of generous feeling.

Shakespeare's sensitiveness extended to the verminous world, his nerves responding acutely to the harmful—

> 'like one that spies an adder
> Wreath'd up in fatal folds just in his way,
> The fear whereof doth make him shake and shudder:'

and equally so to the harmless—

> 'Or, as the snail, whose tender horns being hit,
> Shrinks backward in his shelly cave with pain,
> And there all smother'd up in shade doth sit,
> Long after fearing to creep forth again.'

Sensitiveness is usually and quite erroneously considered a feminine attribute. Apart from this, Shakespeare had certain feminine qualities that endeared him to men: he aroused their protective instincts; he charmed them. We are told that he met 'with many great and uncommon marks of favour and friendship from the Earl of Southampton,' and Davenant reported that the Earl gave him £1,000 'to enable him to go through with a purchase which he heard he had a mind to.' The sum has probably had a nought added to it by Davenant's reporter; but when the Lord Chamberlain's company was formed in 1594, Shakespeare bought a share in it, and from a dedicatory epistle to Southampton prefacing his first published work *Venus and Adonis* (1593) we can guess where the purchase-money came from:

'I know not how I shall offend in dedicating my unpolished lines to your Lordship, nor how the world will censure me for choosing so strong a prop to support so weak a burden; only if your Honour seem but pleased, I account myself highly praised, and vow to take advantage of all idle hours, till I have honoured you with some graver labour.'

Our guess becomes a certainty when *The Rape of Lucrece* (1594) appears with another tribute to Southampton:

' The love I dedicate to your Lordship is without end: whereof this pamphlet without beginning is but a superfluous moiety. The warrant I have of your Honourable disposition, not the worth of my untutored lines, makes it assured of acceptance. What I have done is yours, what I have to do is yours, being part in all I have, devoted yours. Were my worth greater, my duty would shew greater, meantime, as it is, it is bound to your Lordship.'

The gratitude expressed in these addresses shows too urgent a desire to please, and Shakespeare cannot wholly be acquitted of sycophancy: it was the vice of his virtue, the effect of his natural agreeability. His self-depreciation contrasts unfavourably with the rightly proud claim of a contemporary, John Webster, who, in dedicating *The Duchess of Malfi* to Baron Berkeley, informed him that his title was worthless and that his one chance of immortality was to have his name attached to a play by Webster:

'I do not altogether look up at your title; the ancientist nobility being but a relic of time past, and the truest honour indeed being for a man to confer honour on himself . . . . I am confident this work is not unworthy your honour's perusal; for by such poems as this poets have kissed the hands of great princes, and drawn their gentle eyes to look down upon their sheets of paper when the poets themselves were bound up in their winding-sheets. The like courtesy from your lordship shall make you live in your grave, and laurel spring out of it . . .'

That is the way a self-respecting poet ought to address his patron; but it is not the way to rise from penury to prosperity.

Shakespeare's tendency to self-abasement when confronted with a member of the peerage, partly explicable by the effect of worldly magnificence on whatever in his nature responded to the picturesque, accounts for an important and much misunderstood element in his *Sonnets*. We need not here deal with the controversy aroused by those sometimes beautiful but mostly tedious poems. Shakespeare was the exact opposite of Wordsworth, the complete poet-egotist. When expressing himself directly and not through the mouth of a character in a play, Shakespeare is often dull and long-winded. His *Venus* and *Lucrece* cannot be read through with patience, lovely as are some of the lines, especially in the former; and for anyone who is not interested in crossword puzzles, the *Sonnets* are extremely irritating: they are full of conceits, affectations, alliterations, puns, antitheses, and the entire artillery of literary artificialities. Out of all this verbal jumble critics have been able to discover the most extraordinary things, always on the assumption that Shakespeare was writing throughout with absolute sincerity, when it is perfectly clear to anyone but a Shakespearean commentator that an artist does not fool about with words when expressing his true emotions. Most of the sonnets are addressed to a young man, beginning with a supplication that he should marry and have children in order to perpetuate his beauty. Shakespeare had already used the same idea in *Venus and Adonis*. Compare the opening of sonnet 1:

'From fairest creatures we desire increase'

and the laboured appeal through the ensuing sonnets, with this from *Venus*:

'Upon the earth's increase why shouldst thou feed,
Unless the earth with thy increase be fed?
By law of nature thou art bound to breed,
That thine may live when thou thyself art dead;
    And so, in spite of death, thou dost survive,
    In that thy likeness still is left alive.'

Or the lines in sonnet 3:

'Or who is he so fond will be the tomb
Of his self-love, to stop posterity?'

with these in *Venus*:

'What is thy body but a swallowing grave,
Seeming to bury that posterity
Which by the rights of time thou needs must have,
If thou destroy them not in dark obscurity?
    If so, the world will hold thee in disdain,
    Sith in thy pride so fair a hope is slain.'

Most of the *Sonnets* may therefore be read as literary exercises, a number of variations on a theme. There was a craze for that sort of thing when Shakespeare wrote them, especially among the students at the Inns of Court, the chief literary centre of London. From the defeat of the Armada in 1588 sonnets were fashionable for about seven years, Sir Philip Sidney's *Astrophel and Stella* (1591) achieving an extraordinary vogue. Fulke Greville and Michael Drayton joined the chorus. Like Shakespeare, most of the authors of these sonnets did not wish them to be published, and they were handed round in manuscript. They were not meant to be taken too seriously; the love-making in them was literary love-making; and the flattery of some young nobleman was part of the game; as in Richard Barnfield's *Certaine Sonnets*, where a youth of 'worship,' who arouses the correct amount of jealousy in the poet, is addressed 'my love,' 'Nature's fairest work,' 'sweet boy,' whose lips drop honey, at whose beauty the world stands amazed, and all the rest of the nonsense. The male aristocrats of those days must have been more fortunate in appearance than their successors. As in Shakespeare's sonnets, the poet ceaselessly pictures the young man, dreams of him, and

> 'when my sun is absent from my sight,
> How can it choose with me but be dark night?'

It was also considered the thing to surrender one's mistress with a good grace to one's rival and dearest friend, and no sonnet-sequence would have been true to form if the writer did not spend most of his time in Hell, gazing longingly at Heaven from that situation.

Shakespeare's patron, the Earl of Southampton, was a member of Gray's Inn, and of course Shakespeare knew many of his fellow sonneteers at the Inns of Court and could talk their jargon. They were enthusiastic theatregoers, rather too enthusiastic, for their hostile reception of a play sometimes resulted in a riot. They were a boisterous, quarrelsome lot, gaming, drinking and harlot-hunting when not in the mood for playgoing; but they knew most of the players, loudly applauded what they liked, loudly hissed what they disliked, and often entertained their favourite actors. They were the highbrows of their day, starting or nursing the literary fads, and Shakespeare was obviously pandering to their fancy when he wrote *Love's Labour's Lost*. The boom in sonnets was over by 1595, and although Shakespeare's were not published till 1609 they were written for the most part while the demand for such productions was brisk. In 1598, Francis Meres, in his *Palladis Tamia*, referred to 'mellifluous and honey-tongued Shakespeare,' whose 'sugared sonnets' were known among his private friends. Eleven years later, when he was at the peak of his fame, they were issued by a piratical publisher named Thomas Thorpe and inscribed 'To the Onlie Begetter . . . Mr. W. H.'

Countless guesses have been made at the identity of 'Mr. W. H.'—the two men who have received the majority of suffrages being William Herbert, third Earl of Pembroke, and Henry Wriothesley, third Earl of Southampton. Although we know from Shakespeare's fellow-actors and editors, Heminge and Condell, that Pembroke 'prosecuted' him and his works with much favour, there is no proof that he knew the Earl when writing his *Sonnets*. All the available evidence goes to show that 'the Onlie Begetter' was Southampton. Firstly, Shakespeare had said in the dedication to *Lucrece* that his love for the Earl was 'without end.' Secondly, Southampton was at that time being urged by his guardian Lord Burghley as well as his mother to marry Elizabeth Vere, Burghley's grand-daughter, and he was resisting the pressure. Thirdly, it is improbable that Shakespeare was flattering a brace of lords simultaneously: one was quite enough to go on with. The poet's servile admiration for his hero can only be understood if we remember that he was liable to pile it on when his imagination was fired by the nobility, especially when the noble was giving him a lift in the world.

> 'That I in thy abundance am suffic'd
> And by a part of all thy glory live,'

he writes of the man who 'honours' him with 'public kindness.' In those days, too, there was an abyss between the aristocracy and the burgess-class which must have made a youthful Earl seem to a struggling actor like a being from another world. Shakespeare's consciousness of his low social state as an actor comes out again and again in the *Sonnets*:

> 'When, in disgrace with fortune and men's eyes,
> I all alone beweep my outcast state,
> And trouble deaf heaven with my bootless cries,
> And look upon myself, and curse my fate,
> Wishing me like to one more rich in hope,
> Featur'd like him, like him with friends possess'd,
> Desiring this man's art, and that man's scope,
> With what I most enjoy contented least . . .

Let those who are in favour with their stars
Of public honour and proud titles boast,
Whilst I, whom fortune of such triumphs bars . . .

Alas, 'tis true I have gone here and there,
And made myself a motley to the view . . .

So I, made lame by fortune's dearest spite . . .

For I am sham'd by that which I bring forth . . .

O, for my sake do you with Fortune chide,
The guilty goddess of my harmful deeds,
That did not better for my life provide
Than public means which public manners breeds.
Thence comes it that my name receives a brand,
And almost thence my nature is subdu'd
To what it works in, like the dyer's hand:
Pity me then and wish I were renew'd . . .'

We recognise the sincerity of such outbursts because they do not consist of word-play and because they tell us what we already know about him; but that we have to be on our guard against what appear to be personal confessions is proved by sonnet 73:

'That time of year thou mayst in me behold
When yellow leaves, or none, or few, do hang
Upon those boughs which shake against the cold,
Bare ruin'd choirs, where late the sweet birds sang.
In me thou see'st the twilight of such day
As after sunset fadeth in the west;
Which by and by black night doth take away,
Death's second self, that seals up all in rest.
In me thou see'st the glowing of such fire,
That on the ashes of his youth doth lie,
As the death-bed whereon it must expire,
Consumed with that which it was nourish'd by.'

This was written by a man of thirty or thereabouts; and the exaggeration of his age in so sincere a poem shows us how carefully we must discriminate between the serious and 'literary' sonnets. Homosexuals have done their utmost to annex Shakespeare and use him as an advertisement for their own peculiarity. They have quoted sonnet 20 to prove that he was one of themselves. But sonnet 20 proves conclusively that he was sexually normal:

> 'And for a woman wert thou first created;
> Till Nature, as she wrought thee, fell a-doting,
> And by addition me of thee defeated,
> By adding one thing to my purpose nothing.
> But since she prick'd thee out for women's pleasure,
> Mine be thy love, and thy love's use their treasure.'

A pederast who can extract comfort from that must feel that his cause is crumbling. But enough has been said to show that, apart from an over-emphasised affection for a lord who had materially helped him, Shakespeare's *Sonnets* were well 'sugared' and suited to their time. And, of course, like everything of his, they contain lines of spine-thrilling charm, as

> 'And stretched metre of an antique song . . .'

and

> 'Our love was new, and then but in the spring . . .'

After the adulatory sequence devoted to the young man, it is a great relief to come upon those dealing with the poet's black-haired, black-eyed mistress. It must have been a great relief to Shakespeare, too, for no man can write over a hundred eulogistic sonnets without feeling the strain. The poet-dramatist required a contrast in his narrative, a she-devil to balance the he-angel; she provided it, and he let himself go. He sees a thousand errors in her and mentions a few: she is covetous, cruel, a liar, a bore; a seducer, a husband-snatcher, an adulteress, a whore. Even her appearance is against her; her eyes are not bright, her breasts not white, her lips not red enough; her hair is wiry, her complexion poor, her face nothing to speak of. In addition, her voice is unmusical, her carriage is commonplace, most men abhor her, she is as black as hell, and her breath smells. She inspires some of his worst sonnets, in two of which he makes atrocious puns on his Christian name, ending with the information which could have been divined from the preceding lines 'my name is "Will." ' In spite of all, he loves her.

It is practically certain that Shakespeare was infatuated with someone not unlike her. Then, as now, actors had many female admirers, and it is clear enough from his works that he was prone to sensual indulgence. A contemporary, John Manningham, committed to his diary in 1601 a story about Shakespeare which must have been well known at the time. A lady saw Burbage play Richard III and liked him so much that she asked him to call at her house that night, giving the name of Richard III. Shakespeare overheard their conversation, 'went before, was entertained and at his game ere Burbage came.' When the message reached them that Richard III was at the door, Shakespeare sent back word that 'William the Conqueror was before Richard III.'

But that the 'black' mistress[1] had a model is placed beyond doubt by the descriptions of her that are repeated, quite unnecessarily, throughout his work, just as his feelings for Southampton reappear in the relationships between older and younger men in several of the plays; and there is further evidence for her existence in a publication entitled *Willobye his avisa* (1594) written by a young poet named Henry Willoughby. This lad had fallen hopelessly in love with the faithful wife of the host of the George Inn at Sherborne, Dorset. She attracted admirers of all sorts: noblemen, gentlemen, soldiers, ruffians. Willoughby nursed his passion in secret for a while, and then, unable to keep it to himself any longer, unbosomed himself to his 'familiar friend, W.S., who not long before had tried the courtesy of the like passion, and was now newly recovered of the like infection.' Shakespeare treated the youngster's desire in a light-hearted fashion and gave vent to 'a willing conceit,' as might have been expected from the author of the *Sonnets*, 'persuading him that he thought it a matter very easy to be compassed and no doubt with pain, diligence and some cost in time to be obtained':

> 'She is no saint, she is no nun,
> I think in time she may be won,'

said the veteran lover. His counsel gave no comfort to

---

[1] 'Dark Lady' was the romantic appellation popularised by certain late-Victorian writers.

Willoughby, who admired his lady's virtue as much as he yearned to overcome it, and who thought that Shakespeare was laughing at him. Therein he may have been right, for Shakespeare's humour was the least predictable thing about him.

CHAPTER IV

THE PRENTICE PLAYWRIGHT

IN *Love's Labour's Lost*, written just before this time, Shakespeare was in fact laughing at his own sonnets. But much had happened to the poet in the three years' interval between his first batch of sonnets and his second: he had been improving the dramas of other men, had written comedies of his own, and had aroused the envy of another playwright. Also, during that period, Marlowe had flashed across the literary sky like a comet, had attracted the admiration of everyone, including Southampton, with 'the proud full sail of his great verse,' and had suddenly vanished from the sight of men in May, 1593, murdered in a Deptford tavern, leaving behind him a reputation that would have shone like a star down the centuries if it had not been eclipsed by the sun of Shakespeare.

The first work Shakespeare did for the stage was hack-work. He reshaped and largely re-wrote three plays by Marlowe on the Wars of the Roses, slicing out passages and scenes, altering characters, putting in chunks of his own here and there, changing the details and transforming the whole; so that the three parts of *Henry VI* (1590-91),[1] especially the second and third, may almost be regarded as an original work, Shakespeare's earliest attempt at drama. What concerns us here is the appearance in so early a play of some of the author's characteristic traits. Holinshed's *Chronicles* had already become one of his favourite books. He had bought the second and augmented edition, issued in 1587, and, as one would expect from a man who scorned scholarship, had closely followed the story, the portraiture, even Holinshed's libel of Joan of Arc, and the misprints. But where Shakespeare unmistakably shows himself is in the Jack Cade scenes. Humour was his natural element; he revelled in it, and allowed it to take charge of him. In Marlowe's plays the comic scenes are short and it is clear that, like the composer who permits the soloist to show off in a cadenza of his own invention, he let the comedians gag to their hearts'

[1] Most of these play-dates are approximate and have been determined in part by style, in part by external circumstances.

content. Shakespeare was the first playwright to use humour creatively: it was his natural medium for revealing character; and he had a long fight with his comic actors before he succeeded in making them stick to the text. Jack Cade is the precursor of a dramatic epoch; all that is native in British drama springs from him. Comedy, not only as the expression of national character but as a criticism of life, originates on our stage with him.

Instigated by the Duke of York, who wants to be king, Cade soon wants to be king himself. At first he says 'Our enemies shall fall before us, inspired with the spirit of putting down kings and princes,' but inspired with the spirit of his own oratory he jumps the idealistic phases of the successful revolutionist: 'Be brave then,' he exhorts his followers, 'for your captain is brave, and vows reformation. There shall be in England seven halfpenny loaves sold for a penny . . . all the realm shall be in common; and in Cheapside shall my palfrey go to grass: and when I am king, as king I will be . . . there shall be no money; all shall eat and drink on my score; and I will apparel them all in one livery, that they may agree like brothers, and worship me their lord.' We have had several Cades in Europe recently. He condemns a clerk to death because the man can write his name and does not have to make a mark 'like an honest plain-dealing man'; and when Sir Humphrey Stafford comes against him with the king's forces he kneels down, knights himself, and rises as good a man as his opponent. Arrived in London, he commands that at the City's cost 'the pissing-conduit run nothing but claret wine this first year of our reign,' and like all dictators he is down on learning: 'Thou hast most traitorously corrupted the youth of the realm in erecting a grammar school,' he charges Lord Say before having him beheaded: 'and whereas, before, our forefathers had no other books but the score and the tally, thou hast caused printing to be used, and, contrary to the king, his crown and dignity, thou hast built a paper-mill.' When Lord Say pleads for his life, Cade says he must die because he pleads so well, adding 'The proudest peer in the realm shall not wear a head on his shoulders unless he pay me tribute; there shall not a maid be married, but she shall pay to me her maidenhead ere they have it.'

Thus, so early in his life, Shakespeare had little to learn about the motives that drive the average revolutionary leader; and already he had a pretty poor opinion of the mob. 'Was ever feather so lightly blown to and fro as this multitude?' Cade wonders, and Henry VI dwells on the same theme:

> 'Look, as I blow this feather from my face,
> And as the air blows it to me again,
> Obeying with my wind when I do blow,
> And yielding to another when it blows,
> Commanded always by the greater gust:
> Such is the lightness of you common men.'

But the mob is not the only uncertain element and Shakespeare gives us a picture of the vacillating statesmen which so exactly prefigures a similar crew early in 1940 that it must be quoted. The Duke of Exeter asks whether treachery was responsible for the loss of the French provinces. The messenger who has reported the loss replies:

> 'No treachery; but want of men and money.
> Amongst the soldiers this is muttered,
> That here you maintain several factions,
> And whilst a field should be dispatched and fought,
> You are disputing of your generals.
> One would have lingering wars with little cost;
> Another would fly swift, but wanteth wings;
> A third thinks, without expense at all,
> By guileful fair words peace may be obtain'd.'

Shakespeare's opinion of the French, which may have had something to do with their opinion of him for over two centuries, seems to have been arrived at in his youth and to have undergone no revision throughout his career. 'Done like a Frenchman: turn and turn again!' says Joan of Arc. Someone else in *Henry VI* describes them as 'a fickle wavering nation,' whilst a third remarks:

> ''Tis better using France than trusting France:
> Let us be backed with God and with the seas,
> Which He hath given for fence impregnable,
> And with their helps only defend ourselves;
> In them and in ourselves our safety lies.'

Upon which another great Englishman, Dr. Johnson, comments: 'This has been the advice of every man who in any age understood and favoured the interest of England.'

Here, as in his later historical plays, Shakespeare realises that personal vanity has more to do with the shaping of policy and the action of human beings than theories of government, creeds, ideals and what-not. The Queen forms a conspiracy to rid the kingdom of its protector, Humphrey Duke of Gloucester, and by doing so plunges the country into civil war, for the following reason:

> 'Not all these lords do vex me half so much
> As that proud dame, the lord protector's wife.
> She sweeps it through the court with troops of ladies,
> More like an empress than Duke Humphrey's wife:
> Strangers in court do take her for the queen . . .
> Shall I not live to be aveng'd on her?
> Contemptuous base-born callet as she is,
> She vaunted 'mongst her minions t'other day,
> The very train of her worst wearing gown
> Was better worth than all my father's lands . . .'

It is personal pique, too, that makes Warwick 'the kingmaker' change sides and support Henry VI against Edward IV:

> 'Not that I pity Henry's misery,
>   But seek revenge on Edward's mockery.'

The faults in the play are as characteristic of the author as the virtues. His life-long love of puns produced one that would have made Thomas Hood blush: 'For Suffolk's duke, may he be suffocate.' And his prudence took the objectionable form of praising Queen Elizabeth's grandfather through the mouth of Henry VI, who spots the winner and says, as he pats the future Henry VII on the head:

> 'Come hither, England's hope. If secret powers
> Suggest but truth to my divining thoughts,
> This pretty lad will prove our country's bliss.
> His looks are full of peaceful majesty,
> His head by nature fram'd to wear a crown,
> His hand to wield a sceptre, and himself
> Likely in time to bless a regal throne.'

'Shakespeare knew his trade,' is Dr. Johnson's comment.

The play also illuminates Shakespeare's youthful view of life. He was passing through a phase common to many young people in all ages, the phase in which villainy in one form or another has an attractively picturesque quality. The Wars of the Roses were for him what the Wars of the Gangsters have been for the youths of a later period, and his audiences enjoyed the exploits of York and Lancaster as modern audiences have enjoyed the exploits of Chicago racketeers. *Henry VI* is a 'thriller,' a series of crime pictures, full of conspiracy, detection, deeds of blood and daring, double-crossing, jealousy, treachery and sob-stuff. It would make a first-rate film. Like their gangster successors, the nobles in *Henry VI* are cruel, superstitious, greedy and sentimental by turns; their emotions, like their fortunes, are in a state of flux. The ones in power depend on the loyalty and honour of their followers:

> 'Thrice is he arm'd that hath his quarrel just,
> And he but naked, though lock'd up in steel,
> Whose conscience with injustice is corrupted,'

says the king in possession. But the king who wants to be in possession has a different view of honour:

> 'for a kingdom any oath may be broken:
> I would break a thousand oaths to reign one year,'

and makes a different sort of appeal:

> 'Come on, brave soldiers: doubt not of the day,
> And, that once gotten, doubt not of large pay.'

The unfortunate monarch who wanders amiably and impotently through these sanguine scenes is a man after Shakespeare's heart, gentle, sympathetic, patient, dreamy, unworldly, noble-minded and long-winded. Shakespeare saw himself in the part, and probably played it, making a lot of such lines as these:

> 'My crown is in my heart, not on my head;
> Not deck'd with diamonds and Indian stones,
> Nor to be seen: my crown is called content:
> A crown it is that seldom kings enjoy.'

His opposite is the man who afterwards becomes Richard III, the protagonist of a play which Shakespeare wrote about three years later but which may be considered here because it is the sequel to *Henry VI*. The vitality, fun, and light-hearted enjoyment of devilry that Shakespeare put into Richard show that he was still in the 'shocker' stage of his development. Richard was the super-gangster, the Al Capone, of his imagination:

> 'Conscience is but a word that cowards use,
> Devis'd at first to keep the strong in awe,'

cries the man who does not reign long enough to foster conscience in his follwers for his own benefit. To the biographer the interesting thing about *Richard III* is that the future author of *Macbeth* could still have entertained such a juvenile conception of the power-maniac as to explain the motive for his actions in these terms:

> 'And therefore, since I cannot prove a lover,
> To entertain these fair well-spoken days,
> I am determined to prove a villain,
> And hate the idle pleasures of these days.'

Actually of course Richard promptly shows himself more than a match for anyone in the lists of love by winning the widow of a man he has just murdered; and in the third part of *Henry VI* he had given a far more convincing reason for his conduct:

> 'Then, since this earth affords no joy to me,
> But to command, to check, to o'erbear such
> As are of better person than myself . . .'

Nevertheless, Richard III is a schoolboy's notion of a villain, cynical, gay and unrelievedly black. His creator would have made a fortune at Hollywood.

Having polished off the flower of English chivalry in *Henry VI*, Shakespeare turned his attention to works of a less ambitious order. Leaving out *Titus Andronicus*, which reads like a bad burlesque of a bad type of tragedy, containing a few lines suggested by passages in his other works and a few more lifted straight from his pages, Shakespeare tinkered with at least one more play before starting on his own: *The Taming of the Shrew*, which derives from an earlier play he may have touched up called *The Taming of a Shrew*, a skit on Marlowe. Shakespeare's final version is a rollicking farce, the subject appealing to him because he must often have pondered on the problem of how to chasten a woman who was making him suffer. Apart from this, the play's only appeal to the biographer is the mention of Stratford people and places in the Induction.

The first two plays from Shakespeare's unaided pen, written in the years 1591-2, tell us little about him, though *The Two Gentlemen of Verona* proves that he was already an exquisite poet and well on the way to being a master of humorous prose. No man has ever written such a delicious first play. The opening lines suggest one of the reasons why Shakespeare left home:

> 'Home-keeping youths have ever homely wits . . .
> I rather would entreat thy company
> To see the wonders of the world abroad,
> Than, living dully sluggardiz'd at home,
> Wear out thy youth with shapeless idleness.'

There are occasional touches more evocative of love's first rapture than anything in *Romeo and Juliet*:

> 'O, how this spring of love resembleth
>   The uncertain glory of an April day,
> Which now shows all the beauty of the sun,
>   And by and by a cloud takes all away.'

> 'Except I be by Silvia in the night,
>   There is no music in the nightingale.'

Perhaps, too, we catch a glimpse of the poet's black-haired mistress, and of the poet's own glibness and self-assurance:

> 'Flatter and praise, commend, extol their graces;
>   Though ne'er so black, say they have angels' faces.
> That man that hath a tongue, I say, is no man,
>   If with his tongue he cannot win a woman.'

The second play, *The Comedy of Errors*, is a farce, founded on two plays by Plautus, and largely dependent for its fun on the extreme improbability of having two lots of twin-brothers in the cast that performs it. A few lines in the first act remind us that Shakespeare spent some months of 1592 touring the provinces:

'Within this hour it will be dinner-time:
Till that, I'll view the manners of the town,
Peruse the traders, gaze upon the buildings,
And then return, and sleep within mine inn;
For with long travel I am stiff and weary.'

At the beginning of 1592, Lord Strange's men performed several times before Queen Elizabeth at Whitehall, and in the spring of that year they were acting at Philip Henslowe's theatre, the Rose, on Bankside. In June a crowd of apprentices went to a play at one of the innyards of Southwark, and during the performance a riot broke out. It spread to the other side of London Bridge, and the Lord Mayor seized the opportunity to complain to the Privy Council. As a result no plays were allowed to be given in or near London till Michaelmas, and Shakespeare went on tour, his 'art made tongue-tied by authority.' Strange's company appealed to the Privy Council to rescind the order, basing their appeal on the cost of touring a large company (the Lord Admiral's men being with them) and on the plight of the Thames watermen, who depended on theatre-traffic for their living. The request was granted on condition that the town was free from infection; but the plague broke out in August and they were forced to continue their tour.

That autumn Shakespeare received a nasty shock. A dramatist named Robert Greene died in September and his *Groats-worth of Wit bought with a Million of Repentance* was promptly published by a friend, Henry Chettle. Addressing his fellow-dramatists, Marlowe, Nashe and Peele, all of whom like himself had been to the university, Greene advised them to drop play-writing if they did not wish to starve, because the actors no longer wanted their work, having got one of their own number to fulfil their requirements: 'For there is an upstart Crow, beautified with our feathers, that with his *Tigers heart wrapt in a Players hide*, supposes he is as well able to bombast out a blank verse as the best of you: and being an absolute Johannes fac totum, is in his own conceit the only Shake-scene in a country.' This envious attack cut Shakespeare to the quick. 'O tiger's heart wrapped in a woman's hide!' is a line from *Henry VI*, taken by Shakespeare from Marlowe, and Greene was charging the new actor-author with stealing the work of his

social and intellectual superiors and passing it off as his own.
Nothing displays the poet's sensitiveness and anxiety to stand
well with the world so clearly as his line of action the moment
he read Greene's outburst. Instead of taking it as a tribute to
his prowess, he called on Chettle, who accepted an invitation
to the theatre to see him act, and even solicited his patron
Southampton to put in a good word for him; all of which can
be divined from Chettle's apology, printed later in the same
year. Before issuing Greene's book, Chettle confessed, he had
not been acquainted with Shakespeare, 'whom I did not so
much spare as since I wish I had, for that I might have used my
own discretion the author being dead—that I did not I am as
sorry as if the original fault had been my fault; because myself
have seen his demeanour no less civil than he excellent in the
quality[1] he professes. Besides, divers of worship have reported
his uprightness of dealing, which argues his honesty, and his
facetious grace in writing, that approves his Art.' That
Southampton expressed himself strongly on the subject and was
among those 'of worship' who testified to the poet's probity, is
placed beyond doubt in one of Shakespeare's sonnets, where
he made a pun and coined a word which he never repeated:

'Your love and pity doth the impression fill
    Which vulgar scandal stamp'd upon my brow;
For what care I who calls me well or ill,
    So you *o'er-greene* my bad, my good allow?'

That he did care very much who called him well or ill is
another indication that the sonnets addressed to young
Southampton must not be taken too seriously. He poked fun
at them himself in his next play, *Love's Labour's Lost*. Certain
events in the outside world make it plain that this comedy was
not written until the latter part of 1593, though some
chronologists have placed it before the two comedies already
mentioned. It deals satirically with the French king's Court,
and not till July, '93, when Henry of Navarre became a
Catholic, could such a play have been acceptable at the English
Court. Henry's wars against the Catholic League had been
supported by Queen Elizabeth in 1589 with an expeditionary

[1] i.e., as an actor.

force, the English people had fully sympathised with him, and the English church had offered up prayers for his success. In 1591, Elizabeth backed him with another army, placed her new favourite the young Earl of Essex in command of four thousand men, and recommended him to her 'dearest brother' Henry as a very competent lieutenant 'if the rashness of his youth does not make him too precipitate.' This force was for use against the Spaniards in Brittany, and when Elizabeth heard that Henry had used them against the French Catholics she was furious, writing to him: 'Can you imagine that the softness of my sex deprives me of the courage to resent a public affront? The royal blood I boast could not brook from the mightiest prince in Christendom such treatment as you have within the last three months offered to me.' The behaviour of Essex, a headstrong, fiery and rather futile youth, did not mend matters. He rushed about the place making the foolish gestures of a brave but brainless man; he offered to fight the Governor of Rouen single-handed; he did everything possible to assert his chivalry and to demonstrate his incompetence; while disease and desertion reduced his army to a fourth of its original strength. Meanwhile those of his officers who came home on leave spread damaging reports of their trifling, indolent, verbose French allies: Henry himself liked giving and receiving compliments, went hunting when he ought to have been fighting, did nothing to any purpose; his marshal, Biron, loved gallantry, dallying with women and unnecessary trumpet-salutes; Biron's boon companion, a general named Longueville, was addicted to similar pleasantries; and their opposing leader, Le Duce de Mayne, was all that might have been expected of a Frenchman. By the spring of 1593 Henry had become thoroughly unpopular in England, whence no more help could be expected. In July he turned Catholic, Elizabeth exploded 'I cannot now regard myself as your sister,' and Shakespeare wrote *Love's Labour's Lost*.

Though the French leaders in the play are thinly disguised under the names Berowne, Longaville, Dumain, and Henry of Navarre appears as Ferdinand, Shakespeare is naturally far more concerned with the English Court than with the French, but the Gallic names purged the satire of offence at home. If anyone had grounds for being annoyed, it was Elizabeth, who in 1591 had slaughtered some tame deer in Cowdray Park, where Southampton's grandfather lived. Seated comfortably in a pleasant arbour, her musicians playing softly, she received a crossbow from a nymph, accompanied by a song. About thirty deer were then driven into an enclosure; the royal arrows sped; and three or four deer lay gasping out their lives on the ground, pierced by the royal hand. Through the mouth of the Princess of France, Shakespeare told his sovereign what he thought of this kind of 'sport,' even going so far as to play with the name 'Glory' by which she was commonly known at court:

'But come, the bow: now mercy goes to kill,
And shooting well is then accounted ill.
Thus will I save my credit in the shoot:
Not wounding, pity would not let me do't;
If wounding, then it was to show my skill,
That more for praise than purpose meant to kill.
And, out of question, so it is sometimes,
Glory grows guilty of detested crimes,
When, for fame's sake, for praise, an outward part,
We bend to that the working of the heart.'

Love's Labour's Lost is tedious to read. It is Shakespeare's only attempt to write a purely 'literary' comedy, to play up to his witty and poetic friends at the Inns of Court. It is, like the *Sonnets*, full of conceits, quips, quibbles, and intellectual word-play, much of which is now quite meaningless. It might have been written by an Elizabethan George Meredith or an Elizabethan Henry James; indeed the language of Holofernes continually reminds one of the conversational gropings of Henry James. 'He draweth out the thread of his verbosity finer than the staple of his argument,' describes both James and Holofernes, though the latter says it of someone else; and the talk of nearly all the characters is neatly summed up by Moth —'They have been at a great feast of languages, and stolen the scraps'—and by Costard—'O, they have lived long on the alms-basket of words.' Whether Shakespeare would have agreed with Moth and Costard may be doubted, for he makes another character praise these literary somersaults: 'Snip, snap, quick and home! it rejoiceth my intellect: true wit!' He obviously threw himself into the business and enjoyed it, but it was a trying phase in his development, to be partly repeated in *Much Ado About Nothing*, and it is not without significance that we derive the word 'nit-wit' from Costard's remark:

> 'And his page o' t'other side, that handful of wit!
> Ah, heavens, it is a most pathetical nit!'

None the less the play contains valuable material for the biographer. Berowne is very nearly a self-portrait of the dramatist before he began to take a less light-hearted view of the universe:

> 'a merrier man,
> 'Within the limit of becoming mirth,
> I never spent an hour's talk withal:
> His eye begets occasion for his wit;
> For every object that the one doth catch,
> The other turns to a mirth-moving jest,
> Which his fair tongue, conceit's expositor,
> Delivers in such apt and gracious words,
> That aged ears play truant at his tales,
> And younger hearings are quite ravished;
> So sweet and voluble is his discourse.'

We already know that Shakespeare had little use for scholarship. Berowne emphasises his creator's attitude at the beginning of the play:

> 'Small have continual plodders ever won,
> Save base authority from others' books . . .'

and again towards the end:

> 'Why, universal plodding prisons up
> The nimble spirits in the arteries . . .'

But for our present purpose the most important points in the play are the appearance of Shakespeare's black-eyed mistress, and the ridicule he pours on sonnet-making, implying that he has finished with such exercises, which were only to be taken as

> 'courtship, pleasant jest and courtesy,
> As bombast and as lining to the time.'

His mistress appears unmistakably in Berowne's description of Rosaline:

> 'A whitely wanton with a velvet brow,
> With two pitch-balls stuck in her face for eyes;
> Ay, and, by heaven, one that will do the deed,
> Though Argus were her eunuch and her guard.'

The pitch-eyes haunt him: 'I am toiling in a pitch—pitch that defiles: defile! a foul word . . . O, but her eye—by this light, but for her eye, I would not love her; yes, for her two eyes . . . By heaven, I do love: and it hath taught me to rhyme, and to be melancholy . . . . Well, she hath one of my sonnets already . . . .' The king tells Berowne that his love 'is black as ebony,' to which he retorts 'No face is fair that is not full so black,' and then loses himself in a lyric:

> 'O, if in black my lady's brows be deck'd,
> It mourns that painting and usurping hair
> Should ravish doters with a false aspect;
> And therefore is she born to make black fair.
> Her favour turns the fashion of the days,
> For native blood is counted painting now;
> And therefore red, that would avoid dispraise,
> Paints itself black, to imitate her brow.'

As Queen Elizabeth was red-haired, the other characters are made to laugh at Berowne's praise of black; but Shakespeare had already said the same thing in sonnet 127:

> 'In the old age black was not counted fair,
> Or if it were, it bore not beauty's name;
> But now is black beauty's successive heir,
> And beauty slander'd with a bastard shame.
> For since each hand hath put on nature's power,
> Fairing the foul with art's false borrow'd face,
> Sweet beauty hath no name, no holy bower,
> But is profan'd, if not lives in disgrace.
> Therefore my mistress' brows are raven black,
> Her eyes so suited, and they mourners seem
> At such who, not born fair, no beauty lack,
> Slandering creation with a false esteem:
> Yet so they mourn, becoming of their woe,
> That every tongue says beauty should look so.'

All the chief characters in *Love's Labour's Lost* write sonnets to their loves, and even Armado, the absurd Spaniard, is afflicted: 'Assist me some extemporal god of rhyme, for I am sure I shall turn sonnet. Devise, wit; write, pen; for I am for whole volumes in folio.' Their sonnets are as good as the majority of those published under Shakespeare's name, and quite as serious; but by the tongue of Berowne the author condemns them:

> 'This is the liver-vein, which makes flesh a deity,
> A green goose a goddess: pure, pure idolatry.
> God aménd us, God amend! we are much out o' the way.'

And at the end Berowne, alias Shakespeare, bids farewell to sonnetising:

> 'O, never will I trust to speeches penn'd,
>   Nor to the motion of a schoolboys tongue;
> Nor never come in vizard to my friend;
>   Nor woo in rhyme, like a blind harper's song!
> Taffeta phrases, silken terms precise,
>   Three-pil'd hyperboles, spruce affectation,
> Figures pedantical; these summer flies
>   Have blown me full of maggot ostentation:
> I do forswear them . . .'

As if to clarify his design to break with literary affectation, Shakespeare closes the play with two songs of simple, homely beauty, which carry us straight into another world—the wonderful new world he was about to create:

> 'When icicles hang by the wall,
>   And Dick the shepherd blows his nail,
> And Tom bears logs into the hall,
> And milk comes frozen home in pail,
> When blood is nipp'd and ways be foul,
>   Then nightly sings the staring owl,
>   Tu-whit;
> To—who, a merry note,
> While greasy Joan doth keel the pot.

When all aloud the wind doth blow,
 And coughing drowns the parson's saw,
And birds sit brooding in the snow,
 And Marian's nose looks red and raw,
When roasted crabs hiss in the bowl,
Then nightly sings the staring owl,
   Tu-whit;
To—who, a merry note,
While greasy Joan doth keel the pot.'

CHAPTER V

THE POET PLAYWRIGHT

THE summer of 1594 was cold and wet, and Shakespeare reported its inclemency in *A Midsummer Night's Dream*, where for the first time he 'warbled his native wood-notes wild.' A return to Stratford may have inspired the play, which is redolent of the countryside wherein he had learnt to love nature and observe mankind, and which contains a reference to Queen Elizabeth, whose visit to Kenilworth Castle when Shakespeare was eleven years old had been celebrated by an aquatic display. 'The reading of this play,' says Hazlitt, 'is like wandering in a grove by moonlight: the descriptions breathe a sweetness like odours thrown from beds of flowers.' To say that there is no fairy-tale in literature to compare with it is merely to say that it is by Shakespeare. Its simple charm eludes criticism. How can one analyse or explain the sensation communicated by this?

> 'You spotted snakes with double tongue,
>   Thorny hedgehogs, be not seen;
> Newts and blind-worms, do no wrong,
>   Come not near our fairy queen.'

In the bare act of writing it down one's body seems to melt. There is a dissolvent tenderness in Shakespeare absent from the works of other men:

> 'So doth the woodbine the sweet honeysuckle
>   Gently entwist; the female ivy so
>   Enrings the barky fingers of the elm.'

The poet himself, we may be sure, played the part of Theseus, who discusses the imaginative faculty in a manner quite out of keeping with a duke devoted to hunting:

> 'The poet's eye in a fine frenzy rolling,
>   Doth glance from heaven to earth, from earth to
>   heaven;
>   And as imagination bodies forth
>   The forms of things unknown, the poet's pen
>   Turns them to shapes, and gives to airy nothing
>   A local habitation and a name.'

He also speaks of actors in the language of one who has suffered from them: 'The best in this kind are but shadows; and the worst are no worse, if imagination amend them . . . . If we imagine no worse of them than they of themselves, they may pass for excellent men.' Already Shakespeare knew his actors inside out. Bottom is the conceited mummer personified: he wants to play all the leading parts; he does his best to take charge of the production; he dilates on the effect he will produce on the audience; he longs to act a tyrant, 'or a part to tear a cat in, to make all split'; he would like a prologue to be written dealing exclusively with his own performance; he is not concerned with anyone else in the cast; his versatility is such that he will roar as loudly as any lion, or to calm the ladies 'as gently as any sucking-dove'; he wonders whether he ought to wear a straw-coloured, orange-tawny, purple or yellow beard, obviously wanting to try the lot; and he only becomes reconciled to the part he is cast for when the stage-manager describes Pyramus as 'a sweet-faced man; a proper man, as one shall see in a summer's day; a most lovely, gentleman-like man.' Shakespeare was on safe ground. No actor has ever seen himself in the part of Bottom.

Incidentally the actors were having rather a thin time round about the period when Shakespeare was amusing himself at their expense. In 1594 Strange's men became the Lord Chamberlain's men, and Shakespeare bought a share in the company, payment being made to 'William Kemp, William Shakespeare and Richard Burbage' when they performed before the Queen at Greenwich during the Christmas festivities that year. From this we see that the playwright was already as important as the leading comedian and the leading tragedian. On December 28th, '94, they played *The Comedy of Errors* at Gray's Inn; but owing to the crowded state of the hall the Templars walked out, displeased and discontented; the evening developed into a rag; and in a mock trial held a day or two later the 'base and common fellows' from Shoreditch were made responsible for what had happened. The following September the Lord Mayor and Aldermen of the City of London tried to get theatres suppressed on the ground that they were the chief cause of many 'disorders and lewd demeanours

which appear of late in young people of all degrees.'
According to these civic dignitaries the theatres were the sinks
of sin: 'The refuse sort of evil-disposed and ungodly people
about this City have opportunity hereby to assemble together,
and to make their matches for all their lewd and ungodly
practices; being also the ordinary places for all masterless men,
and vagabond persons that haunt the high ways, to meet
together and to recreate themselves.' It was not merely chance
that the flowering of Shakespeare's genius was accompanied
by the stiffening of puritan opposition to the drama: great art
has always been obnoxious to authority. If the actors of those
days had not been under the protection of patrons, they would
have been hounded out of the City; and even the Chamberlain,
Lord Hunsdon, had to beg the Mayor to allow his men to
perform at the Cross Keys in Gracechurch Street a year before
the Aldermen lodged their complaint, just quoted, with the
Privy Council. Thus Shakespeare and his companions were
constantly on the move apart from their summer tours, which
took them to Marlborough in '94, to Cambridge and Ipswich
in '95.

A feeling of uncertainty about the future seems to have crept
into Shakespeare's next play, *The Merchant of Venice* (1595).
As long as he remained an actor Shakespeare wrote parts for
himself, and it is easy enough to detect them because we know
the kind of part he enjoyed playing and recognise some of his
recurring moods and certain personal characteristics in them.
The merchant, Antonio, has the same sort of dog-like devotion
to Bassanio as the author of the *Sonnets* has for his friend.
Antonio is sad and ill-at-ease; and though he says that he is
not worrying over his business ventures (as no doubt
Shakespeare tried to persuade himself that he was not) he is
considerably relieved when he hears that his ships have come
home, saying to Portia 'Sweet lady, you have given me life
and living,' an odd way of expressing indifference to his returns.
But because Antonio has something of his creator within him,
we cannot assume that Shakespeare was anti-semitic. His
dislike of Shylock was due to the man's nature, not his race.
Whenever Shylock speaks as a persecuted Jew he speaks from
the heart of Shakespeare, but when he speaks as a usurer he

provokes the disgust Shakespeare felt for usury. The modern stage method of building up Shylock as a sympathetic character, initiated by Henry Irving, is wholly out of tune with Shakespeare's conception. Shylock's real objection to Antonio is clearly stated:

> 'He lends out money gratis and brings down
> The rate of usance here with us in Venice.'

'Were he out of Venice, I can make what merchandise I like.'

And Antonio is aware of his objection:

> 'I oft delivered from his forfeitures
> Many that have at times made moan to me:
> Therefore he hates me.'

Shylock is replete with avarice, hatred and self-pity. When his daughter runs away with his jewels the loss of a diamond worth two thousand ducats makes him feel that 'the curse never fell upon our nation till now,' and he wants to see his daughter dead at his foot with the ducats in her coffin. These emotions are not essentially Hebraic; they have been shared by many Christian men of business, who however would not confess them so candidly. Much has been written about the ruthless way in which Shakespeare permits the Christians to taunt and fleece Shylock at the end, especially their insistence on his conversion to Christianity. The explanation is that Shakespeare knew how Christians behave when they get a chance of asserting themselves; he was beginning to suffer personally from the Christian merchants of the City, who taunted him as an actor, fleeced him as a manager, and would have liked to enforce his conversion from play-writing to respectability.

He was in fact beginning to take serious stock of his contemporaries, and Portia's comments on her suitors are the result of Shakespeare's observations when performing at Court: on a Frenchman, 'God made him, and therefore let him pass for a man'; on an Englishman, 'Who can converse with a dumb-show?'; on a German, 'When he is best, he is a little worse than a man; and when he is worst, he is little better than a beast.' But the general effect of the play is that of a poetic fairy-tale, closing in music such as one poet alone could compose with words. And more miraculous even than the famous Lorenzo-Jessica duet is the moment when Bassanio chooses the leaden casket at the end of his long speech, and we are made to feel the exaltation of Portia as if it were our own. Shakespeare has a power unique among men of revealing in a few phrases the summits of human emotion. For an instant life is suspended and the desire of the human soul is fulfilled. In that momentary breathless stillness the trembling heart seems to speak from another world:

> 'How all the other passions fleet to air,
>   As doubtful thoughts, and rash-embrac'd despair,
>   And shuddering fear, and green-eyed jealousy!
> O love, be moderate; allay thy ecstasy;
>   In measure rain thy joy; scant this excess!
> I feel too much thy blessing: make it less,
>   For fear I surfeit!'

Shakespeare could do little with the part of Antonio, but in *Richard II*, which soon followed, he probably played the best part of his career. A contemporary, John Davies, addresses him:

> 'Had'st thou not played some Kingly parts in sport,
>   Thou had'st been a companion for a King,
>   And been a King among the meaner sort.'

The kings into whose creation he put most of himself were Henry VI, Richard II and Henry IV, and we need not doubt that he played all three, Richard II being his favourite. It suited both his nature and his quality as an actor to 'tell sad stories of the death of kings.' Obviously he possessed a musical voice, did full justice to long poetical speeches, and a good deal of the sympathy he arouses for Richard was due to the fact that he was writing up a part for himself. When Richard says to his wife:

> 'In winter's tedious nights sit by the fire
>   With good old folks, and let them tell thee tales
>   Of woeful ages long ago betid,'

we catch the modulations of the actor's sad and tuneful

utterance; and we are very close to the man in Richard's last
soliloquy:

> 'My brain I'll prove the female to my soul,
> My soul the father; and these two beget
> A generation of still-breeding thoughts,
> And these same thoughts people this little world
> In humours like the people of this world,
> For no thought is contented . . .
> Thus play I in one person many people,
> And none contented . . .
>
>   . . . but whate'er I be,
> Nor I nor any man that but man is
> With nothing shall be pleased, till he be eased
> With being nothing . . . '

A few years after it was written *Richard II* got Shakespeare
and his company into serious trouble. We shall learn more
about that later. Here we may note that Queen Elizabeth
associated herself with the character. 'I am Richard the Second,
know ye not that?' she once cried. It has been generally
supposed that she took exception to the deposition scene; and
indeed the conspiracies during her reign, and the fear of civil
war in its last decade, were enough to make her feel
uncomfortable when witnessing the discrowning of a monarch
on the stage. But other aspects of the play must have touched
her more nearly. Richard's picture of a ruler's precarious
state cannot have appealed to a woman who loved life, who
lived on flattery, and whose vanity was notorious:

> 'within the hollow crown
> That rounds the mortal temples of a king
> Keeps Death his court, and there the antic sits,
> Scoffing his state and grinning at his pomp,
> Allowing him a breath, a little scene,
> To monarchize, be fear'd and kill with looks,
> Infusing him with self and vain conceit,
> As if this flesh which walls about our life
> Were brass impregnable, and humour'd thus
> Comes at the last and with a little pin
> Bores through his castle wall, and farewell king!

> Cover your heads and mock not flesh and blood
> With solemn reverence: throw away respect,
> Tradition, form and ceremonious duty,
> For you have but mistook me all this while:
> I live with bread like you, feel want,
> Taste grief, need friends: subjected thus,
> How can you say to me I am a king?'

Above all, John of Gaunt's famous speech on England contains a reference to Elizabeth's ancestors which was not complimentary to one who placed security before chivalry, and an implied criticism of her habit of farming out the customs to her favourites, resulting in the plundering of the poor, which was certainly not lost on her:

> 'This royal throne of kings, this sceptr'd isle,
> This earth of majesty, this seat of Mars,
> This other Eden, demi-paradise;
> This fortress built by nature for herself
> Against infection and the hand of war;
> This happy breed of men, this little world,
> This precious stone set in the silver sea,
> Which serves it in the office of a wall,
> Or as a moat defensive to a house,
> Against the envy of less happier lands;
> This blessed plot, this earth, this realm, this England,
> This nurse, this teeming womb of royal kings,
> Fear'd by their breed and famous by their birth,
> Renowned for their deeds as far from home,
> For Christian service and true chivalry,
> As is the sepulchre in stubborn Jewry
> Of the world's ransom, blessed Mary's Son;
> This land of such dear souls, this dear, dear land,
> Dear for her reputation through the world,
> Is now leas'd out, I die pronouncing it,
> Like to a tenement or pelting farm:
> England, bound in with the triumphant sea,
> Whose rocky shore beats back the envious siege
> Of watery Neptune, is now bound in with shame,
> With inky blots and rotten parchment bonds:

That England, that was wont to conquer others,
Hath made a shameful conquest of itself.
Ah, would the scandal vanish with my life,
How happy then were my ensuing death!'

The poet, pure and simple, is still uppermost in *Richard II*, but in *Romeo and Juliet* (1596) the dramatist shares the honours. Modern productions of Shakespeare's plays make it difficult for us to realise that his stagecraft was superb. The Prologue to *Romeo and Juliet* partly explains why his plays were so popular: they were limited to 'the two hours' traffic of our stage,' being performed without a break on a platform that projected into the auditorium, backed by an inner rostrum to sustain variety and continuity. The division of the plays into acts and scenes in modern editions is quite arbitrary, the various changes being shown in the early productions merely by one lot of characters leaving the stage and another lot coming on to it. Scene followed scene without pause, the dialogue being sufficient to suggest the place of action when necessary, and a real impression of the ebb and flow of life was conveyed by the constant exits and entrances, the alternating gloom and animation of the characters, the successive tragic and comic episodes, the bustle of the street and the calm of the closet. Shakespeare was aided, not impeded, by a stage that permitted him to ignore the unities of place, time and action; and we shall never be able to appreciate his skill as a dramatist, nor enjoy the thrills of realism and poetry he could give his contemporaries, until we see his plays performed without intervals on the sort of stage for which he wrote them, by actors who have been specially trained to speak his language.[1] In the meantime we had better read them, for a present-day production on a framed stage is a travesty of the real thing.

Though helped by the simplicity of his stage and the efficiency of his actors, he was handicapped by the fact that his female

---

[1] A life-long job. The modern actor has no notion of how to speak Shakespeare's verse, and is never encouraged to study the art. What Bernard Shaw wrote about Oxford in 1898 is still true of the whole country: 'It is characteristic of the authorities at Oxford that they should consider a month too little for the preparation of a boat-race, and grudge three weeks to the rehearsals of one of Shakespeare's plays. The performance of *Romeo and Juliet* by the Oxford University Dramatic Society naturally did not, under these circumstances, approach the level of skill attained on the Thames.'

parts were played by boys, which is the reason there are so few women in his plays and why he sometimes chose plots that enabled them to dress-up and play male characters, as in the cases of Julia, Portia, Nerissa, Jessica, Rosalind, Celia, Viola and Imogen. The wonder is that he was able to create such essentially female beings as he did. In writing *Romeo and Juliet*, for instance, he must have been able wholly to obliterate from his consciousness the knowledge that Juliet would be played by a boy of fourteen or less, the Nurse by a man of forty or more.

This play was the first of his pre-eminent masterpieces: with it he outshone all his predecessors and contemporaries, and made the lyrical drama a profitless business for his successors. He experienced the emotions of which he sings many years before he gave them to Romeo, for it is the poetry of first love, not the passion of mature love, that he describes. Its soaring celestial quality is revealed not only in the phrase 'A pair of star-crossed lovers, but in Romeo's

> 'I am too bold, 'tis not to me she speaks:
> Two of the fairest stars in all the heaven,
> Having some business, do intreat her eyes
> To twinkle in their spheres till they return.
> What if her eyes were there, they in her head?
> The brightness of her cheek would shame those stars,
> As daylight doth a lamp; her eyes in heaven
> Would through the airy region stream so bright
> That birds would sing and think it were not night.'

And in Juliet's

> 'Come, gentle night, come, loving black-brow'd night,
> Give me my Romeo; and, when he shall die,
> Take him and cut him out in little stars,
> And he will make the face of heaven so fine,
> That all the world will be in love with night,
> And pay no worship to the garish sun.'

Romeo, far more than Juliet, turns feeling into music, reality into ideality:

> 'but come what sorrow can,
> It cannot countervail the exchange of joy
> That one short minute gives me in her sight . . .'

> 'Night's candles are burnt out, and jocund day
> Stands tiptoe on the misty mountain tops . . .'
>> 'all these woes shall serve
> For sweet discourses in our time to come . . .'
>> 'beauty's ensign yet
> Is crimson in thy lips and in thy cheeks,
> And death's pale flag is not advanced there . . .'
>> 'O, here
> Will I set up my everlasting rest,
> And shake the yoke of inauspicious stars
> From this world-wearied flesh.'

Friar Lawrence catches the lyrical infection, the sight of Juliet wringing from him a phrase of heart-arresting poignancy:

> 'Here comes the lady. O, so light a foot
> Will ne'er wear out the everlasting flint.'

It has been suggested that Shakespeare played the Friar, whose speeches expand in a manner dear to an actor who knows how to deliver them; but although the part contains such characteristic reflections as

> 'Two such opposed kings encamp them still
> In man as well as herbs, grace and rude will,'

it is more than likely that Shakespeare picked Mercutio,[1] a development of Berowne, in order to display his versatility after Richard II. The author practically names his part in Mercutio's admission:

> 'True, I will talk of dreams;
> Which are the children of an idle brain,
> Begot of nothing but vain fantasy,
> Which is as thin of substance as the air,
> And more inconstant than the wind, who woos
> Even now the frozen bosom of the north,
> And, being angered, puffs away from thence,
> Turning his face to the dew-dropping south.'

---

[1] Apparently the parts of Mercutio and the Friar are regarded as of equal playing merit, because one well-known actor who had been offered his choice of the two asked me to advise him which to accept: 'Shall I play Mercutio and get off early, or play the Friar and keep my trousers on?'

Of more concern to us than the part Shakespeare played is the reappearance, in name and description only, of Rosaline, whom we last saw in *Love's Labour's Lost* and recognised as his black-eyed mistress. The repetition of the name is significant; for when an author is recording his personal experiences under the guise of fiction, whether consciously or unconsciously, he frequently uses names which resemble the originals, repeats the names so used whenever the subject is called to mind, and never varies his description of the subject. So here. Rosaline, with whom Romeo is in love when the play opens, is described as 'a pale hard-hearted wench' by Mercutio, who further declares that Romeo has been 'stabbed with a white wench's black eye.' Be it noted that Rosaline is dragged into the play; she is quite unnecessary to the plot; and nothing short of Shakespeare's genius could have made Romeo's sudden conversion to Juliet seem inevitable.

The comic element in the street brawls between Capulets and Montagues may have been suggested to Shakespeare by personal experience, for in the year 1596 he took part in something that looks suspiciously like a free fight. On July 22, 1596, Hunsdon, the Lord Chamberlain, died, and Shakespeare's company lost its patron. The puritan Lord Mayor and Aldermen of London took immediate advantage of this, and on the very day that Hunsdon's protection was removed by death plays were prohibited throughout the City and suburbs by the Privy Council, the old excuse being given that sickness would increase 'by drawing of much people together.' At a stroke the actors lost their means of livelihood; they could play neither in the innyards nor at the theatres; and their outlook was gloomy. It is scarcely surprising that Shakespeare, who had moved from Shoreditch and was now living in the parish of St. Helen's, Bishopsgate, neglected to pay a tax of five shillings on his goods, which were valued at five pounds. He left the parish owing the money and crossed over to the Surrey side of the river that autumn, where for some time he resided near the Bear Garden in Southwark. His professional companions left the Shoreditch theatres, at least for a while, crossed the river too, and despite the prohibition began to play at Francis Langley's new theatre, the Swan, in Paris Garden, Southwark, an imposing structure built of flint, with wooden columns painted to resemble marble and seating accommodation for three thousand people. The local Justice of the Peace, a man called Gardiner, instantly proceeded against them, backed by the Lord Mayor and Aldermen on the opposite side of the water. Gardiner was partly actuated by spite, because Langley had called him 'a false knave, a false forsworn knave, and a perjured knave,' the complete justification for such a description making it no less displeasing to the Justice, who sent his stepson William Wayte to close down the Swan. But the actors were desperate, and protected by the new Lord Hunsdon, who however was not Lord Chamberlain as his father had been, they repelled Wayte, telling him roundly that if he attempted to enter the theatre and stop their performances he would do so at the peril of his life. There were probably several rowdy scenes between Wayte's followers and the Langley-Shakespeare contingent, a good deal of the thumb-biting with which we are familiarised in *Romeo and Juliet*, and Wayte was sufficiently scared to appeal for protection to the law. A Writ of Attachment was duly issued to the Sheriff of Surrey, returnable on November 29th, 1596. From it (the original is in Latin) we learn that 'William Wayte begs securities of the peace against William Shakespeare, Francis Langley, Dorothy Soer, wife of John Soer, and Anne Lee, for fear of death, &c.' We have no further details of the quarrel, but from the fact that the actors played before the Court at Whitehall that Christmas, as they had played before the Court at Richmond the previous Christmas, and that they continued to appear in Southwark or Shoreditch, we may conclude that Shakespeare's patron or his company's patron managed somehow to soothe the City fathers.

> 'I am amazed, methinks, and lose my way
> Among the thorns and dangers of this world,'

wrote Shakespeare in the autumn of '96, and he had cause to say so. Not only was his professional future black, but in August of that year he had lost his son Hamnet, aged eleven. The anguish he felt was expressed in *King John*.

He did not go to Holinshed for this play, but obtained all his facts from an old piece called *The Troublesome Raigne of*

King John, reproducing its historical errors, as we should expect, and multiplying them. The chief change he made is of course in the characterisation, especially that of Prince Arthur, who in the old drama is an ambitious intriguing youth but who in Shakespeare's hands becomes an innocent, helpless and pathetic child, his own little boy. Constance speaks these words about her son Arthur, but he is not dead when she speaks them, and they are clearly the cry of an already-bereaved parent:

> 'Grief fills the room up of my absent child,
> Lies in his bed, walks up and down with me,
> Puts on his pretty looks, repeats his words,
> Remembers me of all his gracious parts,
> Stuffs out his vacant garments with his form;
> Then have I reason to be fond of grief.
> Fare you well: had you such a loss as I,
> I could give better comfort than you do . . .
> O Lord! my boy, my Arthur, my fair son!
> My life, my joy, my food, my all the world!'

Shakespeare also refuses to adopt the violently Protestant tone of the old play, wherein Arthur appeals to Hubert's religious feeling. Shakespeare's Arthur appeals to Hubert's humanity. *The Troublesome Raigne* is bitterly anti-Catholic; Shakespeare's play is simply patriotic:

> 'No Italian priest
> Shall tithe or toll in our dominions,'

says King John to Philip of France, adding the only remarks in the play that show what Shakespeare's attitude might have been towards one aspect of Catholicism:

> 'Though you and all the kings of Christendom
> Are led so grossly by this meddling priest,
> Dreading the curse that money may buy out;
> And by the merit of vile gold, dross, dust,
> Purchase corrupted pardon of a man,
> Who in that sale sells pardon from himself,
> Though you and all the rest so grossly led
> This juggling witchcraft with revenue cherish,
> Yet I alone, alone do me oppose
> Against the pope, and count his friends my foes.'

By this time Shakespeare had sized up the type of butcher-despot we have lately seen in Russia, Italy and Germany:

'A sceptre snatch'd with an unruly hand
Must be as boisterously maintain'd as gain'd.'

'For he that steeps his safety in true blood
Shall find but bloody safety and untrue.'

'There is no sure foundation set on blood,
No certain life achiev'd by others' death.'

He saw too that nothing distresses this type of ruler so much as laughter. 'That idiot, laughter,' King John calls it, 'a passion hateful to my purposes.' We are reminded of Philostrate's remark in *A Midsummer Night's Dream*: 'More merry tears the passion of loud laughter never shed.' With Shakespeare, as with all the great humanists, laughter was a passion, equally resented and dreaded by shallow aristocrats and soulless dictators as a criticism of their pretensions.

Shakespeare had also seen enough of public life to realise that the scum always comes to the top, that rulers, politicians and the like are utterly corrupt, and he condemns them in the words of the Bastard, who is intelligent enough to add that himself has not been corrupted because no one has so far tried to corrupt him:

'And why rail I on this Commodity?
But for because he hath not woo'd me yet:
Not that I have the power to clutch my hand,
When his fair angels would salute my palm;
But for my hand, as unattempted yet,
Like a poor beggar, raileth on the rich.
Well, whiles I am a beggar, I will rail
And say there is no sin but to be rich;
And being rich, my virtue then shall be
To say there is no vice but beggary.'

Queen Elizabeth comes in for another jolt. Her elaborate official journeys through England, undertaken with the object of assuring herself of her subjects' loyalty, and her constant state 'occasions' and dressings-up, are glanced at in Salisbury's rebuke to King John, who has just re-crowned himself in order to feel more secure. Incidentally the speech perfectly illustrates a statement by Shakespeare's fellow-actors, Heminge and Condell, who in the preface to his collected works declared that 'His mind and hand went together; and what he thought he uttered with that easiness that we have scarce received from him a blot in his papers.' One can almost see his pen racing across the page in a frantic endeavour to keep pace with his fancies, and the final line reads as if, pausing for breath, he reined in his imagination with a jerk:

> 'Therefore, to be possessed with double pomp,
> To guard a title that was rich before,
> To gild refined gold, to paint the lily,
> To throw a perfume on the violet,
> To smooth the ice, or add another hue
> Unto the rainbow, or with taper-light
> To seek the beauteous eye of heaven to garnish,
> Is wasteful and ridiculous excess.'

The commotions of 1596 are faithfully reproduced in *King John*. Another Armada was expected from Philip of Spain, who had already sent two, neither of which had reached England:

> 'So, by a roaring tempest on the flood,
> A whole armado of convicted sail
> Is scatter'd and disjoin'd from fellowship,'

complains the French King Philip of the play, while King John is informed that a hostile fleet has just been wrecked on Goodwin Sands. The new threat to England in the autumn of '96 produced a state of alarm in high quarters. It was reported that the Spanish fleet had already put to sea, and instructions were issued by the Privy Council that all the forces of the kingdom were to be in readiness against invasion. Gentlemen were ordered to remain at home ('to stay put,' we should now call it), not to leave their shires, to arm themselves and their servants, to disarm suspected persons, to imprison anyone who spread false rumours. The authorities were in fact as nervous as they usually are on such occasions, and Shakespeare, in the guise of the Bastard, told them how the average Englishman who was not nervous expected them to behave:

> 'Be stirring as the time; be fire with fire;
> Threaten the threatener, and outface the brow
> Of bragging horror:[1] so shall inferior eyes,
> That borrow their behaviours from the great,
> Grow great by your example and put on
> The dauntless spirit of resolution.'

Shakespeare closes the play on a clarion note which still has the power to thrill an Englishman and make him conscious of his heritage, in poetry if not in possessions:

> 'This England never did, nor never shall,
> Lie at the proud foot of a conqueror,
> But when it first did help to wound itself.
> Now these her princes are come home again,
> Come the three corners of the world in arms,
> And we shall shock them. Nought shall make us rue,
> If England to itself do rest but true.'[2]

---

[1] To Shakespeare 'bragging horror' meant Philip of Spain; to us it has meant Hitler & Co.

[2] Even now Shakespeare speaks for the man in the street and the man in the field. At 1 o'clock on June 17th, 1940, I was sitting in the Half Moon Inn at Storrington, Sussex, when the news came over the Wireless that the French army had surrendered to the German. After a moment's silent stupefaction, followed by some whistling and muttering, a countryman drained his tankard, got up, shook himself, said, 'Oh, well! Come the three corners of the world in arms!' and went out.

CHAPTER VI

In the autumn of 1596 Shakespeare became a gentleman; at least his father did. A few months earlier, after an interval of nearly twenty years, John Shakespeare had again applied for his coat-of-arms, and on October 20th the application was granted. Obviously the father had been incited thereto by the son, who paid the necessary expenses. Although it is more than a little painful for us to realise that the world's greatest genius wished to become a gentleman in the technical sense of the term, we must take into consideration his social ups and downs as a youth, the stigma of being an actor (which in those days meant being a rogue and vagabond), and his poetic response to the glamour of worldly distinctions when such trumpery was at any rate ornamental. His desire to be a gentleman is the worst thing we know about him; and, being the genius he was, it is quite bad enough, for it means that his sense of values was warped. Everything that is weak and paltry in his works springs from that defect: his false rhetoric, his pomposity, his affectations, his cheap sallies of wit, some of his later bitterness, his self-humiliating dedications and sonnets. But such was the transcendent power of his genius that, at the very moment when his worldly thoughts were engaged by the prospect of gentility, his imagination was employed in the creation of a character that reduced all social distinctions to absurdity. Falstaff is the comment of the genius on the coat-armour of the gentleman.

The two Parts of *Henry IV* and *Henry V* are grounded on Holinshed and an earlier play entitled *The Famous Victories of Henry the Fifth*, in which one of Prince Hal's tavern companions is called Sir John Oldcastle. That Shakespeare originally used Oldcastle's name for his amazing creation of Falstaff is not open to question, because the Prince refers to him in Part I as 'my old lad of the castle,' the prefix 'Old' is printed at the beginning of a speech by Falstaff in the quarto of Part II, and the mistake is rectified in the Epilogue: 'For Oldcastle died a martyr, and this is not the man.' What happened was that Oldcastle's descendants kicked up a fuss, and as they were people of some social standing Shakespeare did what Falstaff would have done: used his discretion.

Nothing at all comparable with *Henry IV*, Part I (1597) had ever been seen in a theatre. Real life, the life of the road and the tavern, a world that every playgoer could instantly recognise as his own, appeared for the first time on the stage. The effect was shattering; people laughed as they had never laughed before; the sayings of Falstaff and his companions went into the common speech and were quoted in the streets, in private letters, in other people's works; pirated editions of the play sold like hot cakes; the theatre was packed at every performance:

> ' . . . let but Falstaff come,
> Hal, Poins, the rest—you scarce shall have a room,
> All is so pestered,'

wrote a contemporary. No such outburst of unmitigated delight has occurred in the history of the drama. It was as if the true genius of a nation had suddenly been revealed to itself, as if a blessing had been granted to the people which everyone could enjoy. Here was not a barren victory of arms, the spoils of which would be grabbed by profiteers and politicians: it was a fruitful victory of the spirit, the unconquerable spirit of Humour, the essential spirit of England. Falstaff instantly became, and still remains, the symbolic figure of the race. He is not a comic character: he is the spirit of Comedy incarnate. We do not laugh at him: we share his laughter at everything. He 'lards the lean earth as he walks along' and mirth springs from it. The English imagination expresses itself naturally in humour; its native poetry is acclaimed by 'the passion of loud laughter'; and Falstaff is the greatest achievement of the national muse. While creating him Shakespeare was standing 'on the top of happy hours,' a phrase he had coined to describe the condition of his young patron in the *Sonnets*; he was drunk with life, and under the influence he told the truth. Never before had so clear a fountain of irresponsible fun bubbled out of him, and never again would his love of life lift his imagination into so serene an air. Surveying the universe through the eyes of Falstaff, he laughed until his sides ached. He could turn his eyes inward and laugh at himself too, because his spirits were high, his health was good, and creatively he was at the top of his form. Even the serious parts of *Henry IV* have a vigour and a naturalness he had not previously exhibited. Nowhere else in his work does his verse move so easily: it is the perfection of conversational poetry. We note his growing acquaintance with Court circles, where ladies swear 'a good mouth-filling oath' and gentlemen are 'perfumed like a milliner.' More interesting still is the knowledge he had gained of the men of action who crowded round the Queen. Hotspur is an Elizabethan firebrand, his rashness and intemperate wordiness having been taken straight from Essex. People who fondly imagine that born men of action are strong and silent may learn the truth from Shakespeare. Northumberland accuses Hotspur of 'Tying thine ear to no tongue but thine own,' and he is a typical specimen. Most of the famous men of action in history have been incurable windbags, swayed by childish passions, weakly stubborn and vainglorious.

Henry IV, Part I, was such a huge success that in May, 1597, Shakespeare was able to buy the best house in Stratford, New Place, for sixty pounds, whither presumably he removed his parents, wife and children, the old house in Henley Street being thenceforth occupied by sister Joan, who had married a hatter named William Hart. A few weeks prior to this purchase the office of Lord Chamberlain was bestowed on Lord George Hunsdon, the son of their old patron, and Shakespeare's company once more became 'The Chamberlain's men.' In the summer of '97, following another purity drive by the City fathers, they went on tour, visiting Faversham, Rye, Dover, Marlborough, Bath and Bristol, receiving thirty shillings for a performance in the Gild Hall of the latter in September. That winter they played before the Court at Whitehall; but Shakespeare was more interested in his new property than in acting just then. He had bought a fine brick and timber house, consisting of ten rooms, with a frontage of sixty feet, a height of twenty-eight feet, and a breadth in one place of seventy feet. With it went two barns, two gardens and two orchards. The property had been neglected and he was compelled to spend a lot of money on restoration, which meant taking a personal interest in the craft of building. It is rather amusing to see the amateur mason airing his new-bought knowledge in his next play, *Henry IV*, Part II (1598):

> 'When we mean to build,
> We first survey the plot, then draw the model;
> And when we see the figure of the house,
> Then must we rate the cost of the erection;
> Which if we find outweighs ability,
> What do we then but draw anew the model
> In fewer offices, or at least desist
> To build at all?'

This is not the only bit of autobiography discernible in the play. Shakespeare had recently been enjoying the sea at Dover and Rye, and apart from a little topographical slip in the folio edition of *Henry V*, where 'Dover pier' was printed for 'Hampton pier,' we can guess he had been watching the breakers from the shore when reading Henry the Fourth's reproval of the 'dull god,' Sleep:

> 'Wilt thou upon the high and giddy mast
> Seal up the ship-boy's eyes and rock his brains
> In cradle of the rude imperious surge,
> And in the visitation of the winds,
> Who take the ruffian billows by the top,
> Curling their monstrous heads, and hanging them
> With deafening clamour in the slippery clouds,
> That with the hurly death itself awakes?
> Canst thou, O partial sleep! give thy repose
> To the wet sea-boy in an hour so rude,
> And in the calmest and most stillest night,
> With all appliances and means to boot,
> Deny it to a king? Then, happy low, lie down!
> Uneasy lies the head that wears a crown.'

Our certainty that Shakespeare played the King in both Parts of *Henry IV* is established by the emergence of the poet's nature in a character mostly at variance with his own. That

Shakespeare suffered from insomnia is certified by his deeply-felt outbursts on the theme, in the *Sonnets*, in *Henry IV*, and above all in *Macbeth*. That he loved music is written all over his work:

> 'Music do I hear?
> Ha, ha! keep time: how sour sweet music is
> When time is broke and no proportion kept!'

cries Richard II, while Lorenzo in *The Merchant of Venice* feels that the entire universe is set to song, and that only evil people are unmusical:

> 'Look how the floor of heaven
> Is thick inlaid with patines of bright gold:
> There's not the smallest orb which thou beholdst
> But in his motion like an angel sings,
> Still quiring to the young-eyed cherubins;
> Such harmony is in immortal souls;
> But whilst this muddy vesture of decay
> Doth grossly close it in, we cannot hear it.
>
> .   .   .   .   .
>
> The man that hath no music in himself,
> Nor is not mov'd with concord of sweet sounds,
> Is fit for treasons, stratagems, and spoils . . .
> Let no such man be trusted.'

And even that astute politician Henry IV, who on his deathbed is far-sighted enough to tell his son

> 'For all the soil of the achievement goes
> With me into the earth,'

and crafty enough to advise him

> 'Be it thy course to busy giddy minds
> With foreign quarrels,'

is nevertheless given the poet's susceptibility

> 'Let there be no noise made, my gentle friends;
> Unless some dull and favourable hand
> Will whisper music to my weary spirit,'

and speaks with all the yearning of the poet's soul:

> 'Will Fortune never come with both hands full,
> But write her fair words still in foulest letters?
> She either gives a stomach and no food;
> Such are the poor, in health; or else a feast
> And takes away the stomach; such are the rich,
> That have abundance and enjoy it not.'

The character of Prince Hal has annoyed many lovers of Falstaff because of his treatment of his old companions on becoming Henry V. But Shakespeare took the facts from history and stuck to them. His job was to paint human nature as it is, not as sentimentalists would like it to appear. He explained Hal's behaviour by the simple method of exhibiting him as a prig in a soliloquy at the beginning of the play; and he had seen quite enough of the aristocrats of his time to know that, however much they might relax amongst their social inferiors in leisure hours, they would very rapidly assert their position if their inferiors attempted to take advantage of their condescension: the social order had to be maintained. Shakespeare was not a moralist; he portrayed people as they were; and as a rule the moralist does not like him and cannot understand him. Dr. Johnson, otherwise one of his most perceptive critics, is constantly stumbling over the moral obstacle. Concerning the cold-blooded treachery of Prince John of Lancaster towards the end of *Henry IV*, Part II, Johnson writes: 'It cannot but raise some indignation to find this horrible violation of faith passed over thus slightly by the poet, without any note of censure or detestation.' But why should the poet hold up the action of his drama with a moral dissertation? Shakespeare was an artist, and Lancaster's action is made intelligible by none other than Falstaff. 'This same sober-blooded boy doth not love me; nor a man cannot make him laugh,' says Sir John. Whereupon Dr. Johnson, unaware that he is answering his criticism of Shakespeare's indifference to Lancaster's treachery, makes a note: 'He who cannot be softened into gaiety cannot easily be melted into kindness.'

But few men could have enjoyed *Henry IV* more than Johnson, who almost bursts forth into blank verse when he tries to do justice to Falstaff and whose summary of the work is sound: 'Perhaps no author has ever in two plays afforded so much delight . . . the incidents are multiplied with wonderful fertility of invention, and the characters diversified with the utmost nicety of discernment, and the profoundest skill in the nature of man.' Falstaff is more marvellous and lovable than ever in Part II, which is still further enriched by the Shallow scenes, to which no words could do justice. 'The true spirit of humanity,' writes Hazlitt, 'the thorough knowledge of the stuff we are made of, the poetical wisdom with the seeming fooleries in the whole of the garden-scene at Shallow's country-seat, and just before in the exquisite dialogue between him and Silence on the death of old Double, have no parallel anywhere else.' The tavern scene at the end of Act 2 is the finest example in all Shakespeare of another of Hazlitt's sayings: 'He had only to think of anything in order to become that thing, with all the circumstances belonging to it . . . all the persons concerned must have been present in the poet's imagination, as at a kind of rehearsal; and whatever would have passed through their minds on the occasion, and have been observed by others, passed through his, and is made known to the reader.' To leave the theatre of Shakespeare for, say, the world of Charles Dickens, is sometimes like leaving the real world for the theatre.

Falstaff brought his creator both wealth and reputation. Evidence of his fame and affluence is provided in the autumn of '98. Francis Meres, a clerical schoolmaster of Cambridge, published his *Palladis Tamia*, containing a 'Comparative Discourse of our English Poets,' wherein we read that 'as Plautus and Seneca are accounted the best for comedy and tragedy among the Latins, so Shakespeare among the English is the most excellent in both kinds for the stage . . . As Epius Stolo said that the Muses would speak with Plautus's tongue if they would speak Latin, so I say that the Muses would speak with Shakespeare's fine-filed phrase if they would speak English.' On the heels of this publication a leading citizen of Stratford, Richard Quyney, whose son Thomas in due time married Shakespeare's daughter Judith, arrived in London to appeal on behalf of his fellow-citizens against the taxes which parliament had just levied for the defence of the realm on land, goods and personality. Stratford had been 'twice afflicted and almost wasted by fire' in the course of the last few years, and its inhabitants were petitioning the Chancellor of the Exchequer to exempt them from these taxes. Quyney himself was kept hanging about in London and ran short of cash; so he wrote to Shakespeare, whose financial position was such that he had recently been considering the purchase of his wife's old home at Shottery, begging for a loan of thirty pounds (over four hundred pounds in modern money) to tide him over. The letter, addressed to 'my loving good friend and countryman Mr. William Shakespeare,' was dated the 25th October, 1598, and written at the Bell Inn, Carter Lane. Although engaged in a dangerous and costly operation at the time, Shakespeare managed to oblige Quyney, whose appeal to the Court was favourably considered by the Queen and allowed by the Chancellor.

Owing to the continued opposition of the City puritans the Shoreditch theatres were in danger of being 'plucked down,' so Shakespeare and the two young Burbages decided to anticipate the authorities and do the plucking. Old Burbage died early in '97, leaving the Theatre to his eldest son Cuthbert and some property he had bought at Blackfriars to Richard. The lease of the Theatre expired in March, '97, and the ground-landlord not only refused to renew it but claimed the building. Shakespeare and his friends, unwilling to prolong negotiations which they knew would be futile, acted with promptitude. On December 26th, '98, two days after they had performed before the Court at Whitehall, twelve of them descended upon Shoreditch, armed with daggers, swords and battle-axes, and under the direction of a builder named Peter Street began to pull down the Theatre. The ground-landlord was away, but his servants did their best to resist these 'riotous persons,' who however were more than a match for them and managed to convey the structure, in pieces, across the Thames to Southwark. With the timber thus transported they began to erect a new playhouse called the Globe on the north side of Maiden Lane, described by Stow as 'a long straggling place with ditches on each side, the passages to the houses being over little bridges,

with little garden-plots before them.' Peter Street was temporarily lodged in gaol for his part in the business, but as the
actors again played at Court on New Year's Day it is clear
that they were not molested. On January 20th, '99, they
revisited Shoreditch and carted off the rest of the material,
appearing once more before the Court, then at Richmond, on
February 20th. The piece of ground on which the Globe was
being built had been leased by its owner, Sir Thomas Brend,
for thirty-one years from Christmas '98, to the two Burbages,
William Shakespeare, John Heminge, Augustine Phillips,
Thomas Pope[1] and William Kemp; but that Shakespeare
was considered the chief person in the transaction is proved by
the post-mortem inquisition on Brend in May, '99, which refers
to 'a building of late erected in the occupation of William
Shakespeare and others.'

The new theatre was circular in shape ('this wooden O');
it had galleries, the top one being covered with thatch, but no
roof. A large stage, also covered with thatch, projected well into
the pit, so that the performers were surrounded on three sides
by the spectators. The first play to be produced there, in the
spring of 1599, was a pageant, a historical panorama, and a
patriotic pot-boiler: Shakespeare's *Henry V*.[2] The author would
not have allowed anyone else to speak the Chorus, which
contains the best poetry in the piece, and our assurance that
he played it is made trebly sure by the appropriateness of his
appearance in such a part at the opening of the new theatre and
by the reference to 'our bending author' in the Epilogue, which
must have brought down the house. The most moving lines in
the Chorus reveal Shakespeare's own uneasiness over the
Fifth Columnists of his time:

> 'O England! model to thy inward greatness,
> Like little body with a mighty heart,
> What mightst thou do, that honour would thee do,
> Were all thy children kind and natural!'

It was absolutely necessary that the Globe should open with
a resounding success, and Shakespeare determined to play to

---

[1]Pope was probably the original Falstaff, because Kemp evidently played
Shallow.
[2]His last play to be produced there, *Henry VIII*, was of the same kind.

the gallery. But though he never had the smallest compunction about producing pot-boilers whenever the occasion called for them, he was incapable of producing anything that did not contain good poetry and honest characterisation; and even at his worst the excitement of creation gave him a zest that almost persuades us that he admired Henry the Fifth, whose speech before the battle of Agincourt has a ringing sincerity:

> 'Old men forget: yet all shall be forgot,
>   But he'll remember with advantages
>   What feats he did that day. Then shall our names,
>   Familiar in his mouth as household words . . .
>   Be in their flowing cups freshly remembered.
>
>   This story shall the good man teach his son,
>   And Crispin Crispian shall ne'er go by,
>   From this day to the ending of the world,
>   But we in it shall be remembered;
>   We few, we happy few, we band of brothers;
>   For he to-day that sheds his blood with me
>   Shall be my brother . . .'

With uncanny insight Shakespeare makes Henry foreshadow Napoleon, who delivered himself of similar sentiments after the battle of Austerlitz: 'Soldats! . . . Vous avez décoré vos aigles d'une immortelle gloire . . . Mon peuple vous reverra avec joie, et il vous suffira de dire *J'etais a la bataille d'Austerlitz*, pour que l'on réponde *Viola un brave*!' Shakespeare also anticipates another of Napoleon's sayings, after the battle of Waterloo, 'Tout est perdu!' And Henry has something in common with Hitler, whose threats have a like ferocity. For instance this:

> 'France being ours, we'll bend it to our awe,
>   Or break it all to pieces:'

And this, telling the Governor of Harfleur what will happen to his people if he does not capitulate:

> 'in a moment, look to see
>   The blind and bloody soldier with foul hand
>   Defile the locks of your shrill-shrieking daughters;
>   Your fathers taken by the silver beards,
>   And their most reverend heads dash'd to the walls;

> Your naked infants spitted upon pikes,
> Whiles the mad mothers with their howls confus'd
> Do break the clouds, as did the wives of Jewry
> At Herod's bloody-hunting slaughtermen.'

Henry's religion is tribal: he promises God a fair return for favours received; and like Cromwell (to whom he presents a key-phrase 'And bids you, in the bowels of the Lord') he has a high opinion of the Almighty's military skill:

> 'And be it death proclaimed through our host
> To boast of this or take that praise from God
> Which is his only.'

The finest passage in the play is Mistress Quickly's description of Falstaff's death, and, echoing Bardolph, we wish we were with him 'wheresome'er he is, either in heaven or in hell.' Not all his companions put together, plus a new set of comics thrown in, make up for his absence, though Fluellen has some good moments: 'If the enemy is an ass and a fool and a prating coxcomb, is it meet, think you, that we should also, look you, be an ass and a fool and a prating coxcomb? in your own conscience, now?' But Falstaff's presence would have wrecked the play, and Shakespeare as a manager was taking no chances. The first three plays he wrote for the Globe were pot-boilers, *Henry V* being followed pretty closely by *The Merry Wives of Windsor* and *Much Ado About Nothing*.

There is a tradition that Queen Elizabeth, delighted with Falstaff, commanded the author to show him in love. We may accept the truth of it without demur, for if ever a work was written in contempt of an order *The Merry Wives of Windsor* is that work. 'You wish to see Falstaff made a fool of?' one can imagine Shakespeare saying to the Queen, beneath his breath: 'Very well, but you shan't see Falstaff.' She was so eager to witness the play, goes the story, that she gave the author a fortnight in which to finish it. That too we may believe. He probably rattled it off in less than a week; he could have written it in his sleep. Unlike his other plays, its plot was entirely invented by himself, which is conclusive evidence that it was written to order in a hurry. He tells us exactly what he thought about this degradation of his glorious creation. 'See now how wit may be made a Jack-a-Lent, when 'tis upon ill employment!' he makes his pseudo-Falstaff say, and again 'Have I laid my brain in the sun and dried it, that it wants matter to prevent so gross o'er-reaching as this? . . . 'Tis time I were choked with a piece of toasted cheese.' And then, very unexpectedly, the only flash of the authentic Falstaff in the play: 'This is enough to be the decay of lust and late walking through the realm,' which is a sufficient comment on the buffoon who had taken his name in vain. We are told that Shakespeare paid the Queen a handsome compliment in the last scene. But this is questionable. 'Worthy the owner, and the owner it,' says Mistress Quickly of Windsor Castle, which could have been taken in two ways and was not the class of compliment to which Elizabeth was accustomed. Shakespeare had wandered about the Windsor district, for there are references to Frogmore and Datchet, and he got the names of Ford and Page from the latter. The Cotswold hills which he knew so well are mentioned; the shrieks of women when bears were led through the Southwark streets close to where he lived are noticed; and an ironic allusion to a recent action by his company must have amused the Globe audiences: 'Like a fair house built on another man's ground; so that I have lost my edifice by mistaking the place where I erected it.'

Whether Shakespeare played Benedick in his third money-maker for the Globe, *Much Ado About Nothing*, we do not know, but the character is closely related to Berowne, and both of them are portraits of the man as he believed the world saw him, not as he saw himself. Benedick suits himself to his company, 'a lord to a lord, a man to a man.' He has 'every month a new sworn brother,' who 'will hang upon him like a disease.' He is 'sooner caught than the pestilence, and the taker runs presently mad.' This faithfully describes Shakespeare as a social magnet, one whose wit and charm made him exceedingly attractive to young men, who found him irresistible until, tired of their society, he showed them a different side of himself, 'for what his heart thinks his tongue speaks.' Beatrice calls Benedick 'the prince's jester' and Benedick reflects 'It may be I go under that title because I am merry.' Shakespeare was naturally merry in company and he must often have resented the imputation that because he talked a lot of nonsense he was shallow and scatter-brained. They 'only are reputed wise for saying nothing,' is Gratiano's criticism of long-faced silent folk, whom Shakespeare distrusted so much that he makes his villain Don John a man of few words. On the other hand there was a type of talkativeness that disgusted him: the boisterous, hectoring, swaggering conversation of the aristocrats he met in taverns or at Court. In *Much Ado About Nothing* he lets off steam in the character of Antonio, a name he used in three plays to cover an aspect of himself:

> 'What, man! I know them, yea,
> And what they weigh, even to the utmost scruple—
> Scambling, out-facing, fashion-monging boys,
> That lie, and cog, and flout, deprave, and slander,
> Go antiquely, and show outward hideousness,
> And speak off half a dozen dangerous words,
> How they might hurt their enemies, if they durst;
> And this is all.'

Once again Shakespeare tells us what he thinks of a play written with an eye to the box-office, this time by the simple method of labelling it *Much Ado About Nothing*, which is his personal opinion of the stuff and must not be confused with his attitude to the audience implied in two later titles, *As You Like It* and *What You Will* (*Twelfth Night*). The Dogberry and Verges scenes have been highly praised, but Dickens might have written them, whereas the incomparable Shallow and Silence scenes in *Henry IV*, Part 2, belong to a different order of creation and are utterly beyond the compass of anyone else. Shakespeare, by the way, came across Dogberry at Grendon in Buckinghamshire, while journeying from London to Stratford. He was always on the look-out for odd characters, and a certain constable of that place was rapidly transferred by him to Messina. Will Kemp played the part, but his incorrigible habit of 'gagging,' which had been steadily getting on Shakespeare's nerves, caused more friction than usual between actor and author. Shakespeare was now part-owner of a theatre where his plays were the chief popular attractions, and he could exercise considerable authority in it. The upshot was that

Kemp sold his interest in the Globe, cleared out, and went dancing and japing about the continent. Apparently he fancied that he had got the better of Shakespeare, for in a Cambridge play called *The Return from Parnassus* (1602) he is represented as saying to the students who are welcoming him home from his trip abroad: 'Is it not better to make a fool of the World (i.e. the Globe) as I have done, than to be fooled of the World, as you scholars are?' Which reminds us of Greene's complaint that the actors had produced a playwright who was putting the scholars out of business. Shakespeare's judgment of Kemp was later delivered by Hamlet. The passage, which was drastically revised and abbreviated in later editions after Kemp's death, originally ran as follows:

'Let not your clowns speak more than is set down. There be of them, I can tell you, that will laugh themselves to set on some quantity of barren spectators to laugh with them, albeit there is some necessary point in the play then to be observed. O 'tis vile, and shows a pitiful ambition in the fool that useth it. And then, you have some again that keep one suit of jests as a man is known by one suit of apparel, and gentlemen quote his jests down in their tables before they come to the play, as thus—*Cannot you stay till I eat my porridge*? and *You owe me a quarter's wages*: and *My coat wants a cullisen*, and *Your beer is sour*; and blabbering with his lips and thus keeping in his cinque pace of jests, when, God knows, the warm clown cannot make a jest unless by chance, as the blind man catcheth the hare: Masters, tell him of it.'

Kemp was succeeded at the Globe by Robert Armin, whose more fantastic personality must have been partly responsible for the Court jesters who appear in some of Shakespeare's plays, beginning with *As You Like It*.

A German visitor to London, Thomas Platter of Basle, saw Shakespeare's next play in the autumn of 1599: 'On the 21st of September, I, with my companions, after dinner, somewhere about two o'clock, was rowed across the River to see, in the straw-thatched House there, the tragedy of the first Emperor, Julius Cæsar, acted extremely well by scarcely more than fifteen players.' But *Julius Cæsar* belongs to a different story,

which shall be told in the next chapter.[1] Before the effect of
the outside world on Shakespeare's abnormally impressible
nature had finally turned him into a writer of grim comedies
and stark tragedies, he gave expression to his gay and easy
disposition in two more plays, the first being an attempt to
escape from a life which was becoming increasingly burdensome, the second a wonderful epitome of the beauty and
humour that had been his, made all the more poignant because
they were slipping from his grasp.

In *As You Like It* he frankly went back to his youth and to
the countryside where he had grown up. The forest of Arden
is the Warwickshire forest he had known, with a lioness thrown
in for the sake of the plot. There his romantic imagination
could easily picture a state of society for which he was beginning to yearn, wherein one could 'fleet the time carelessly, as
they did in the golden world.' The whole spirit of the play, and
his own desire, are in the songs:

> 'Who doth ambition shun,
>   And loves to live i' the sun,
>   Seeking the food he eats,
>   And pleased with what he gets,
> Come hither, come hither, come hither:
>   Here shall he see
>   No enemy
> But winter and rough weather.'

> 'Blow, blow, thou winter wind,
>   Thou art not so unkind
>   As man's ingratitude;
>   Thy tooth is not so keen,
>   Because thou art not seen,
>   Although thy breath be rude.
> Heigh-ho! sing, heigh-ho! unto the green holly:
> Most friendship is feigning, most loving mere folly.
>   Then heigh-ho! the holly!
>   This life is most jolly.'

---

[1]Shakespeare sometimes revised his plays, either to bring them up to date for
reproduction on the stage, or to improve their poetry, or to fit parts for fresh
actors in revivals, or to strengthen and point the characterisation when it was safe
to do so. It cannot be doubted that the *Julius Caesar* we now have is very different
from the play seen by Herr Platter late in 1599, before the rebellion and death of
Essex.

Re-living his youth, he saw the meadows where love had first come to him, where he and Anne had kissed and held hands, while the hours sped by but time stood still in his heart:

'It was a lover and his lass,
   With a hey, and a ho, and a hey nonino,
That o'er the green corn-field did pass,
   In the spring time, the only pretty ring time,
When birds do sing, hey ding a ding, ding;
Sweet lovers love the spring.

Between the acres of the rye,
  .   .   .   .

These pretty country folks would lie,
  .   .   .   .

This carol they began that hour,
  .   .   .   .

How that a life was but a flower
  .   .   .

And therefore take the present time,
  .   .   .   .

For love is crowned with the prime.'
  .   .   .   .

The world he had longed to see in those far-off days seemed very artificial when viewed from the green shades of Arden. Touchstone swears he has been a courtier: 'If any man doubt that, let him put me to my purgation. I have trod a measure; I have flattered a lady; I have been politic with my friend, smooth with mine enemy; I have undone three tailors; I have had four quarrels, and like to have fought one.' As for the greater world beyond England that he had not seen, that too was scarcely worth visiting if the value of travel appeared in the globe-trotters he had met. 'And your experience makes you sad,' says Rosalind to Jaques: 'I had rather have a fool to make me merry than experience to make me sad; and to travel for it too! . . . Farewell, Monsieur Traveller: look you lisp and wear strange suits, disable all the benefits of your own country, be out of love with your nativity, and almost chide God for making you that countenance you are; or I will scarce think you have swam in a gondola.' Shakespeare was so fond of the word 'Rose,' which he mentions more often than any other flower, and its amplifications 'Rosaline' and 'Rosalind,' that one cannot help wondering whether his raven-haired mistress was not called by some such name; but the Rosalind of *As You Like It* does not resemble her: in fact she teases the girl whose description shows that Shakespeare could not quite banish his mistress even from a retrospect in which she had no part:

> ' 'Tis not your inky brows, your black silk hair,
> Your bugle eyeballs, nor your cheeks of cream,
> That can entame my spirits to your worship,'

says Rosalind to Phoebe. Then, turning to Silvius, she adds:

> ' 'Tis not her glass, but you, that flatters her;'

which is precisely what Shakespeare told his mistress in the *Sonnets*. Two more personal points in the play are worth noting. As the colour of Shakespeare's hair was reported to be reddish, Celia's description of Orlando's is interesting: 'Your chestnut was ever the only colour.' Also, it seems, the poet played Adam, donning a long beard for the part and rather overacting the senility. At the time he wrote the comedy he was suffering from nostalgia for the past and doing his best to obliterate the present; so playing Adam would have suited his mood of self-pity.

> 'O good old man, how well in thee appears
> The constant service of the antique world!'

Such lines, which explain the play's popularity among sentimentalists, came naturally to Shakespeare at a moment in his life when, if he had not been a great poet, he might have developed into something horribly like Sir James Barrie.

While on the subject of this woodland comedy, we may as well destroy a popular illusion. Donnish dreamers, who like to live in a past that does not make them feel uncomfortable instead of a present that does, never tire of telling us that Shakespeare's England was a far more beautiful place than ours. A moment's reflection will dispose of that dream. England in Shakespeare's time was a country of broad heaths, rough commons and straggly woods, even the cultivated patches being divided by stones, ditches and fences more often than by hedges. But as the common lands were gradually filched from the people in the seventeenth, eighteenth and nineteenth centuries, hedges sprouted up all over the place, and the peculiar beauty of England to-day, wherever the towns do not thrust out their hideous claws, lies in the garden-like aspect of the countryside, partitioned like a chessboard, the green lush fields separated by the various-tinted foliage and seasonable colours of the hedgerows. Thus the rape of the land has made it lovelier. As Shakespeare said:

> 'There is some soul of goodness in things evil,
> Would men observingly distil it out.'

The opening lines of *Twelfth Night* lift us at once into a world where Orlando and Rosalind and their humdrum relations could scarcely have breathed:

> 'If music be the food of love, play on;
> Give me excess of it, that, surfeiting,
> The appetite may sicken, and so die.
> That strain again! it had a dying fall:
> O! it came o'er my ear like the sweet sound
> That breathes upon a bank of violets,
> Stealing and giving odour. Enough! no more:
> 'Tis not so sweet now as it was before.'

As for the humour in the play, Jaques and Touchstone are not worthy to get drunk in the company of Sir Toby Belch and Sir Andrew Aguecheek, nor to keep sober in the company of Malvolio.

Twelfth Night is Shakespeare's last happy play, but one can feel all through it that he is bidding farewell to youth and the joys of a good digestion: it is a sort of autumnal happiness, all the more beautiful because of the lowering atmosphere. Its spirit is flawlessly caught in the lyrics:

> 'What is love? 'tis not hereafter;
> Present mirth hath present laughter;
>   What's to come is still unsure:
> In delay there lies no plenty;
> Then come kiss me, sweet and twenty,
>   Youth's a stuff will not endure.'

'Come away, come away, death,
    And in sad cypress let me be laid;
Fly away, fly away, breath;
    I am slain by a fair cruel maid.
My shroud of white, stuck all with yew,
    O! prepare it.
My part of death, no one so true
    Did share it.'

'A great while ago the world begun,
    With hey, ho, the wind and the rain;
But that's all one, our play is done,
    And we'll strive to please you every day.'

The Clown also hits the note in 'pleasure will be paid, one time
or another,' which reminds us of 'Pain pays the income of each
precious thing' in *Lucrece*.

Shakespeare probably set out with the intention of ridiculing
puritanism, from which he and his fellows had suffered, in the
character of Malvolio. 'Dost thou think, because thou art
virtuous, there shall be no more cakes and ale?' Sir Toby asks
him. 'He brought me out o' favour with my lady about a bear-
baiting here,' complains Fabian. 'Sometimes he is a kind of
puritan,' says Maria. But at that point Shakespeare had a
qualm of caution. The Earl of Essex was popular among the
puritans of the City, and as Southampton was devoted to
Essex it would not have been wise to attack the Earl's adherents;
so when Aguecheek says that if he thought Malvolio was a
puritan he'd beat him like a dog, Maria is made to contradict
herself: 'The devil a puritan that he is, or any thing constantly,
but a time-pleaser' (a safe way of calling him a puritan), and
thenceforward Malvolio is ridiculed merely for his self-love.
Shakespeare reserved puritanism for later treatment, after the
City people had let down Essex. But as he again refers to the
aristocratic bullies who made themselves conspicuous in the
streets and at Court, most of them probably followers of Essex,
it is permissible to guess that they had caused him some
personal inconvenience: 'For it comes to pass oft that a terrible
oath, with a swaggering accent sharply twanged off, gives manhood more approbation than ever proof itself would have

earned him.' This is said by Sir Toby, who at least has the courage to use his sword—dutch courage, of course, for as a rule 'his eyes were set at eight i' the morning.'

Though the scene of the play is in Illyria, our author cannot resist mentioning a famous London tavern—'In the south suburbs, at the Elephant'—and though the plot does not demand it he makes another Antonio display the same dog-like devotion to Sebastian as his namesake does for Bassanio in *The Merchant of Venice*, the poet for his patron in the *Sonnets*.

Shakespeare's plays were now in demand at the centres of law and learning as well as at Court. We find his company performing before the Queen at Richmond through the winter of 1599-1600, visiting Oxford in 1600, performing before the Queen at Whitehall through the winters of 1600-1 and 1601-2, and visiting Oxford again in 1601. In February, 1602, *Twelfth Night* was presented at Middle Temple Hall, and in the winter of 1602-3 the Lord Chamberlain's men appeared for the last time before the Queen at Whitehall and Richmond. She was to see no more plays by Shakespeare after *Twelfth Night*:

> 'Those flights upon the banks of Thames,
> That so did take Eliza and our James,'

were over for Eliza.

CHAPTER VII

ROMANS AND GREEKS

It has been assumed by many writers, because the assumption pleases them, that Shakespeare had as high an opinion of Queen Elizabeth as she had of him. The picture of monarch and poet chanting pæans in each other's honour flatters both monarchs and poets and satisfies the ordinary person that all's for the best in the best of all worlds. But such a picture is a distortion of life. Monarchs like to gain the praise of poets, and poets like to catch the attention of monarchs; but they never coalesce and usually fear one another. 'The love of power in ourselves, and the admiration of it in others, are both natural to man,' says Hazlitt; 'the one makes him a tyrant, the other a slave.' Elizabeth was a tyrant, but Shakespeare was a free man; and free men hate tyrants. It is not too much to say that Shakespeare loathed Queen Elizabeth.

For a man of his sensitiveness there was very little in her to like. She was stingy, greedy, vain, cruel, tortuous, tyrannical, and apparently a virgin. We have already noted his criticisms of her public character, and we can but faintly conceive the disgust he felt for her when she committed his fellow-author John Hayward to the Tower for writing a History of Henry IV, merely because it contained a description of Richard the Second's deposition. She wanted to have him tried for treason and put upon the rack to force a confession from him that her own deposition was hinted at: but she was advised not to do so and contented herself with keeping the unfortunate fellow under lock and key for the rest of her life. Shakespeare disliked her private character too. Her absurd behaviour with her favourites, the capricious use of her power, the way she played off one man against another, the well-nigh incredible vanity which caused her to interfere with the personal lives of those dependent upon her: everything about her seemed to him preposterous and warped. Her treatment of his patron in 1598 must have been the last straw. Southampton had fallen in love with Elizabeth Vernon, one of the Queen's ladies-in-waiting, which annoyed the Queen so much that she ordered him from the Court. Though he had leave to return, she treated him so badly that he obtained permission to travel abroad, and on February 10th he accompanied Sir Robert Cecil to France, leaving Elizabeth Vernon pregnant and sorely distressed. Cecil's Father, Lord Burghley, the Queen's chief counsellor, died on August 4th, and on the 29th there was a state funeral at Westminster, when London was crammed with peers and their retinues. Southampton took advantage of the prevailing bustle, came back to England in great secrecy, married Mistress Vernon, returned at once to France, and wrote to break the news to Cecil, desiring him 'to find the means of acquainting her Majesty therewith in such sort as may least offend.' But before Cecil received this letter her Majesty had been acquainted with the facts and was 'grievously offended,' instructing Cecil to order Southampton's instant return to London, 'and advertise your arrival, without coming to the Court until her pleasure be known.' The Queen was so angry that she did not attend divine service that day at her chapel, unable perhaps to reconcile her feelings with her faith, and stamped about the place threatening the Southamptons with the Tower. In the meantime she imprisoned her peccant maid-of-honour. Southampton funked the ordeal of facing the Queen and stayed away; but at the beginning of November his wife bore a daughter, he returned home, and the Queen promptly sent him to join her in prison. Through the influence of his friend Essex he regained his liberty before the month was out.

Such senile explosions of vexed vanity were not lost on Shakespeare, whose interest in Southampton's welfare naturally embraced the actions of Southampton's kinsman, the Earl of Essex. After Burghley's death the two parties at Court were more sharply divided than ever. Those who thought that Cecil held the future in his hands grouped themselves round him; those who believed in the star of Essex followed him. Essex had an extraordinary vogue. Not only was he Earl Marshal and the Queen's favourite, but he was popular with the puritans, and the Catholics rallied to him. He favoured the succession of King James of Scotland to the English throne. James supported him, and he was the idol of everyone in the country who, tired of Elizabeth's tricky policy, was responsive to brave gestures, impulsive actions and a chivalrous character. Even Shakespeare appears to have been impressed by him, for he was obviously thinking of Essex when painting Hotspur:

> 'by his light
> Did all the chivalry of England move
> To do brave acts: he was indeed the glass
> Wherein the noble youth did dress themselves:
> He had no legs that practis'd not his gait;
> And speaking thick which nature made his blemish,
> Became the accents of the valiant;
> For those that could speak low and tardily,
> Would turn their own perfection to abuse,
> To seem like him: so that, in speech, in gait,
> In diet, in affections of delight,
> In military rules, humours of blood,
> He was the mark and glass, copy and book,
> That fashion'd others.'

After it was all over, Shakespeare makes Ophelia speak of Hamlet in exactly the same way as Lady Percy speaks of Hotspur, and again we seem to see Essex as he appeared to those like Shakespeare who had once admired him:

> 'O! what a noble mind is here o'erthrown:
> The courtier's, soldier's, scholar's, eye, tongue, sword;
> The expectancy and rose of the fair state,
> The glass of fashion and the mould of form,
> The observed of all observers, quite, quite down!'

Following several quarrels, which had been patched up, the Queen decided, partly on the advice of his enemies, to make Essex her Lord Deputy in Ireland. No one had been able to tranquillise that country, and everyone, including Essex, felt that he was the man for the job. The Queen had another motive for letting him go: his popularity irked her; and knowing his incompetence as a leader she guessed that he would fail in his mission and return home less popular than when he set forth. The conspiratorial atmosphere that surrounded him was another reason for sending him away. Thrust forward by his eager companions, he might at any moment start a rebellion, and under pretence of removing Cecil, remove her. In spite of his protestations of eternal devotion, his temperament was a danger to her state, and many of those who egged him on were violent fanatics or ambitious place-hunters. 'He goeth not forth to serve the Queen's realm, but to humour his own revenge,' wrote a close observer of events, and Elizabeth observed events more closely than anyone around her.

Before his departure Essex had trouble with his rival Cecil and with the Queen: the former persistently put difficulties in his way, the latter flatly refused to let him make Southampton his General of the Horse. The fact that Southampton had married one of her maids-of-honour without asking her permission naturally made him an incalculable cavalry leader. Southampton therefore followed Essex to Ireland in a private capacity; and the moment he arrived Essex appointed him General of the Horse. While they were in Ireland together Lady Southampton stayed with the Essex family and kept her husband in touch with society gossip, one item of which proves the popularity of Shakespeare's plays in Court circles: 'All the news I can send you that I think will make you merry is that I read in a letter from London that Sir John Falstaff is by his mistress, Dame Pintpot, made father of a goodly miller's thumb, a boy that is all head and very little body. But this is a secret.'[1]

Essex left London on the afternoon of March 27th, 1599. He mounted his horse in Seething Lane, and, himself plainly dressed for dramatic effect, he passed through Gracechurch Street, Cornhill and Cheapside, accompanied by many noblemen in gorgeous apparel, and acclaimed by the people, who 'pressed exceedingly to behold him . . . for more than four miles' space, crying and saying, *God bless your lordship*! *God preserve your honour*! etc., and some followed him until the evening only to behold him.' As was to be expected, he bungled the Irish business. Tyrone, the leader he was supposed to quell,

---

[1] Falstaff addresses Mistress Quickly 'Peace, good pint-pot!' A 'miller's thumb' is a small fish with a large head. Falstaff's body was so large that his head was relatively small. The real names of the parties nominated remain a secret.

remained in Ulster, while he frittered away his forces during a three months' campaign in Leinster and Munster, doing all the heroic and stupid things he had done on previous occasions. When he realised that he had achieved nothing, he blamed everyone but himself, wrote frantic letters to the Queen complaining of his enemies at home, and vented his spleen on several hundreds of soldiers convicted of cowardice by degrading their officers and executing a tenth of their number. Back in Dublin at the end of July he amused himself by creating fifty-nine knights. Elizabeth became sarcastic. Why had he not attacked Tyrone? She was spending a thousand pounds a day on the expedition and ordered him to march at once into Ulster. The reply came that his force of sixteen thousand had been reduced to four thousand. She sent another two thousand. He pleaded that operations would be difficult in the winter months. She answered that as he had wasted both the spring and the summer 'none of the four quarters of the year will be in season for you,' and she hinted that he had no intention of finishing the war. Suddenly Essex heard that Cecil had been given a lucrative post which he had coveted and expected. Completely losing his head, he threatened to return home, dispose of the Cecil crew, and force the Queen to act in accordance with his own wishes. Then he calmed down and decided to march against Tyrone. But that wily gentleman was quite ready for him. A parley was proposed. Essex consented, and Tyrone suggested a six weeks' truce. Essex, sick of the whole affair, fell in with the suggestion, and that was that. Although he had received a command from the Queen that he should remain in Ireland, he deserted his post, and with a crowd of officers arrived in London on September 28th. The Court was at Nonesuch. Should he capture the Queen by force or win her to him by words? He was in two minds about it. The weaker mind prevailed. He galloped down to Nonesuch, and with the mud of travel on his face flung himself at her feet.

Some months before this ignominious return Shakespeare had expressed his own feeling of disquietude in *Henry V*, where the Chorus, in describing the City's reception of the victor of Agincourt, hopes that the vanquisher of Tyrone will be well received:

'But now behold,
In the quick forge and working-house of thought,
How London doth pour out her citizens . . .
As, by a lower but loving likelihood,
Were now the general of our gracious empress,—
As in good time he may,—from Ireland coming,
Bringing rebellion broached on his sword,
How many would the peaceful city quit
To welcome him! much more, and much more cause,
Did they this Harry.'

Clearly Shakespeare did not think so highly of Essex as of
Henry V; while the phrases 'by a lower but loving likelihood'
and 'as in good time he may' are not those of an enthusiastic
and optimistic supporter. In fact Shakespeare, though attracted
by the picturesque personality of Essex and concerned over the
fate of Southampton's leader, had already seen through these
restless figures in public life, making full use of his observations
in a tragedy that he wrote and produced while Essex was still
in Ireland. Elizabethan London seethed with revolutionary
firebrands: Shakespeare saw them in taverns, rubbed shoulders
with them at Court, and talked with them at the house of
Southampton, a meeting-place for discontented nobles and
gentlemen. He sensed rebellion in the air, and the time was ripe
for a political drama. He was not much interested in politics,
but the types of conspirators he had come across gave him the
material he wanted for a play founded on the story of Julius
Cæsar, which he had read in Plutarch. 'Types' is the word. He
soon perceived that they and their like were not 'characters.'
There was no richness in the nature of the kind of man who was
drawn to public life; nearly always he was at the mercy of some
one passion: conceit, idealism, envy, hatred, ambition, avarice:
he was a taker, not a giver; a busybody; one who wished to
dominate, to interfere with the lives of others; not one who
was content to live and let live, to enrich the world by being
in harmony with it. And so Shakespeare's *Julius Cæsar*, the
greatest study of political types in literature, is cold and
rhetorical compared with his other tragedies: it is the result of
his observation, not his emotion. But his observation is more
acute than that of any other son of man.

Coleridge used to say, whenever he found fault with anything in Shakespeare, that he was almost certainly wrong and
Shakespeare right; because past experience had taught him
that whatever he had considered to be imperfect in Shakespeare
had, on further reflection and experience, turned out to be
perfect. The two greatest dramatic critics in the English
language, William Hazlitt and Bernard Shaw, should have
remembered Coleridge's warning when they found fault with
Shakespeare's conception of Julius Cæsar. Perhaps it is only
now, after a lapse of 340 years and the sprinkling of Europe
with Cæsars, that we are able to do justice to Shakespeare's
unerring insight. According to Hazlitt, Cæsar in the play
makes 'several vapouring and rather pedantic speeches' and
does not resemble 'the portrait given of him in his
Commentaries.' According to Shaw, 'it is impossible for even
the most judicially minded critic to look without a revulsion of
indignant contempt at this travestying of a great man as a silly
braggart . . . . There is not a single sentence uttered by
Shakespeare's Julius Cæsar that is, I will not say worthy of him,
but even worthy of an average Tammany boss.' Writing exactly
three hundred years after the first production of the play, Shaw
asserted that 'Cæsar was not in Shakespeare, nor in the epoch,
now fast waning, which he inaugurated.' Well, we know all
about the Cæsar type now, and Shakespeare is justified of his
'travesty.' We have heard Cæsar braying and bragging over the
wireless; we have read his commentaries and are aware that the
portrait in them is not like himself because he got someone else
to write them; we have felt his 'strength' in his bombs, his
'greatness' in his indifference to human life; and we realise that
when God wishes to scourge the world he makes people go
mad, set up an idol called Cæsar, whom civilised folk recognise
as Satan, and worship it.

How, then, did Shakespeare know all about Cæsar, making
him speak in the very accents with which we are now so familiar?
Without one-tenth of the knowledge of statecraft possessed by
those shrewd political observers, Hazlitt and Shaw, he nevertheless perceived what they did not: that a Cæsar would 'keep
us all in servile fearfulness,' that 'When Cæsar says "do this,"'
it is performed,' that he talks pompous platitudes because he is

by temperament a criminal and can only rule by hoodwinking, that the dictator type dislikes men who read and think for themselves, pretends to fear nothing but is frightened by omens, 'would not be a wolf but that he sees the Romans are but sheep,' is flattered most when told that he hates flatterers, asserts his will on every occasion yet calls himself the servant of the State, claims to be superior to ordinary men, not subject to common emotions, and

> 'constant as the northern star,
> Of whose true-fix'd and resting quality
> There is no fellow in the firmament.'

The explanation is that Shakespeare had studied a Cæsar at first-hand, and the Cæsar type does not vary much down the ages. His Cæsar's other name was Queen Elizabeth, whose senility and vacillation are added to the portrait.[1] Let us now do belated justice to the man who understood Cæsar, Cromwell, Napoleon, Hitler, Mussolini and other criminal lunatics by keeping a watchful eye on Elizabeth.

The revolutionists in *Julius Cæsar* were revealed to him with equal clarity; they were all part of the Essex faction, some animated by hatred, some by ambition, some by envy, some by love of mischief, some by an abstract sense of justice; and such was the range of his understanding that he was able to re-create them for all time as types of their various passions. We are given Brutus, the liberal idealist, who loves the name of honour more than he fears death, who kills Cæsar from the highest motives, whose mere reputation makes the action respectable, and who excuses the deed to himself on the ground that Cæsar *might* have abused his position. He hates the thought of conspiracy, and because he believes others to be as high-minded as himself he is unfitted to deal with a world of evil. He recoils from bloody and intemperate action, seizes every opportunity to preach a moral sermon, refuses to dirty his fingers with 'base bribes,' has an exalted opinion of himself, and is ready to die when he has ceased to be of use:

> 'Night hangs upon mine eyes; my bones would rest,
> That have but labour'd to attain this hour.'

[1]Hugh Kingsmill was the first person to spot this.

The Brutus type has reappeared since Shakespeare's time as Hampden in the English Revolution, Brissot in the French Revolution, and Kerensky in the Russian Revolution. But Shakespeare humanised it, making Brutus tender and compassionate.

If Brutus is the typical Girondin of revolutions, Cassius is the typical Jacobin: he groans beneath the age's yoke; he hates Cæsar because he thinks himself a better man; he never smiles, never indulges in recreation;

> 'Such men as he be never at heart's ease
> Whiles they behold a greater than themselves.'

He plays up to the nobility in Brutus, whom he flatters cunningly; he is an adept at propaganda, throwing anonymous letters into Brutus's windows; himself untrustworthy, he distrusts everyone; he is bloody-minded and far-sighted, advising the death of Antony and the right action at Philippi, and realising the danger of allowing Antony to make a funeral oration; he knows how to buy over his opponents:

> 'Your voice shall be as strong as any man's
> In the disposing of new dignities;'

and when he finds he cannot have his own way he wallows in self-pity like a spoilt child. His type has reappeared, with qualifications, under the names of Marat, Robespierre, Lenin, and countless others; in fact every crisis produces a Cassius.

The most vivid portrait in the play is that of Antony, who is almost a character. Shakespeare expends the full force of his rhetoric upon him and obviously liked him better than the rest because, although an out-and-out opportunist, he enjoys life. After Cæsar's death he puts up a magnificent bluff, because he knows it will not be called by Brutus, and his Forum speech, with its well-timed appeal to the cupidity of the mob, is a gorgeous bit of acting. Shakespeare had witnessed the effect of a popular orator on an audience. Says Bassanio to Portia:

> 'Only my blood speaks to you in my veins;
> And there is such confusion in my powers,
> As, after some oration fairly spoke
> By a beloved prince, there doth appear
> Among the buzzing pleased multitude;

> Where every something, being blent together,
> Turns to a wild of nothing, save of joy,
> Express'd and not express'd.'

But Shakespeare has no illusions about Antony, who promptly starts murdering his enemies the moment he is in the ascendant, and who has the born politician's shrewdness in estimating the material values of those about him. Mirabeau had much of Antony in him, and Lloyd George had more.

The tough, blunt-spoken, sarcastic, disillusioned sort of politician, more common in England than elsewhere, though France produced a good sample in Clemenceau, is hit off in Casca; while the cold calculating machine-man, who was to be elaborated in *Antony and Cleopatra* and who in Shakespeare's time was Sir Robert Cecil, is seen in Octavius. We cannot linger over the incidental gleams of insight in the play, except to mention that there is a Cicero in every village—

> 'For he will never follow any thing
> That other men begin;'

that Shakespeare knew how art is handled by democracy, Cinna being lynched because he is a poet; and that no one in all history but Shakespeare could have convinced us that he was present and made an exact report of what took place when Cæsar's Ghost appeared to Brutus:

Brutus: Why comest thou?
Ghost: To tell thee thou shalt see me at Philippi.
Brutus: Well, then I shall see thee again?
Ghost: Ay, at Philippi.
Brutus: Why, I will see thee at Philippi then.

The revolt Shakespeare had foreseen broke out a little more than a year after the production of *Julius Cæsar*, with Essex as the Brutus. The two had few points in common, though both were popular, both were supposed to be disinterested, and Cæsar's *Et tu, Brute* might have been spoken by Elizabeth to Essex. After the return from Ireland, when the Queen realised she was in no danger, Essex was kept under guard at York House, whence he wrote contrite epistles to Elizabeth, who declined to read them. The news went round that he was ill, and his partisans became active, publishing pamphlets in which he was praised and his enemies blamed. The Star Chamber assembled and condemned his behaviour in the Irish business; meanwhile he and Southampton were corresponding with King James, telling him that Cecil was hostile to his claim and putting forward a plan whereby the succession to the English throne could be settled in the Scottish king's favour by military action. James replied evasively. At last Elizabeth, after confining Essex to his own house, set up a disciplinary court, before which Essex was charged with various misdemeanours. He went through the necessary grovelling formalities, and eleven months after his return from Ireland received his freedom. He continued to write letters to the Queen protesting his undying devotion, but when she took from him the monopoly of sweet wines, that had brought him in a fat income for ten years, he lost control of himself and threatened revenge. 'He uttered strange words, bordering on such strange designs that made me hasten forth and leave his presence,' wrote Sir John Harington. One of his outbursts, concerning the Queen's conditions—'Her conditions are as crooked as her carcase!'—was reported to her and she did not relish it. Again he wrote to King James, whose reply was a little more encouraging than usual. His supporters, incited by his own spurts of rage and resentment, were now driving him on. They circulated rumours that Cecil was intriguing with Spain, that Sir Walter Raleigh had sworn to kill Essex, and that the Queen intended to imprison the Earl in the Tower. Essex had worked himself up into such an excitable condition that at moments he believed the rumours his partisans had started and talked wildly of attacking the Court, of capturing the Queen, and of raising a revolt in the City.

On Thursday or Friday, the 5th or 6th of February, 1601, a curious thing happened. Some of Essex's followers, including Sir Charles and Sir Jocelyn Percy, younger brothers of the Earl of Northumberland, and Lord Monteagle, visited Shakespeare, Augustine Phillips and the Burbages, to request a special performance of *Richard II* at the Globe on Saturday, the 7th. The actors objected that the play was stale, that they had not played it for years, that no one would come to see it. Their visitors insisted, offering them forty shillings over and above the takings to put the play on. The actors then agreed. Apparently these followers of Essex believed that the 'deposition' scene would encourage playgoers to view another deposition in a becoming frame of mind. On Saturday the 7th, after dining in Fleet Street, Lord Monteagle, Sir Charles Percy, Edward Bushell, Sir Christopher Blount, Sir Gelly Meyrick, Captain Thomas Lee and others, ferried across the river and witnessed *Richard II* at the Globe. If Shakespeare played the leading part, he must have suffered more than an actor's first-night nervousness. The imprisonment of John Hayward for writing a description of Richard's deposition in a History of Henry IV would have warned him of Elizabeth's feelings on the subject, and he knew quite well that rebellion was ripe.

After the performance the conspirators, unpurged by poetry, re-crossed the river and went to Essex House, where a messenger arrived from the Queen summoning the Earl to a meeting of the Council. He asumed that this was a plot to seize him and returned word that he was ill. Asking everyone present to sleep at his house, he despatched messages to all his supporters. By Sunday morning some three hundred armed men had assembled, and the Queen sent the Lord Chief Justice and other dignitaries to demand the reason for it. Essex, now quite at the mercy of the fanatical faction, allowed the Queen's officers to be locked up and found himself in the Strand, his ears deafened by the cries of his supporters. Having heard that Charing Cross was barricaded, he made for the City, entering it by Lud Gate. Shouting 'For the Queen!' 'A plot is laid for my life!' 'The Crown is sold to the Infanta of Spain!' etc., and waving his sword, he marched up the hill towards St. Paul's, where the Lord Mayor and Aldermen were listening to a sermon. The citizens gaped at him and many cheered him, but as they did not know what he wanted them to do they contented themselves with gaping and cheering. Then a herald arrived, proclaiming him a traitor, and the citizens felt that the safest place was indoors. Down Cheapside he went, his face streaming with perspiration, a hunted look in his eyes. He arrived at the house of a friend in Gracechurch Street and went in. The friend made an excuse and left him. When he came out he saw that many of his people had already deserted him. He lost hope and decided to return, but Lud Gate had been closed and a company of pikemen and musketeers barred his retreat. A clash, a few casualties, and Essex led a faithful fifty down to the Thames, by which he returned to Essex House, where he shortly gave himself up. Essex, Southampton and several others were condemned to death. Southampton was spared but remained in the Tower until the accession of James I.

Augustine Phillips, representing the players at the Globe, was closely examined concerning the performance of *Richard II*. He managed to satisfy the authorities that the actors were innocent of offence; but the Queen had her revenge on them. On the evening of Shrove Tuesday, February 24th, Shakespeare and his company were commanded to appear before her. On the following morning, Ash Wednesday, Essex was beheaded. No doubt she got some grim pleasure out of their discomfort; no doubt Shakespeare got some, too, if the play was *Julius Cæsar*. His hatred of her was now qualified by contempt, and when she died about two years later he resolutely refused to notice the fact, though called upon by other poets to do so:

'You poets all, brave Shakespeare, Jonson, Greene, [1]
Bestow your time to write for England's Queen,'

was the appeal of one rhymster; while another, Henry Chettle, addressed Shakespeare in these terms:

'Nor doth the silver-tongued Melicert
Drop from his honey'd muse one sable tear
To mourn her death that graced his desert
And to his lays open'd her royal ear.
Shepherd, remember our Elizabeth
And sing her "Rape," done by that Tarquin, Death.'

Shakespeare remained aloof and silent.

Beyond question the Essex affair made a deep and permanent effect on Shakespeare, and therefore on his art. For more than a month the fate of his patron remained uncertain, and Southampton's imprisonment in the Tower, which lasted for two years, would have been continued indefinitely if the Queen

[1] Greene, by the way, had been dead for some years.

had lived. What made the situation almost unbearable to Shakespeare was that he could not give whole-hearted support to either party, seeing the revolt and its consequences with the impartial eye of an artist yet feeling affection for individuals whose actions irritated and distressed him, heartily disliking the leading members of the Government gang, the Queen, Cecil, Bacon and the rest, yet realising that they were more prudent guardians of the realm than their opponents, because they were more watchful of their own interests. A further cause for exasperation lay in Shakespeare's unwilling implication in the rising and the possible financial collapse of a concern he had so laboriously built up. For some time he must have been the victim of changing moods, despair alternating with hope, anger with sorrow, but in the end a feeling of bitterness, cynicism and life-weariness was uppermost, and this became the dominant note in his next play. Gradually he absorbed the experience, and the scope of his art widened and deepened under its influence, but he was to write no more joyous comedies, and we may date his increasingly sombre view of life from the Essex catastrophe.

Other troubles, coming at the turn of the century, intensified his mortification. The revival of the boy companies was not the least of them. From 1599 onwards the choir-boys of St. Paul's, who played in their singing-school close to the Cathedral, and the choir-boys of the Chapel Royal, who played in a theatre at Blackfriars, became more and more popular, and by 1602 they were rivalling the Chamberlain's men. Satire and singing were their specialities, and society flocked to hear them. It almost looks as if Shakespeare thought of retiring from business, because in 1602 he paid £320 for a freehold property in the manorial fields of Old Stratford, west of the hamlet of Welcombe, consisting of one hundred and seven acres of arable land and twenty acres of pasture and rights of common; he also bought a cottage in Chapel Lane for the use of his gardener. Certainly for a year or so he wrote nothing, and when he did at last produce something it was quite unlike his previous work. Later on, in *Hamlet*, when the rivalry of the boy-actors was diminishing and his own creative powers were reviving, he dealt with the subject; and as we happen to know that his company had been forced to tour the provinces in 1602 because London playgoers were patronising the boys at Blackfriars, we can appreciate the following dialogue:

Hamlet: What players are they?

Rosencrantz: Even those you were wont to take delight in, the tragedians of the city.

Hamlet: How chances it they travel? their residence, both in reputation and profit, was better both ways.

Rosencrantz: I think their inhibition comes by the means of the late innovation.

Hamlet: Do they hold the same estimation they did when I was in the city? Are they so followed?

Rosencrantz: No, indeed they are not.

Hamlet: How comes it? Do they grow rusty?

Rosencrantz: Nay, their endeavour keeps in the wonted pace: but there is, sir, an eyrie of children, little eyases, that cry out on the top of question, and are most tyranically clapped for 't: these are now the fashion, and so berattle the common stages—so they call them—that many wearing rapiers are afraid of goose-quills, and dare scarce come thither.

Hamlet: What! are they children? who maintains 'em? how are they escoted? Will they pursue the quality no longer than they can sing? will they not say afterwards, if they should grow themselves to common players—as it is most like, if their means are not better—their writers do them wrong, to make them exclaim against their own succession?

Rosencrantz: Faith, there has been much to-do on both sides: and the nation holds it no sin to tarre them to controversy: there was, for a while, no money bid for argument, unless the poet and the player went to cuffs in the question.

Hamlet: Is it possible?

Guilderstern: O! there has been much throwing about of brains.

Hamlet: Do the boys carry it away?

Rosencrantz: Ay, that they do, my lord; Hercules and his load too.

The 'throwing about of brains' refers to the controversy between the dramatists that broke out with the rise of the juvenile actors. John Marston and Thomas Dekker wrote for the boys of St. Paul's, Ben Jonson for those of the Chapel Royal. Jonson quarrelled with Marston, and both did their best to drag Shakespeare into the fray, Marston by ridiculing his coat of arms in a play produced by the St. Paul's boys, Jonson with a joke about his motto 'Non Sanz Droict' in *Every Man out of his Humour*, where one character asks 'But ha' you arms? ha' you arms?' another replies 'I' faith, I thank God, I can write myself "Gentleman" now; here's my patent, it cost me thirty pound, by this breath,' and the first suggests 'Let the word be, *Not Without Mustard.*' As Shakespeare would not be drawn, Jonson caricatured the actors at the Globe in *The Poetaster*, which included attacks on Dekker and Marston and another smack at Shakespeare: 'He is a gentleman, parcel-poet . . . his father was a man of worship, I tell thee . . . he pens high, lofty, in a new stalking strain, bigger than half the rhymers in the Town again . . . he will teach thee to tear and rand. Rascal, to him, cherish his Muse . . . he shall write for thee, slave! If he pen for thee once, thou shalt not need to travel with thy pumps full of gravel any more, after a blind jade and a hamper, and stalk upon boards and barrel-heads to an old cracked trumpet.' In this passage Jonson displays envy of Shakespeare's success as a dramatist; but in time honesty got the better of envy and Ben was great enough to pay homage to a greater than himself.

Their friendship for one another was strong and they must have had a lot in common,

> 'for in companions
> That do converse and waste the time together,
> Whose souls do bear an equal yoke of love,
> There must be needs a like proportion
> Of lineaments, of manners and of spirit.'

Yet it is difficult to resist the feeling that their companionship was not always a comfortable one. Jonson was quarrelsome and over-bearing, Shakespeare was conciliatory and submissive. Jonson was constantly in hot water with the authorities and on at least three occasions was imprisoned for his outspokenness. In 1597 his participation in a play that satirised eminent personages got him into gaol. The following year he killed a fellow-prisoner and fellow-actor in a duel. Pleading guilty he suffered another term of imprisonment, during which he was visited by a priest and became a Roman Catholic, professing that faith for about twelve years. Released by benefit of clergy he forfeited his 'goods and chattels' and was branded on his left thunb with the letter T (for Tyburn). Before this episode he had been associated with a rival company, but in 1598 his comedy *Every Man in his Humour* was produced by the Lord Chamberlain's men, with Shakespeare in the part of Old Knowell. Jonson, when quite unknown, had sent one of his early plays to Shakespeare's company. It suffered the common fate of plays sent to managements by unknown authors. Someone glanced it over carelessly, turned it down, and in due course the author would have received it back, with the usual note that it was not the sort of thing the Chamberlain's men were looking for, if Shakespeare himself had not caught sight of a sentence or two that encouraged him to read more. He liked it, persuaded his company to perform it, and Jonson's name was made. After that they were often together, and though Thomas Fuller's account of their wit-combats is from hearsay it is clearly an authentic picture of the two: Jonson being likened to a huge Spanish galleon; Shakespeare to an English man o' war, lesser in bulk but lighter in sailing, turning with all tides, tacking about and taking advantage of every wind; such was the quickness of his wit and invention.

No doubt Jonson was inclined to patronise Shakespeare, whose genius was independent of scholarship, which annoyed the scholar in Jonson, whose high opinion of his classical attainments was often the subject of the other's wit. Shakespeare acted as godfather to one of Jonson's children and after the christening fell into a pensive mood. Jonson wanted to know whether he felt melancholy. 'No, faith, Ben, not I, but I have been considering a great while what should be the fittest gift for me to bestow upon my godchild, and I have resolved at last.' 'I prithee, what?' 'I' faith, Ben, I'll e'en give him a dozen Latin Spoons, and thou shalt translate them.'[1] But despite Jonson's vexation he could not help recognising Shakespeare's superiority even to his classical favourites, writing:

> 'Or, when thy Socks were on,
> Leave thee alone for the comparison
> Of all that insolent Greece or haughty Rome
> Sent forth, or since did from their ashes come.'

And after Shakespeare's death he paid a handsome tribute in poetry and a more personal tribute in prose, wherein we can detect the voice of the pedant:

> 'I remember the players have often mentioned it as an honour to Shakespeare that in his writing (whatsoever he penned) he never blotted out line. My answer hath been, would he had blotted a thousand. Which they thought a malevolent speech. I had not told posterity this but for their ignorance, who choose that circumstance to commend their friend by, wherein he most faulted. And to justify mine own candour (for I loved the man and do honour his memory on this side idolatry as much as any). He was indeed honest, and of an open and free nature: had an excellent phantasy; brave notions and gentle expressions: wherein he flowed with that facility that sometime it was necessary he should be stopped.'

Jonson's phrase 'of an open and free nature' echoes a passage in *Troilus and Cressida*, and we may therefore take the description of Troilus by Ulysses as a description of Shakespeare by himself:

> 'Not soon provok'd nor being provok'd soon calm'd;
> His heart and hand both open and both free;
> For what he has he gives, what thinks he shows;[2]
> Yet gives he not till judgment guide his bounty,
> Nor dignifies an impure thought with breath.'

Reserving judgment on the last line, the knowledge we have so far gained of the man testifies to the truth of the rest. In *Troilus*

[1] The authority for this story is John Donne, the poetic dean of St. Paul's.
[2] Of Benedick, too, it is said 'What his heart thinks his tongue speaks.'

and *Cressida* we are also given Shakespeare's opinion of Jonson (which may be why Jonson remembered it so well), though the view was jaundiced by Jonson's attacks on him in the two plays already mentioned. In the Cambridge play, *The Return from Parnassus*, Will Kemp is made to say of academic writers: 'Why here's our fellow Shakespeare puts them all down, aye, and Ben Jonson too. O that Ben Jonson is a pestilent fellow; he brought up Horace giving the poets a pill; but our fellow Shakespeare hath given him a purge that made him bewray his credit.' Jonson had introduced the Augustan poets, with himself as Horace, into *The Poetaster*. Shakespeare's 'purge' was *Troilus and Cressida*, in which Jonson appears as Ajax: 'He is as valiant as the lion, churlish as the bear, slow as the elephant; a man into whom nature hath so crowded humours that his valour is crushed into folly, his folly sauced with discretion . . . he is melancholy without cause and merry against the hair . . . he is a gouty Briareus, many hands and no use, or purblind Argus, all eyes and no sight.' We learn that Ajax struck down Hector in the battle, 'the disdain and shame whereof hath ever since kept Hector fasting and waking.' Recalling Shakespeare's sensitiveness to criticism, his insomnia when troubled, and Jonson's success with the boy-players, we can easily guess who 'Hector' was. Ajax, 'who wears his wit in his belly and his guts in his head,' grumbles and rails at Achilles (Shakespeare again), is full of envy at his greatness, and wants to know whether Achilles 'thinks himself a better man than I am?' He ascribes all his own weaknesses to Achilles and is so eaten up with conceit that he cannot tell when his leg is being pulled. Jonson, we know, was always praising his schoolmaster, to whom he owed the education of which he was so proud, and Shakespeare makes Ulysses refer ironically to Ajax's teacher:

> 'Fam'd be thy tutor, and thy parts of nature
> Thrice-fam'd beyond all erudition.'

Altogether a biting portrait, which Shakespeare would have sweetened if he had dealt with Jonson at a period when his mood was less sour.

But there is nothing sweet about *Troilus and Cressida*, which is a thoroughly disagreeable play. It was written in 1602, and entered on February, 1603, in the Stationers' register: 'The Book of Troilus and Cressida, as it is acted by my Lord Chamberlain's men.' It was probably performed once or twice and quickly forgotten, for when it appeared in print in 1609 the writer of the preface anounced it as 'a new play', never staled with the stage, never clapper-clawed [1] with the palms of the vulgar.'

After the Romans, the Greeks; but much had happened between *Julius Cæsar* and *Troilus and Cressida*, and Shakespeare's style had become as involved as his mind. The detachment with which he had portrayed the Romans in *Julius Cæsar* is wholly lacking in *Troilus and Cressida*. He had been through the hoop, the passage had left him crumpled, and in Chapman's translation of the *Iliad* he found the material which sorted with his present disillusionment: a lot of venomous bragging idiots squabbling over nothing. So much out of tune with himself was he that he appears by fits and starts in several characters. Sometimes he speaks with the tongue of Ulysses, as when, with the Essex revolt in mind, he says:

'The heavens themselves, the planets and this centre,
  Observe degree, priority and place:
          . . . O, when degree is shak'd,
  Which is the ladder to all high designs,
  The enterprise is sick! . . .
  Take but degree away, untune that string,
  And hark, what discord follows!
  Then every thing includes itself in power,
  Power into will, will into appetite;
  And appetite, a universal wolf,
  So doubly seconded with will and power,
  Must make perforce an universal prey,
  And last eat up himself.'

Again through the mouth of Ulysses he tells himself (Achilles now) that he can beat Jonson and all the other dramatists who are writing for the boy-actors if only he will pull himself together:

[1] Thersites in the play says 'Now are they clapper-clawing one another.'

'One touch of nature makes the whole world kin,
That all with one consent praise new-born gawds . . .
The present eye praises the present object:
Then marvel not, thou great and complete man,
That all the Greeks begin to worship Ajax;
Since things in motion sooner catch the eye
Than what not stirs. The cry went once on thee,
And still it might, and yet it may again,
If thou wouldst not entomb thyself alive,
And case thy reputation in thy tent . . .
The fool slides o'er the ice that you should break.'

Then it is Patroclus who advises Achilles (Shakespeare):

'Those wounds heal ill that men do give themselves.'

And, as Achilles, the poet mourns the fact that

'greatness, once fall'n out with fortune,
Must fall out with men too . . .
And not a man, for being simply man,
Hath any honour, but honour for those honours
That are without him, as places, riches, and favour,
Prizes of accident as oft as merit.'

Another mouthpiece of Shakespeare in his bitterest mood
is Thersites, who spits impartially at everyone. Through him
Shakespeare got rid of much of his bile and a lot of sex-nausea
that accompanied his phase of disgust with life in general.
As we have seen, he appears for a moment in the character of
Troilus, and it seems fairly certain that false Cressida is a
sketch of his bugle-eyed mistress at her worst, for Pandarus
remarks that her hair is 'somewhat darker' than Helen's,
Ulysses speaks of her wantonness, and she is as quickly faithless
to Troilus as the woman in the *Sonnets* is to the poet. But,
quite apart from his mistress, a good deal of Shakespeare's
sex-nausea at ·this date, closely connected with his cynical
attitude to the world at large, and expressed through Pandarus
and Thersites, was due to the neighbourhood in which he
lived and earned his living. The Bishop of Winchester had his
Palace between London Bridge and the Globe Theatre and
owned most of the land in that district, fattening himself on

the rents of sin; for it was a region of brothels, the women of which were known as Winchester Geese, and Pandarus refers to their 'hold-door trade' in the last lines of *Troilus and Cressida*:

'Brethren and sisters of the hold-door trade,
Some two months hence my will shall here be made:
It should be now, but that my fear is this,
Some galled goose of Winchester would hiss.
Till then I'll sweat, and seek about for eases;
And at that time bequeath you my diseases.'

A suspicion, steadily growing as they read on, that the play would not repeat the success of *Julius Cæsar*, must have amounted to conviction when Shakespeare's fellow-shareholders in the Globe reached those last lines.

All's Well That Ends Well marks the beginning of Shakespeare's recovery from his bitter mood. Another title for the play might have been *The King's Fistula*, because the plot hangs on Helena's cure of the King's disease, which was symbolic of the author's mental state. The King embodies several characteristics of Shakespeare, who probably played the part, and that his own spiritual condition caused him to dramatise the tale by Boccaccio is evident throughout. Doctors had proved useless for his complaint; they had

'worn me out
With several applications: nature and sickness
Debate it at their leisure . . .
                    and
The congregated college have concluded
That labouring art can never ransom nature
From her inaidable estate.'

Although she believes her medicine will cure him, Helena's appeal to the King is therefore frankly religious:

'He that of greatest works is finisher,
Oft does them by the weakest minister.'

'But most it is presumption in us when
The help of heaven we count the act of men.'

Lafeu also criticises the scientific view: 'They say miracles are past; and we have our philosophical persons, to make modern and familiar, things supernatural and causeless.' But Shakespeare was fully aware of the need for personal effort, since he could depend neither on prayers nor on pills:

> 'Our remedies oft in ourselves do lie
> Which we ascribe to heaven: the fated sky
> Gives us free scope; only doth backward pull
> Our slow designs when we ourselves are dull.'

There is a good deal about fathers in the play, the reason being that Shakespeare had just lost his: John Shakespeare died in September, 1601. When Helena weeps for her father, Lafeu says 'Moderate lamentation is the right of the dead; excessive grief the enemy of the living.' The King, in speaking at length of Bertram's father, is Shakespeare speaking of the old puritan with whom he had cracked jests:

> 'In his youth
> He had the wit which I can well observe
> To-day in our young lords; but they may jest
> Till their own scorn return to them unnoted
> Ere they can hide their levity in honour . . .
>   Such a man
> Might be a copy to these younger times.'

Again Shakespeare girds at the courtier-like soldier whose boasting and clothing had once imposed upon him: 'I will never trust a man again for keeping his sword clean, nor believe he can have every thing in him by wearing his apparel neatly.' He realises at last that people are what they make of themselves, not what creed, birth, titles, money, attire, and such extraneous accidents appear to make them. The Clown, the King and the braggart come to the same conclusion:

> 'If men could be contented to be what they are, there were no fear in marriage; for young Charbon the puritan and old Poysam the papist, howsome'er their hearts are severed in religion, their heads are both one.'

'Our bloods,
Of colour, weight, and heat, pour'd all together,
Would quite confound distinction . . .
honours thrive
When rather from our acts we them derive
Than our foregoers.'
'Simply the thing I am
Shall make me live.'

Shakespeare is trying hard to look on the bright side of things:
'The web of life is of a mingled yarn, good and ill together:
our virtues would be proud, if our faults whipped them not;
and our crimes would despair, if they were not cherished by
our virtues.' And therefore, since life is so difficult for everyone,
'though you are a fool and a knave, you shall eat.'

It seems indeed as if our poet were doing his utmost to excuse
the wickedness in man, his determination to forgive everybody
being due to his desire to make the best of things, because
he had recently been making the worst of things. He creates
characters that are unnecessarily treacherous for the sole
purpose of exhibiting a large toleration. 'I cannot reconcile
my heart to Bertram,' writes Dr. Johnson; 'a man noble
without generosity, and young without truth; who marries
Helena as a coward, and leaves her as a profligate: when she
is dead by his unkindness, sneaks home to a second marriage,
is accused by a woman whom he has wronged, defends himself
by falsehood, and is dismissed to happiness.' In the same way
Parolles, a wholly contemptible character, is treated with more
clemency than was Falstaff, an entirely commendable character.
The explanation is that their creator was in a state of convalescence, too weak to feel revengeful. When health was
restored he made up for this period of mildness in the last-act
hecatombs of the great tragedies, which included the good and
bad with indiscriminate impartiality.

In *Measure for Measure* the Duke's amnesty is so outrageous
that Jesus Christ would have challenged it. A few years before
it was written the Lord Chief Justice, Sir John Popham,
'played *rex* of late among whores and bawds, and persecutes
poor pretty wenches out of all pity and mercy.' Shakespeare

portrayed just such a man in Angelo, and the brothel-atmosphere of Southwark is faithfully reproduced in the play. Angelo condemns Claudio to death for the very act Shakespeare himself had committed:

> *Claudio* Thus stands it with me: upon a true contract
> I got possession of Julietta's bed:
> You know the lady; she is fast my wife,
> Save that we do the denunciation lack
> Of outward order: this we came not to,
> Only for propagation of a dower
> Remaining in the coffer of her friends,
> From whom we thought it meet to hide our love
> Till time had made them of us. But it chances
> The stealth of our most mutual entertainment
> With character too gross is writ on Juliet.
>
> *Lucio*: With child, perhaps?
>
> *Claudio*:   Unhappily, even so.

Angelo is the full-length picture of a puritan that Shakespeare had cautiously refrained from painting in *Twelfth Night*. Essex's popularity with the puritans of the City no longer mattered, so Shakespeare let himself go. Angelo

> 'scarce confesses
> That his blood flows, or that his appetite
> Is more to bread than stone: hence shall we see
> If power change purpose, what our seemers be.'

> 'a man whose blood
> Is very snow-broth; one who never feels
> The wanton strings and motions of the sense,
> But doth rebate and blunt his natural edge
> With profits of the mind, study and fast.'

Lucio describes him more compactly—'it is certain that when he makes water, his urine is congealed ice'—and declares that 'sparrows must not build in his house-eaves, because they are lecherous.' Isabella sees him, not as a puritan, but as Everyman in office:

'but man, proud man,
Drest in a little brief authority,
Most ignorant of what he's most assur'd,
His glassy essence, like an angry ape,
Plays such fantastic tricks before high heaven
As make the angels weep.'

But then Isabella herself is a puritan. 'More than our brother
is our chastity,' says she, after Angelo has promised that, if
she will go to bed with him, he will spare her brother; and when
Claudio, terrified of death, begs her to save him by giving
herself to Angelo, she screams at him

'Is't not a kind of incest, to take life
From thine own sister's shame?'

and is so revolted by his eminently reasonable request that she
wants him to be killed as quickly as possible. At the end she
even asks the Duke to spare the man who condemned her
brother to death, excusing Angelo in these terms:

'I partly think
A due sincerity govern'd his deeds,
Till he did look on me: since it is so,
Let him not die.'

This is too much for Dr. Johnson, who writes: 'I am afraid
that our Varlet Poet intended to inculcate, that women think
ill of nothing that raises the credit of their beauty, and are
ready, however virtuous, to pardon any act which they think
incited by their own charms.' Undoubtedly our Varlet Poet
intended to inculcate this; moreover our Varlet Poet was
undoubtedly right.

The Duke forgives Angelo; indeed he forgives everyone
except Lucio, who has been saying a few nasty things about the
Duke behind his back. 'Perhaps the poet intended to show,
what is too often seen, that men easily forgive wrongs which
are not committed against themselves,' remarks Dr. Johnson.
One is unwilling to contradict Johnson when he is praising
Shakespeare, but the mournful truth is that Lucio suffers
because he has been guilty of 'slandering a prince.' In this way
did Shakespeare welcome James I to the throne of England.

CHAPTER VIII

'LIFE'S FITFUL FEVER'

FEARING trouble in the country the Cecil clique wasted no time after the Queen's death, proclaiming James within six hours of it. Elizabeth had not thought much of him, informing her Council that he was a child, a fool and a coward. His wife and son despised him, and he had not been long in England before his courtiers were making little jokes about King Elizabeth being succeeded by Queen James. He spent fabulous sums on his favourites, more than his grandson Charles II spent on mistresses, but perhaps in James's case their functions were identical. A fool who is also a child and a coward is open to flattery, and the sycophants of his reign laid it on with a trowel. 'Undoubtedly your Majesty speaks by the special assistance of God's Spirit,' said Archbishop Whitgift. 'I protest my heart melteth for joy that Almighty God, of His singular mercy, hath given us such a King as since Christ's time hath not been,' said Bishop Bancroft, who naturally succeeded Whitgift as Archbishop of Canterbury. 'There hath not been since Christ's time any king or temporal monarch which hath been so learned in all literature and erudition, divine and human,' said Francis Bacon, who naturally became Lord Chancellor.

Shakespeare did not record his judgment of James, which was sensible of him, because the King promptly became the patron of his company, the members of which were henceforth known as 'the King's men.' The letters patent were issued on May 19th, 1603, *pro Laurentio Fletcher et Willielmo Shakespeare et aliis*, and gave them permission to perform plays 'as well for the recreation of our loving subjects as for our solace and pleasure when we shall think good to see them during our pleasure.' The licence was practically a carte-blanche, for it allowed them to play not only 'within their now usual house called The Globe,' plague permitting, but also 'within any town-halls or moot-halls or other convenient places in any city, university, town or borough whatsoever'; and all Justices, Mayors, Sheriffs, Constables, Headboroughs and other officers were commanded 'to aid and assist them,' which meant the end of puritan interference. The following names were included in the licence: Lawrence Fletcher, who had played before the King in Edinburgh and was therefore named first, William Shakespeare, Richard Burbage, Augustine Phillips, John Heminge, Henry Condell, William Sly, Robert Armin and Richard Cowley. The King's men became officers of the Royal Household, as Grooms of the Chamber without fee, which gave them the right, on ceremonial occasions, to wear the royal livery; red doublet, hose, and cloak adorned on the sleeve with the royal arms. Household duties were not expected of them, though in August, 1604, as we shall see, Shakespeare wasted over a fortnight playing the part of a Groom.

James's coronation was postponed owing to a violent outbreak of the plague in London. In Southwark alone 1,355 people died from it during August and September; and the King's men went on tour, visiting Ipswich, Maldon, Coventry, Shrewsbury, Bath, Cambridge, Oxford and other towns. Though crowned at Westminster on July 25th, the King put off his procession through the City until 'the angry hand of God had worked the will of His all-commanding power,' or in other words until the drainage system had taken its full toll of deaths, and went about the country creating knights, barons and earls, becoming quite popular with the earls, barons and knights he had created. From October to December he was staying with the Countess of Pembroke at Wilton, near Salisbury, and hunting in the park. On Friday, December 2nd, he witnessed a performance of *As You Like It* there.

The King's men, having finished their tour, were staying at Mortlake, where Augustine Phillips had a house. Two of their one-time associates, Will Kemp and Thomas Pope, had succumbed to the plague, and they still remained away from London, though by November the danger of infection had been much reduced. While at Mortlake they received a summons to appear before the King at Wilton. Whether this was a direct command from the King or an invitation from the Countess's son, who admired both Shakespeare and his work, we do not know; but it was probably the latter, because the Countess wrote to her son asking him to bring the King from Salisbury, where he was on a temporary visit, in order to see *As You Like It* at Wilton, adding as an inducement, 'We have the man Shakespeare with us.'[1] Evidently James enjoyed the play for the actors received thirty pounds, a large sum even allowing for the expenses of their journey. But their new patron was unlike Elizabeth in every respect: as long as he lived they were treated generously. It is also greatly in his favour that, like his son Charles I, he appreciated the plays of Shakespeare; and at some later date wrote 'with his own hand' an 'amicable' letter to the poet, which came into the possession of Sir William Davenant, who showed it to several friends. After the performance at Wilton the King's men played before James at Hampton Court and Whitehall; and on March 15th, 1604, Shakespeare with eight other members of the company took part in the 'royal entry,' walking or riding in the procession from the Tower to Westminster, dressed in their red liveries.

By this time Shakespeare was sick of the Southwark stews and the neighbouring prison, the Clink. With the reopening of the Globe in April, 1604, he crossed the river and settled in lodgings at the house of his wig-maker, one Christopher Mountjoy, a Huguenot, who lived close to the City wall, at the corner of Silver Street and Monkwell Street in Cripplegate. Mountjoy had an apprentice named Stephen Bellott, and both he and his wife were anxious that Bellott should marry their daughter Mary; so anxious indeed that Mountjoy's wife 'did solicit and entreat' Shakespeare 'to move and persuade'

[1]The authenticity of this letter, which unaccountably vanished round about 1870, is assured in the Pembroke family. I learn from Lord Herbert that his grandfather's brother had seen and handled it, and often spoke of the famous reference to Shakespeare. There was also a great-aunt, who lived into the 1920's, and who when young had seen the letter. It may seem surprising that so precious a document should have been so carelessly looked after that the precise time of its disappearance is uncertain. But it should be remembered that the care of family documents is a comparatively recent development. A century ago country gentlemen were, perhaps wisely, more concerned with their port than their papers. The original MS. of Boswell's Journal of *A Tour to the Hebrides* turned up a few years ago in an old croquet-box at Malahide Castle and the attics of country houses still yield (or did as long as Americans would buy them) rare and valuable documents. An indication of the manner in which Shakespeare's visit to Wilton was assumed in the Pembroke family is given by an extant eighteenth century catalogue of Wilton House in which the room Shakespeare had occupied is specified.

Bellott 'to effect the said marriage.' Shakespeare was quite willing, his efforts were successful, and the marriage took place in November, 1604.

This year saw the publication of *Hamlet*, 'newly imprinted and enlarged to almost as much again as it was, according to the true and perfect coppie.' A pirated edition had been issued the previous year, but the masterpiece we know first appeared in 1604. The story of *Hamlet* is an old one, and a pre-Shakespearean play on it had been performed. After the Essex tragedy, while still at odds with life, Shakespeare produced his first version, which instantly became popular. His company performed it at the Globe, in Oxford, Cambridge and other places. But it did not satisfy him. He saw that he had failed to do the subject justice, and as soon as he felt equal to the effort he started working on it again. One of the books with which he tried to solace himself during the painful period through which he had just passed was Florio's translation of Montaigne's *Essays*.[1] He could not at such a time have made a better choice. Montaigne's good humour, even temper and genial toleration were the right tonics for him, and *Hamlet* shows that he had profited from the Frenchman's sceptical outlook on life.

The play's extraordinary popularity for nearly three and a half centuries is easily explained. 'It is *we* who are Hamlet,' says Hazlitt. But if he had said 'It is we who *wish* to be Hamlet' he would have been nearer the mark; and if he had added that even Hamlet's shortcomings flatter our self-esteem, he would have hit it. Hamlet's courage appeals to the coward, his lovableness to the unlovable, his philosophising to the un-philosophical, his politeness to the unpolished, his poetical nature to the prosaic; whilst those who are resolute, normal, healthy, gregarious and practical, are delighted to find that a charming and intelligent Price can be irresolute, eccentric, morbid, unsociable and dreamy. Then, too, Hamlet appeals to the elements common to most human beings; who enjoy pretending to be what they are not, acting a part, playing up to their friends, scoring off their enemies; who see themselves as mysterious, misunderstood, victimised, alone in the world, different from those about them; who feel themselves capable

[1]His autographed copy is now in the British Museum.

of a love so deep that it can never be wholly reciprocated; who believe that they are in the right and those who disagree with them in the wrong; who are convinced that their sorrows are greater than their neighbours', their duties more burdensome, their loyalties more dependable, their reasons for self-pity more reasonable. *Hamlet* is the best example in Shakespeare's work of the author's adaptability; he was by nature all things to all men; and the play is his most characteristic tragedy, though certainly not his greatest.

Out of this welter of emotional attitudinising the biographer must restrict himself to what reveals the man behind the actor, and the first thing to note is that Shakespeare shows his own prudence in the advice Polonius gives to Laertes, which in places recalls the description of Troilus by Ulysses, though it is 'lifted' from Montaigne:

> 'Give thy thoughts no tongue,
> Nor any unproportioned thought his act.
> Be thou familiar, but by no means vulgar;
> The friends thou hast, and their adoption tried,
> Grapple them to thy soul with hoops of steel;
> But do not dull thy palm with entertainment
> Of each new-hatch'd, unfledg'd comrade. Beware
> Of entrance to a quarrel, but, being in,
> Bear't that th' opposed may beware of thee . . .
> Neither a borrower nor a lender be;
> For loan oft loses both itself and friend,
> And borrowing dulls the edge of husbandry.
> This above all: to thine own self be true,
> And it must follow, as the night the day,
> Thou canst not then be false to any man.'

Next, in Hamlet's speech to Horatio, we learn the qualities in a man that Shakespeare admired, the opening lines here quoted being a piece of self-criticism:

> 'No, let the candied tongue lick absurd pomp,
> And crook the pregnant hinges of the knee
> Where thrift may follow fawning.

> . . . thou hast been
> As one, in suffering all, that suffers nothing,
> A man that fortune's buffets and rewards
> Hast ta'en with equal thanks; and bless'd are those
> Whose blood and judgment are so well commingled
> That they are not a pipe for fortune's finger
> To sound what stop she please. Give me that man
> That is not passion's slave, and I will wear him
> In my heart's core, ay, in my heart of heart,
> As I do thee.'

The effort Shakespeare had made to live his own life, above the brawls of parties and sects, is disclosed in a remark by Rosencrantz:

> 'The single and peculiar life is bound
> With all the strength and armour of the mind
> To keep itself from noyance.'

But that he had failed to maintain his detachment is apparent in the King's

> 'O limed soul, that struggling to be free
> Art more engaged!'

and in Hamlet's

> 'But thou wouldst not think how ill all's here
> About my heart: but it is no matter:'

and again in Hamlet's last words to Horatio:

> 'O good Horatio, what a wounded name,
> Things standing thus unknown, shall live behind me.
> If thou didst ever hold me in thy heart,
> Absent thee from felicity awhile,
> And in this harsh world draw thy breath in pain,
> To tell my story.'

As an actor himself, and one whose living depended on the theatre, Shakespeare naturally took a great interest in the welfare of actors and the art of production. His thorough knowledge of the theatre is shown in every play he wrote, and such terms as 'stage,' 'scene,' 'part,' 'cue,' 'act,' 'entrance,' 'exit,' in their metaphorical as well as their professional sense, are scattered all over his writings. He was from the first, and remained to the end, a man of the theatre. In *Hamlet* his interest in stage matters is shown to the detriment of the plot. First of all there is the discussion between Hamlet and Rosencrantz on the boy-actors. Then the players arrive, Hamlet makes an elaborate criticism of a play he has once seen, and the First Player recites a long speech from it. After which Hamlet tells Polonius to see that the players are properly treated:

> *Hamlet*: Good my lord, will you see the players well bestowed? Do you hear, let them be well used; for they are the abstracts and brief chronicles of the time: after your death you were better have a bad epitaph than their ill report while you live.
>
> *Polonius*: My lord, I will use them according to their desert.
>
> *Hamlet*: God's bodikins, man, much better: use every man after his desert, and who should 'scape whipping? Use them after your own honour and dignity: the less they deserve, the more merit is in your bounty. Take them in.

A little later Hamlet holds up the drama with a lecture to the players on the art of acting, from which we realise that Shakespeare was forever drumming it into the heads of the company at the Globe that they must be (1) natural, and (2) not too natural—

> 'Speak the speech, I pray you, as I pronounced it to you, trippingly on the tongue; but if you mouth it, as many of your players do, I had as lief the town-crier spoke my lines. Nor do not saw the air too much with your hand, thus; but use all gently: for in the very torrent, tempest, and, as I may say, whirlwind of passion, you must acquire and beget a temperance that may give it smoothness. O, it offends me to the soul to hear a robustious periwig-pated fellow tear a passion to tatters, to very rags, to split the ears of the groundlings, who for the most part are capable of nothing

but inexplicable dumb-shows and noise: I would have such a fellow whipped for o'er-doing Termagant; it out-herods Herod: pray you, avoid it . . . Be not too tame neither, but let your own discretion be your tutor: suit the action to the word, the word to the action; with this special observance, that you o'er-step not the modesty of nature; for anything so overdone is from the purpose of playing, whose end, both at the first and now, was and is, to hold, as 'twere, the mirror up to nature; to show virtue her own features, scorn her own image, and the very age and body of the time his form and pressure. Now, this overdone, or come tardy off, though it make the unskilful laugh, cannot but make the judicious grieve; the censure of which one must in your allowance o'er-weigh a whole theatre of others. O, there be players that I have seen play, and heard others praise, and that highly, not to speak it profanely, that, neither having the accent of Christians nor the gait of Christian, pagan, nor man, have so strutted and bellowed that I have thought some of nature's journeymen had made men, and not made them well, they imitated humanity so abominably.'

The actor who played Hamlet was obviously not in need of this advice. He was Richard Burbage, who had risen to the front rank of tragedians in the name part of Shakespeare's *Richard III*. As he played all Shakespeare's great tragic roles, and as Shakespeare would not have been such a fool as to create them without knowing that his leading man could do full justice to them, we may safely assert that Richard Burbage was the greatest actor who ever lived. Of course he had the inestimable advantage of being rehearsed by Shakespeare; but even allowing for that, he must have been an interpretative genius of the highest order. We merely know that his movements were exquisitely graceful, that his naturalness charmed everybody, that his voice was musical enough to make commonplace poetry sound beautiful, and that when he was on the stage the audience was rapt. 'Sit in a full theatre,' reports a contemporary, 'and you will think you see so many lines drawn from the circumference of so many ears while the actor is the centre.' Though less has been recorded of him than of any great player in the history of the English stage, he must be awarded the palm of pre-eminence, for what other actor has had a Hamlet, an Othello, a Lear and a Macbeth written for him?

Shakespeare himself was seen as the Ghost in *Hamlet*, another 'kingly' role. It was considered 'the top of his performance' as an actor. More in this part than in any other we perceive his peculiar quality on the stage. He was really a born reciter; he could give the right value to every syllable. The Ghost's speeches, like those of Richard II and Henry IV, are more musical than dramatic, and in the poet's voice 'buried Denmark' would have lost none of his majesty. It may be doubted whether Shakespeare appeared in any of his later plays. We know that he was in Ben Jonson's *Sejanus* in 1603, and he may occasionally have played his old parts at the Globe or on tour when called upon to do so; but the success of *Hamlet* would have released him from the necessity of continuous acting, and his intense preoccupation with tragic themes after *Hamlet* would have made mummery extremely distasteful to him. Possibly, too, he was tired of the familiarity with which he was treated by audiences, who called the actors by their christian names, usually abbreviated, or by nicknames, and he had a low opinion of the 'groundlings.' Heywood wrote in 1635

'Mellifluous Shakespeare, whose enchanting Quill
Commanded Mirth and Passion, was but Will'

to the occupants of the pit.

With the final version of *Hamlet* Shakespeare managed to purge himself of the mental condition in which he had written the three preceding plays. He could now disentangle good from evil and see the conflict between them as a straight fight between innocence and guilt, beauty and ugliness, truth and falsehood, right and wrong. He over-simplified the issue, with the result that *Othello*, though a triumph of dramatic technique and the most fiery love-poem in the English language, lacks the quality we most closely associate with him: its chief characters are not human beings: Othello is too noble, Iago too vile.

These creatures we see moving before us are living in a hot-house, untouched by the fresh winds of heaven, unaffected by the common things of earth; they are automatons, whose energy is simply that of their master-manipulator. It may be that if he had breathed life into them the intensity of their passion would have been dissipated, used up by the exertion of living. As it is, the emotion generated in the course of the play is almost unbearable, making the murder of Desdemona horrible and unnatural, because, as Hugh Kingsmill points out, 'she is a living person strangled by a symbol.' It is curious to consider that while this terrific battle was being fought in his soul the dramatist was waiting, as Groom of the Chamber, on the Constable of Castile, then in London to ratify a treaty of peace with Spain. From the 9th to the 27th of August, 1604, Shakespeare and eleven of his fellows danced attendance on an ambassador, who was entertained with exhibitions of bear-baiting, rope-dancing, bull-baiting, tumbling, and so on. The King's men received £21 12s. for their services, which means that Shakespeare was paid at the rate of 2s. a day for being obsequious to a diplomatic dago.

Certain hints of Shakespeare's character are discernible in Othello himself, whose isolation as a black man in a white civilisation reflects Shakespeare's own isolation as an actor and a poet. This touches his pride:

> 'I fetch my life and being
> From men of royal seige . . .'

and it is made clear that Desdemona had become his wife after refusing

> 'The wealthy curled darlings of our nation.'

Once more we have the qualities Ben Jonson ·gives to Shakespeare, and Ulysses to Troilus, in

> 'The Moor is of a free and open nature,
> That thinks men honest that but seem to be so.'

Further, Othello's astonishing outburst on seeing Desdemona safe after the storm is Shakespeare's memory of some unimaginable rapture. It recalls Portia's ecstasy, and goes as far as language is capable of expressing a purely spiritual emotion, the material world ceasing to be as the words fall from a figure entranced:

> 'It gives me wonder great as my content
> To see you here before me. O my soul's joy!
>   . . . If it were now to die,
> 'Twere now to be most happy, for I fear
> My soul hath her content so absolute
> That not another comfort like to this
> Succeeds in unknown fate . . .
> I cannot speak enough of this content;
> It stops me here; it is too much of joy.'

It was Shakespeare again who had felt the physical pain of carnal desire in Othello's

>   'O thou weed,
> Who art so lovely fair and smell'st so sweet
> That the sense aches at thee . . .'

and had experienced the loss of something quite beyond valuation :

>   ' had she been true,
> If heaven would make me such another world
> Of one entire and perfect chrysolite,
> I'ld not have sold her for it.''

Finally the poet is appealing to his own biographer in some of Othello's last lines:

> 'Speak of me as I am; nothing extenuate,
> Nor set down aught in malice: then must you speak
> Of one that lov'd not wisely but too well;
> Of one not easily jealous, but, being wrought,
> Perplexed in the extreme.'[1]

Shakespeare, we recall, would not be debauched and gave the excuse of illness when asked to drinking parties. He lends

---

[1] 'Not soon provoked, nor being provoked soon calmed,' is how Ulysses describes Troilus.

this peculiarity, as it then was, to Cassio, who has 'very poor and unhappy brains for drinking,' is 'unfortunate in the infirmity,' wishes 'courtesy would invent some other custom of entertainment,' and breaks out 'O God, that men should put an enemy in their mouths to steal away their brains! that we should, with joy, pleasance, revel and applause, transform ourselves into beasts!' It is left to Iago to comment sanely on this: 'Come, come, good wine is a good familiar creature, if it be well used: exclaim no more against it.'

Iago has been a stumbling-block to critics. Coleridge talks of his 'motiveless malignity,' but malignity is motiveless. Shakespeare knew, says Hazlitt, 'that the love of power, which is another name for the love of mischief, is natural to man. He would know this as well or better than if it had been demonstrated to him by a logical diagram, merely from seeing children paddle in the dirt or kill flies for sport.' This is true, but it is not the whole truth about Iago, who is easily understood if regarded, not as an evil man, but as the incarnated spirit of evil. Much had happened to Shakespeare since his creation of the silent villain, Don John. In those days evil had been for him either an inexplicable incident in life which he disliked and dismissed (*Much Ado About Nothing*) or the effect of high spirits which he enjoyed (*Richard III*) or the natural result of oppression which he partly sympathised with (*The Merchant of Venice*) or the outcome of ambition which he understood (*King John*). Now he saw evil as a main ingredient of life, as something inherent in mankind, and the perception of this made him create a purely diabolical figure whose one object is to destroy what is simple and good, solely because it is simple and good.

> 'He hath a daily beauty in his life
> That makes me ugly,'

is the reason Iago gives for wanting to kill Cassio. True though it is, Emilia explains his disease more accurately when she says that jealous souls

> 'are not ever jealous for the cause,
> But jealous for they are jealous: 'tis a monster
> Begot upon itself, born on itself.'

Substitute 'evil' for 'jealous' and Iago becomes compre-
hensible. As if to place the point beyond dispute, Shakespeare
makes Othello look at Iago's feet to see if he is cloven-hoofed
like a devil.

Othello was performed before the King at Whitehall on
November 1st, 1604. Other plays by Shakespeare were given
before the Court that winter: *The Merry Wives of Windsor*,
Measure for Measure, *The Comedy of Errors*, *Henry V* and
The Merchant of Venice, the last of which was repeated by
command of the King. The company received £110 for performing these and two other plays. The Queen also witnessed
Love's Labour's Lost during the Christmas festivities, which were
prolonged until the middle of January, and we catch a glimpse
of how 'star' actors were treated then in a letter from Sir
William Cope to Robert Cecil:

> 'I have sent and been all this morning hunting for players,
> jugglers, and such kind of creatures, but find them hard to
> find; wherefore leaving notes for them to seek me, Burbage
> is come, and says there is no new play that the Queen hath
> not seen, but they have revived an old one called *Love's
> Labour's Lost*: which for wit and mirth, he says, will please
> her exceedingly; and this is appointed to be played to-morrow
> night at my Lord of Southampton's: unless you send a
> writ to remove the *corpus cum causa* to your house in Strand.
> Burbage is my messenger, ready attending your pleasure.'

In May, 1605, Augustine Phillips died at Mortlake, leaving
'to my fellow, William Shakespeare, a thirty shilling piece in
gold.' A pleasant token of friendship but hardly needful, for
two months later Shakespeare bought half a leasehold interest
in the corn and hay tithes of Old Stratford, Welcombe and
Bishopston, for £440, which shows that he was doing pretty
well. There was another outbreak of the plague that year and
the King's men toured; we hear of them at Oxford, Barnstaple
and Saffron Walden. While they were away London was scared
by the disclosure of the Gunpowder Plot.

Before coming to the throne James I had promised to stop
the persecution of the Roman Catholics and to make life easier
for them. For a while he did, but as the Jesuits continued their

plots after his accession he reverted to Elizabeth's policy of repression. During the period of leniency, however, one Robert Catesby, for whom no bread was better than half a loaf, determined to hurry things up. In May, 1604, he and three others, including a Yorkshire squire named Guy Fawkes, an enthusiastic Catholic who had fought for the Spaniards in Flanders, formed their plan of action, took an oath of secrecy, and received the sacrament from a Jesuit priest. Hiring a building adjoining the House of Lords, they began to mine from the cellar on December 11th, and had got half-way through the wall by March, 1605, when they learnt that a vault immediately beneath the House of Lords was to let. They rented it and stored over one and a half tons of gunpowder there, covering the barrels with coal and wood. When everything was ready they dispersed in order to obtain help for the cause after the King and parliament had been blown up. But several others were now privy to the 'deed of dreadful note,' some of whom were weak enough to ask Catesby if they might warn those of their friends, relations or fellow-Catholics who were doomed to destruction when parliament was opened by the King. Catesby was firm. For the good of the faith it was necessary that Catholics and Protestants should commence their upward journey together, though of course it was clearly understood that they would arrive at different destinations. Thereupon one conspirator, with a sickly conscience or a squeamish stomach, wrote to Lord Monteagle advising his absence from parliament. Monteagle showed the letter to Cecil (now Lord Salisbury) who decided to have the cellar beneath the Lords searched when the time was ripe. The conspirators got to know of the letter sent to Monteagle; but hearing from Fawkes, who was guarding the cellar, that nothing had been touched, Catesby went ahead with the arrangements. On November 4th the King, who had seen the letter, ordered the Lord Chamberlain to explore the building. The door of the cellar was opened by Fawkes, who explained that the large piles of faggots belonged to Thomas Percy, one of the conspirators. The name of a well-known Catholic aroused suspicion and that night a Westminster magistrate discovered the gunpowder and arrested Fawkes, who named his accomplices under the persuasion of torture. The conspirators fled when they heard that the game was up. Those who were not killed during the flight were executed.

Shakespeare took a keen interest in the story of the plot as it was unravelled at the trial. He had known Catesby from childhood and most of the others came from his native county. In London the plotters frequented the Mermaid tavern, which was kept by his friend William Johnson, and a crowd of them, disguised as a hunting-party, spent a fortnight during October at Clopton House, just outside Stratford-on-Avon. Strange though it may seem, the relief in the country over the escape of King and parliament was considerable, James himself becoming for a while quite popular. Not unmindful of the trend of public feeling, Shakespeare set the scene of his next play in the King's native country; and since the King was interested in evil spirits, and had written a book on witchcraft, he used a story in Holinshed that contained the background and the sibylline ingredients he required.

In *Othello* he had dealt with unalloyed evil as a driving-force in the universe. But this did not satisfy him: it was an artless explanation of men's actions. Moreover he was far more interested in human beings than in symbols. So he meditated on the ruling desires of men, from which evil sprang, each of the tragedies that followed *Othello* being a study of the corrupting effect of an overmastering passion; though his genius took possession of him in *King Lear* and transcended the original theme. The most obvious of these obsessions, the picturesqueness of which had appealed to him in his youth, but which he now saw as the cause of more wickedness and unhappiness than all the rest put together, was public ambition, the desire to achieve glory and to exercise power. In *Macbeth* he gives us an imaginative picture of a man of action, with the result that unimaginative critics, having observed that soldiers are not poets, cannot perceive the essential truth of the picture. Frank Harris, for example, proved to the satisfaction of many literary men that Macbeth was simply Hamlet in kilts. But then Harris would have failed to distinguish between a wolf and a spaniel because they both barked. Macbeth and Hamlet speak Shakespearean English, their resemblance ending there.

Pure evil is here embodied in the Witches, its existence in Macbeth being manifested by the spiritual degradation of ambition in its worst form: the desire for domination over others. Though a warrior who does not know the meaning of fear in battle and who rips open his enemies in the heat of action without a qualm, his conscience at first makes a coward of him:

> 'Present fears
> Are less than horrible imaginings,'

because, as his wife says, he is

> 'not without ambition, but without
> The illness should attend it;'

and she reproves him

> 'Art thou afeard
> To be the same in thine own act and valour
> As thou art in desire?'

Having 'screwed his courage to the sticking-place,' he murders the King, and is instantly smitten with remorse, though the extremity of his reaction owes a lot to Shakespeare's own nervous condition caused by insomnia:

> 'the innocent sleep.
> Sleep that knits up the ravelled sleave of care,
> The death of each day's life, sore labour's bath,
> Balm of hurt minds, great nature's second course,
> Chief nourisher in life's feast—'

and

> 'How is't with me when every noise appals me?'

The deed being done, the inevitable hardening process sets in. One man being out of the way, another must follow; the sense of security must be buttressed by butchery:

> 'To be thus is nothing;
> But to be safely thus.'

He gets two men to murder Banquo by the well-known method of playing on their resentment. The modern totalitarian state is created with the help of such men as these:

> 'I am one, my liege,
> Whom the vile blows and buffets of the world
> Have so incensed that I am reckless what
> I do to spite the world.'

> 'And I another
> So weary with disasters, tugged with fortune,
> That I would set my life on any chance,
> To mend it or be rid on't.'

Macbeth is still cautious; he is feeling his way; carelessness will come a little later, as it always does with a dictator; so he tells the murderers why he is relying on them:

> 'though I could
> With bare-fac'd power sweep him from my sight
> And bid my will avouch it, yet I must not,
> For certain friends that are both his and mine,
> Whose loves I may not drop, but wail his fall
> Whom I myself struck down.'

Like all power-maniacs, he can only see one step ahead of him, fancying that when Banquo is dead he will be happy, mentally wretched until then, careless whether the whole universe is wrecked so long as he can satisfy his single whim:

> 'But let the frame of things disjoint, both the worlds suffer,
> Ere we will eat our meal in fear, and sleep
> In the affliction of these terrible dreams
> That shake us nightly. Better be with the dead,
> Whom we, to gain our peace, have sent to peace,
> Than on the torture of the mind to lie
> In restless ecstasy. Duncan is in his grave;
> After life's fitful fever he sleeps well;
> Treason has done his worst: nor steel, nor poison,
> Malice domestic, foreign levy, nothing
> Can touch him further.'

He also believes, as so many autocrats do, that the harmful effect of evil can be rectified by more evil:

> 'Things bad begun make strong themselves by ill.'

The moment he learns that Banquo's son has escaped the
murderers, he finds that Banquo's death means nothing to him:

> 'But now I am cabin'd, cribb'd, confin'd, bound in
>   To saucy doubts and fears;'

and in his imagination, because the Witches have prophesied
that Banquo's children shall be kings, he sees Banquo's Ghost
sitting in his own seat at the banquet.

The man who rules by ruthlessness trusts nobody:

> 'There's not a one of them but in his house
>   I keep a servant fee'd':

and Macbeth has now reached a point from which he cannot
retreat:

> 'I am in blood
> Stepp'd in so far that, should I wade no more,
> Returning were as tedious as go o'er.'

This reason for his later actions, which Frank Harris thought
absurd, is one of the poet's most brilliant rays of insight. The
hardening process is almost completed, and Macbeth explains
away his early scruples, which had been due to 'the initiate fear
that wants hard use.' He will in future act promptly, his fell
purpose unshaken by 'compunctious visitings of nature':

> 'from this moment
> The very firstlings of my heart shall be
> The firstlings of my hand.'

But he remains true to type, visiting the Witches to steady his
resolution; and then, fortified by superstition, he 'makes
assurance double sure' by slaughtering the Macduff family,
so that he may 'sleep in spite of thunder.'

At the end life itself ceases to have any value for him, not
only because he has never valued the lives of others, but
because dominion over others, which must continually increase
to appease the appetite of the fool who wants it, brings no
consolation. He is fretful, regretful, weary and furious by
turns. The world is barren because he is sick at heart. He

curses the servant whose white face pictures the fear in his own breast. At one moment he feels that a final spurt of energy will bring him comfort; at the next he realises that he were better dead:

> 'I have liv'd long enough: my way of life
> Is fallen into the sear, the yellow leaf;
> And that which should accompany old age,
> As honour, love, obedience, troops of friends,
> I must not look to have; but, in their stead,
> Curses, not loud but deep, mouth-honour, breath,
> Which the poor heart would fain deny, and dare not.'

He turns to the doctor for help:

> 'Canst thou not minister to a mind diseas'd,
> Pluck from the memory a rooted sorrow,
> Raze out the written troubles of the brain,
> And with some sweet oblivious antidote
> Cleanse the stuff'd bosom of that perilous stuff
> Which weighs upon the heart?'

Spurning the doctor's drugs, he calls for his armour; wants it put on; a few seconds later wants it pulled off; he is on the see-saw of unsatisfied desire. The cry of women leaves him unmoved, though

> 'The time has been my senses would have cool'd
> To hear a night-shriek, and my fell of hair
> Would at a dismal treatise rouse and stir
> As life were in't. I have supp'd full with horrors.'

His wife's death is as meaningless as life:

> 'Out, out, brief candle!
> Life's but a walking shadow, a poor player
> That struts and frets his hour upon the stage,
> And then is heard no more; it is a tale
> Told by an idiot, full of sound and fury,
> Signifying nothing.'

Not wishing to live himself, he would welcome the end of all things:

> 'I 'gin to be a-weary of the sun,
>   And wish the estate o' the world were now undone.'

But being a soldier, not a civilian in uniform, he intends to die game:

> 'Ring the alarum-bell! Blow, wind! come, wrack!
>   At least we'll die with harness on our back.'

And, after a last pang of fear, does so:

> 'Lay on, Macduff,
>   And damned be him that first cries "Hold, enough!"'

The darkness that shrouds the soul of a human being whose peace of mind can only be procured by the death or discomfort of others is emphasised in *Macbeth* by the prevailing atmosphere of the outer world:

> 'Light thickens, and the crow
> Makes wing to the rooky wood:
> Good things of day begin to droop and drowse,
> Whiles night's black agents to their preys do rouse,'

> 'The west yet glimmers with some streaks of day:
> Now spurs the lated traveller apace
> To gain the timely inn . . . '

Except for the silly scene in England between Malcolm and Macduff, which Shakespeare presumably put in because the tragedy needed padding or because the actor playing Malcolm complained that his part was too short for a 'juvenile lead,' *Macbeth* is beyond criticism. In saying that Shakespeare did not write the soliloquy of the Porter, Coleridge merely disqualified himself as a critic: it is the most characteristically Shakespearean thing in the play, though the humour is not of his best. If the dramatist made a personal appearance, it would have been in the part of Duncan, who had 'borne his faculties so meek.' The date of *Macbeth* is fixed for us by three external circumstances. In October, 1605, just before the discovery of the

Gunpowder Plot, there were eclipses of the sun and moon. Ross refers to both Plot and eclipses:

> 'Thou seest, the heavens, as troubled with man's act,
> Threaten his bloody stage: by the clock 'tis day,
> And yet dark night strangles the travelling lamp.
> Is't night's predominance, or the day's shame,
> That darkness does the face of earth entomb,
> When living light should kiss it?'

One of the plotters, a Jesuit priest named Henry Garnett, had been partly responsible for a book entitled *The Defence of Equivocation*, which put forward the plea that persecuted Catholics were justified in lying. Hence the Porter's comment in *Macbeth*: 'Here's an equivocator, that could swear in both scales against either scale; who committed treason enough for God's sake, yet could not equivocate to heaven'. Thus *Macbeth* was written after November 5th, 1605; and it was produced before March 24th, 1606, because on that date parliament sanctioned a Bill prohibiting the use of God's name on the stage. It was probably among the ten plays seen by the Court at Whitehall between Christmas, 1605, and March, 1606, for which the King's men got one hundred pounds. James I saw them frequently in 1606. The King of Denmark was in England on a visit to his sister Queen Anne, and Shakespeare's company appeared before the royal party twice at Greenwich in July, and once at Hampton Court in August, receiving thirty pounds. The plague kept them on tour in the summer and autumn: we catch sight of them at Marlborough, Leicester, Dover, Maidstone and Oxford.

For several years, when passing through Oxford on his way to and from Stratford or when acting there, Shakespeare had stayed with John Davenant and his wife. They kept a tavern in the Cornmarket.[1] John was 'a very grave and discreet citizen,' who seldom or never laughed, a puritan 'of a melancholy disposition,' who nevertheless loved plays, particularly Shakespeare's. His wife was a very beautiful witty and vivacious woman, whose conversation was 'extremely agreeable.' They had seven children, four boys and three girls, all born between

---

[1] The Crown, now No. 3, on the east side.

the years 1600-1609. One of them, Robert, who became a clergyman, told John Aubrey that Shakespeare had given him 'a hundred kisses,' and there can be no doubt that the poet was on very familiar terms with the family. The second son, William, was born early in 1606, and had Shakespeare as a godfather. Eventually William achieved fame as a poet and dramatist, succeeded Ben Jonson as laureate, was knighted by Charles I for bravery in the Civil War, saved Milton's life at the Restoration in 1660 (Milton having saved his when he had been captured nine years previously), became a Roman Catholic, introduced scenery and women performers to the stage and the word 'operas' to the language, and was the friend of many actors who had been coached by Shakespeare. In later life Sir William Davenant confided to several friends, including Thomas Betterton the actor and Samuel Butler the author of *Hudibras*, that he was Shakespeare's natural son, and he told them a story. Shakespeare had stopped at the Davenant's on one of his journeys through Oxford and wished to see his godson, who was at school. A message was sent, and the boy started to run home, meeting on the way a clergyman who wanted to know where he was going in such haste. 'O, sir, my godfather is come to town and I am going to ask his blessing,' replied the lad. 'Hold, child, thou must not take the name of God in vain,' said the parson. We need not assume that Sir William was ignorant of his parentage, although we should have preferred to hear his mother on the subject. We know from his work that Shakespeare was extremely susceptible to the charm of pretty women who happened to be witty. We also know that William Davenant was the only child in the family who inherited his mother's conversational ability. Further, Davenant had just the amount of talent we should expect from one whose father was a genius, the record of great men's sons showing a considerable declension of similar gifts. Finally, Davenant committed the essentially filial crime of botching some of Shakespeare's plays, with the object of popularising them after the Restoration.

Conceivably the birth of this natural son prompted Shakespeare to create the bastard Edmund in *King Lear* (1606). Edmund's mother was 'fair' and provided 'good sport at his making,' while his legitimate brother advises 'commit not with man's sworn spouse,' and sums up:

> 'The gods are just, and of our pleasant vices
> Make instruments to plague us.'

At any rate it seems to have struck Shakespeare that an illegally begotten child might owe his characteristics to social censure.

The story of *King Lear* is in Holinshed, its period being heathen; but in a play called *King Leir and his Three Daughters*, performed in 1594, the setting is Christian. Owing to the recent Bill in parliament Shakespeare returned to the earlier period, his Lear swearing by Jupiter, Apollo, Juno, and so on. The late eclipses of the sun and moon are brought in, both for the purpose of laughing at astrological superstitions and to emphasise the non-Christian character of the play; though the dramatist is in two minds on the subject, making Kent, one of his mouthpieces, say

> 'It is the stars,
> The stars above, govern our conditions.'

There is an unmistakable reference to the condition of King James's Court, of which Shakespeare had been seeing more than enough. The visit of the Danish monarch had been celebrated with such a riot of drunkenness and fornication that even Sir John Harrington was shocked: 'The sports began each day in such manner and such sort as well nigh persuaded me of Mahomet's paradise.' Men who had once refused to taste good liquor now 'wallow in beastly delights. The ladies abandon their sobriety, and are seen to roll about in intoxication,' the lower hall being invaded by 'sick and spewing' females. The King of Denmark had to be carried to bed. 'I ne'er did see such lack of good order, discretion and sobriety . . . we are going on as if the Devil was contriving every man should blow up himself by riot, excess and devastation of time and temperance. The great ladies do go well masked, it be the only show of their modesty.' Shakespeare had witnessed these scenes of debauchery at Greenwich and Hampton Court, and makes Goneril describe them:

'Men so disorder'd, so debosh'd, and bold,
That this our court, infected with their manners,
Shows like a riotous inn: epicurism and lust
Make it more like a tavern or a brothel
Than a grac'd palace. The shame itself doth speak
For instant remedy.'

One more detail from the outside world may be noted: Shakespeare had just been with his company to Dover, their third visit, had looked down from the tallest cliff, and had been sufficiently impressed with what he saw to describe it in the play.

The particular obsession he intended to grapple with in *King Lear* was greed, the commonest and most bestial of human passions, with its attendant callousness and ingratitude. But his imagination ran away with him, and in the finished play the whole tragedy of life lay revealed, its meaning clarified, its consolation imparted. The main theme, as it developed in his mind, is concisely set forth by Hugh Kingsmill:

'The question which Shakespeare confronted in *Lear* was the loneliness of man, the final question, to which the family, the nation, and God are the imperfect answers framed by the mass of men as substitutes for their deepest desire, the perfect love of two individuals . . .

'Lear's sin was the selfishness and vanity in which his desire for love had been entangled. The greater sin of his enemies was that they had ceased to feel their isolation in life, or, rather, cherished it, and saw in love a menace to the power based on their isolation.

'The last truth which those who love men learn about their fellow-creatures is the first and only truth which the majority of men trouble to master. What his youthful contemporaries in Stratford already knew before he left them, that self-interest is the directing force of most men, is the truth which Shakespeare fully felt only when he made Lear break his heart against it. Lear's daughters are the custodians of the social system, Their rejection of him is the rejection of passion by organised self-interest . . .'[1]

[1] 'The return of William Shakespeare' 1929.

The Fool, whose comments are the only promptings to sanity
the demented King hears with patience because they come
from a fool, puts the matter thus:

> 'That sir which serves and seeks for gain,
>   And follows but for form,
> Will pack when it begins to rain,
>   And leave thee in the storm.'

Shakespeare believes that man is at the mercy of Fate, and
makes Gloucester say:

> 'As flies to wanton boys, are we to the gods;
>   They kill us for their sport.'

But this does not dishearten him, and it is Gloucester who
agrees with the ultimate verdict:

> 'Men must endure
> Their going hence, even as their coming hither:
> Ripeness is all.'

Whether evil comes directly from the gods or through their
human instruments does not matter; what does matter is that
good may be the fruit of evil, for suffering, by releasing
sympathy, creates understanding. It is always the ingenuous
and the innocent who suffer, partly from their thoughtlessness,
partly from their trustfulness. Lear believes his wicked
daughters; Gloucester believes his wicked son; Edgar believes
his wicked brother: all are 'more sinned against than sinning.'
The nature of each

> 'is so far from doing harms
> That he suspects none;'

but Regan's hard saying is true of all:

> 'O, sir, to wilful men
> The injuries that they themselves procure
> Must be their schoolmasters.'

Because Lear is innocent of anything worse than vanity,
demanding as a right the love that can only be freely given,
he imagines the Creator as a sort of super-Lear:

> 'O heavens,
> If you do love old men, if your sweet sway
> Allow obedience, if yourselves are old,
> Make it your cause; send down, and take my part!'

But his own plight soon forces him to rise above himself, and for the first time he sees that others are more to be pitied than he:

> 'Poor naked wretches, wheresoe'er you are
> That bide the pelting of this pitiless storm,
> How shall your houseless heads and unfed sides,
> Your loop'd and window'd raggedness, defend you
> From seasons such as these? O, I have ta'en
> Too little care of this! Take physic, pomp;
> Expose thyself to feel what wretches feel,
> That thou mayst shake the superflux to them,
> And show the heavens more just.'

Gloucester loses his eyes, and gains a similar vision:

> 'that I am wretched
> Makes thee the happier: heavens, deal so still!
> Let the superfluous and lust-dieted man,
> That slaves your ordinance, that will not see
> Because he doth not feel, feel your power quickly;
> So distribution should undo excess,
> And each man have enough.'

By awaking pity, suffering arouses perception, and Lear realises that human beings are at the mercy of knaves, hypocrites and fools:

> 'A man may see how this world goes with no eyes. Look with thine ears: see how yond justice rails upon yond simple thief. Hark, in thine ear: change places, and, handy-dandy, which is the justice, which is the thief? . . . a dog's obeyed in office.'

> 'Thou rascal beadle, hold thy bloody hand!
> Why dost thou lash that whore? Strip thine own back;
> Thou hotly lust'st to use her in that kind
> For which thou whipp'st her. The usurer hangs the
> cozener,

> Through tatter'd clothes small vices do appear;
> Robes and furr'd gowns hide all. Plate sin with gold,
> And the strong lance of justice hurtless breaks;
> Arm it in rags, a pigmy's straw doth pierce it.
>   . . . Get thee glass eyes,
> And, like a scurvy politician, seem
> To see the things thou dost not.'

Yet such is the nature of things, and the 'poor, bare, forked animal' man must endure them as well as he can:

> 'Thou must be patient; we came crying hither:
> Thou know'st the first time that we smell the air
> We waul and cry . . .
> When we are born, we cry that we are come
> To this great stage of fools.'

When at last, purged of vanity, he sees Cordelia again, his humility is that of a child:

> 'I am a very foolish fond old man,
> Fourscore and upward, not an hour more or less;
> And, to deal plainly,
> I fear I am not in my perfect mind . . .
> If you have poison for me, I will drink it . . .
> Pray you now, forget and forgive . . .'

Later, the old man finds happiness in the prospect of imprisonment with Cordelia; and so fervid is Shakespeare's religious feeling at this moment, expressing in one sentence the desire of the mystic, that he forgets the act of parliament forbidding the mention of God on the stage:

> 'Come, let's away to prison;
> We two alone will sing like birds i' the cage:
> When thou dost ask me blessing, I'll kneel down,
> And ask of thee forgiveness: so we'll live,
> And pray, and sing, and tell old tales, and laugh
> At gilded butterflies, and hear poor rogues
> Talk of court news; and we'll talk with them too,
> Who loses and who wins; who's in, who's out;

> And take upon's the mystery of things,
> As if we were God's spies: and we'll wear out,
> In a wall'd prison, packs and sects of great ones
> That ebb and flow by the moon.'

In spite of all that man may have to undergo, Shakespeare knows that life is worth the anguish of living:

> 'O, our lives' sweetness:
>   That we the pain of death would hourly die
>   Rather than die at once!'

though he is aware that no one who has been freed from suffering will embrace it again for the sake of life:

> 'Vex not his ghost: O, let him pass! he hates him
> That would upon the rack of this tough world
> Stretch him out longer.'

King Lear, the most passionate expression of the human spirit in poetry, was performed before James I at Whitehall on December 26th, 1606. We are not told what the leering King and his lewd Court thought of Shakespeare's contribution to the Christmas junketings.

CHAPTER IX

GREEKS AND ROMANS

THE King's men put on nine plays at Whitehall in the winter of 1606-7, earning £90, and Shakespeare saw rather more of Court life than he could stomach after *Lear*. The extravagance, debauchery and sexual promiscuity in the Palace caused a public scandal. The royal servants, who went wageless while money was thrown away on futile favourites, mobbed the Lord Treasurer, demanding their dues; and the King was forced to promise Parliament that he would turn over a new leaf. But no sooner had he done so than a new favourite popped up, a pretty youth from Scotland named Robert Carr, whose brogue delighted the courtiers (whom it paid to be delighted) and who was given a lesson in Latin every morning by the King; so it was said. In time Carr became Groom of the Bedchamber (£600 a year), managed to collect some £200,000 in cash and jewels, was created a knight, earned in addition about £19,000 a year, and was doing so well that even Robert Cecil, Lord Salisbury, jibbed. The King had given a handsome estate to Cecil, who was therefore on shaky ground; but when in a moment of infatuation James presented Carr with £20,000 Cecil placed four tables in a room through which the King had to pass, with £5,000 in silver on each table. James was staggered, never having seen so much money before, and asked Cecil why it was there. Cecil gently replied that it was the sum he had given to Carr. 'Swounds, man, but five thousand should serve his turn!' exclaimed the King. Information as to whether the balance of £15,000 went to swell the Salisbury estate is lacking.

Some months before Carr had reached these glittering heights, Shakespeare wrote *Timon of Athens*, in which parasitism, gorging, swilling, whoring, and other Court pastimes, are placed in an unfavourable light. The fact that he could no longer make dramatic use of names from the Christian mythology sent him back to Greece and Rome for his next group of plays; but in any case it was safer to deliver a general attack on human bestiality in a remote setting. The venom, bitterness and raving animosity of the attack make it certain that Shakespeare was mentally unbalanced when he wrote it. Interesting biographically, the play is negligible as art; it is as if the sediment in *King Lear* had come to the top and spilt over. We need not feel surprise that the author of *Lear* should have broken down after that stupendous effort. Any one of his great tragedies would have been sufficient to kill any other poet, had any other poet been capable of the emotional blaze in which *Hamlet*, *Othello*, *Macbeth* and *King Lear* were generated. The most astounding thing in the history of literature is that Shakespeare somehow contrived to pull himself together after this breakdown and write another masterpiece, *Antony and Cleopatra*, which, alone, would have given him the crown of poetry.

But the collapse was extremely grave, and there are places in *Timon* where he gibbers. The disgust he felt for the Court could not of itself have been responsible for the tone of *Timon*. Men of genius do not go crazy because society is misbehaving itself or the social system is out of gear. If they did, every man of genius would have to be locked up. We owe *Timon* primarily to its author's personal feelings, which were naturally conditioned by his observation of the outside world. Timon's hatred reflects Shakespeare's self-dissatisfaction; he had been too servile; he had 'crooked the pregnant hinges of the knee'; and so prickly was his conscience that he now felt ashamed even of his juvenile dedications. In the opening scene of *Timon* we get this:

> *Painter*: You are rapt, in some work, some dedication
> To the great lord.
> *Poet*:   A thing slipped idly from me.
> Our poesy is as a gum, which oozes
> From whence 'tis nourished.

And in the last act the Poet says that he will tell Timon 'of an intent that's coming toward him,' just as Shakespeare had told Southampton in the *Venus and Adonis* dedication that he intended to honour him 'with some graver labour.' The Painter replies: 'To promise is most courtly and fashionable: performance is a kind of will or testament which argues a great sickness in his judgment that makes it.' A little later Shakespeare is ironical at his own expense in Timon's remark to the Poet:

> 'Why, thy verse swells with stuff so fine and smooth
> That thou art even natural in thine art.'

He was sick of hearing that his writing was 'natural,' the implication usually being that he was unscholarly and could turn out his stuff by the yard without stopping to think. He had become accustomed to being patronised by Ben Jonson, but it was annoying to hear the younger generation taking the same line. One of them Francis Beaumont, condescended in this fashion:

> 'Here I would let slip,
> If I had any in me, scholarship,
> And from my learning keep these lines as clear
> As Shakespeare's best are, which our heirs shall hear
> Preachers apt to their auditors to show
> How far sometimes a mortal man may go
> By the dim light of Nature.'

A man only realises that he is extraordinary when he compares himself with ordinary men. Shakespeare was not conceited by nature, but he must have known by the time he wrote *Hamlet* that peers and politicians, the Southamptons and Cecils of life, were for the most part imbeciles and humbugs, while he was—well, Shakespeare. The recollection of the amount of time and polite attention he had been compelled to give such men, whose patronage spelt both security and comfort to a player, was a constant source of irritation and resentment; while the delicacy with which he had treated the feelings of others, the constant adapting of himself to his company, the continual strain of being pleasant and amusing when he did not feel equal to it, of doing things that bored him because he was too considerate to complain: the memory of all this must have exasperated him beyond endurance when feeling utterly played out after the unparalleled struggle that ended with *Lear*, and when, longing for rest and sympathy, he found instead that he was still expected to run after fools, to be tactful, generous, genial, adaptable, self-effacing, and so on. His hypersensitive soul rose in revolt, and *Timon* was the result. He had wasted the riches of his nature on a harsh, ungrateful and indifferent world; and the virulence of his invective was in proportion to the liberality of his disposition.

Greed, ingratitude, callousness, which had become subsidiary components of *Lear*, are the principal elements in *Timon*; but never having felt greed and its offshoots within himself, Shakespeare could not show the process whereby they degraded character, and contented himself with exhibiting and denouncing them. 'Men shut their doors against a setting sun' is the text from which he preaches, or rather curses, and he arrives at the conclusion that

> 'The strain of man's bred out
> Into baboon and monkey,'

which is not Darwin's conception of evolution. He hits out in every direction, and though mankind is the object of his wrath, his aim improves when he deals with a section of it. The simple soldier, Alcibiades, sees the truth about the politicians of every age and country, men in whom 'policy sits above conscience':

> 'I have kept back their foes,
> While they have held their money and let out
> Their coin upon large interest, I myself
> Rich only in large hurts:'

and he decides:

> ' 'Tis honour with most lands to be at odds.'

One detail in the play shows clearly that Shakespeare was not in command of himself even while he was writing sanely. He allows one of these despicable politicians to define the virtue he most admired in a man, the virtue that Hamlet sees in Horatio, that Timon lacks and Shakespeare envied:

> 'He's truly valiant that can wisely suffer·
> The worst that man can breathe, and make his wrongs
> His outsides, to wear them like his raiment, carelessly,
> And ne'er prefer his injuries to his heart,
> To bring it into danger.'

Timon's imprecations are so widely distributed that their general effect is comical, as a person in a perpetual rage is comical. He actually anathematises the man who defames everybody, Apemantus, though he shows a soft side here, sincerely wishing that Apemantus were better: 'Would thou wert clean enough to spit upon!' Timon's loathing of the world is frequently expressed in sexual images, and his pre-occupation with venereal diseases would seem excessive in one who does not appear to have been libidinous if we did not remember an earlier play; but the disgust that was a feature of *Troilus and Cressida* has become a scream of hate in *Timon of Athens*:

> 'Of man and beast the infinite malady
> Crust you quite o'er!

> 'To general filths
> Convert o' the instant green virginity.'

> 'Lust and liberty
> Creep in the minds and marrows of our youth.'

> 'Itches, blains,
> Sow all the Athenian bosoms, and their crop
> Be general leprosy!'

Timon warns Alcibiades that his companion Phyrnia 'hath in her more destruction than thy sword,' and advises another lady present

> 'Be a whore still: they love thee not that use thee;
> Give them diseases, leaving with thee their lust.
> Make use of thy salt hours: season the slaves
> For tubs and baths; bring down rose-cheek'd youth
> To the tub-fast and the diet.'

Both the women are a little short with him until he gives them gold, when they are anxious to hear more and he is willing to oblige:

> 'down with the nose,
> Down with it flat; take the bridge right away . . .
> make curl'd-pate ruffians bald;

> And let the unscarr'd braggarts of the war
> Derive some pain from you: plague all;
> That your activity may defeat and quell
> The source of all erection. There's more gold:
> Do you damn others, and let this damn you,
> And ditches grave you all!'

It was perhaps as well for Shakespeare that in June, 1607, his daughter Susanna married Dr. John Hall, a physician with a large practice in and around Stratford-on-Avon. If the poet was in need of medical advice and attendance when he went home, he would have had the best procurable from his son-in-law. There is indirect evidence, in a tragedy he tinkered with at this period, that Hall saved his life, though he may have over-valued the doctor's ministrations. No doubt his companions at the Globe wanted a new play from him, *Timon* having 'failed to attract.' He did not feel equal to it, but agreed to revise someone else's work and put his name to it. The play they brought to him, *Pericles*, was a feeble performance, and as he was in a feeble condition he could not make much of it. We see signs of his workmanship here and there, but little need detain us. His mood during convalescence is conveyed in these lines:

> 'Why should this change of thoughts,
> The sad companion, dull-eyed melancholy,
> Be my so us'd a guest as not an hour,
> In the day's glorious walk, or peaceful night,
> The tomb where grief should sleep, can breed me quiet?'

His rather childish belief in his son-in-law's skill is suggested by:

> 'Death may usurp a nature many hours,
> And yet the fire of life kindle again
> The o'erpressed spirits;'

and by

> 'Reverend sir,
> The gods can have no mortal officer
> More like a god than you.'

Doubtless the brothel scenes attracted him in his then frame of mind, and perhaps he touched them up; while his authentic voice, speaking in accents that recall the transports of Portia and Othello, comes to us in:

> 'O Helicanus, strike me, honour'd sir;
> Give me a gash, put me to present pain;
> Lest this great sea of joys rushing upon me
> O'erbear the shores of my mortality,
> And drown me with their sweetness:'

and in

> 'no more, you gods! your present kindness
> Makes my past miseries sports: you shall do well,
> That on the touching of her lips I may
> Melt, and no more be seen.'

Perhaps these bursts of peace and happiness, which are those of a weak man regaining his strength, were due to a sudden realisation that his recovery was certain and to a fresh revelation of the world's beauty.

Driven from London by the plague, Shakespeare's company visited the provinces in the summer of 1607. Marlborough, Barnstaple, Dunwich, Cambridge and Oxford saw them, and of course other places of which we have no record. The King's men were not the only actors who performed his works that year, and if at all capable of pleasure he would have heard with some amusement and satisfaction that in September *Hamlet* was given on board the East Indiaman *Dragon* at Sierra Leone for the entertainment of four negro visitors. Later in the same month the crew acted *Richard II*; but they preferred *Hamlet*, which they repeated the following March. Their captain, Hawkins, permitted such innocent recreations 'to keep my people from idleness and unlawful games or sleep.'

While the *Dragon* was sailing eastwards, Shakespeare's imagination was soaring in much the same direction. By a miracle he temporarily recovered from the mental and physical condition in which he had written *Timon* and revised *Pericles* and produced another great tragedy, but one that has a serenity, a detachment and an opulence lacking in its predecessors;

qualities that were the result of an illness which separated him
from the spiritual turmoil wherein the others had been created.
Antony and Cleopatra stands with *Macbeth* as one of those very
rare works that entirely justify man's existence on earth, works
in which a godlike understanding is exactly balanced by a
divine sympathy, brain and heart in perfect unison. A comparison between the two is instructive. In *Macbeth* the disintegrating motive is the lust for power; in *Antony and Cleopatra*
it is the power of lust. The first means the assertion of self and
is joyless in its exercise; the second means the abandonment of
of self and is joyful in its exercise. These causes and effects are
mirrored in the atmosphere and treatment of the two plays,
Macbeth being gloomy, confined, rapid, *Antony and Cleopatra*
being cheerful, spacious, leisurely. It has often been urged that
Antony and Cleopatra is not a good stage-play because of its
numerous scene-transitions. But the truth is that Shakespeare
perfected not only his more complex poetic diction in it but
also his peculiar dramatic technique, in which the richness and
variety of life is captured by the constantly changing pageant of
characters and the sudden variations of mood, as scene follows
scene in uninterrupted succession.

In *Antony and Cleopatra* Shakespeare's intelligence kept
level with his emotion, and the effect is dazzling. It is as if, from
a golden autumnal sky, the rays of the setting sun were filling
the universe with vivid shifting colours. We owe this wealth
of beauty to reasons wholly unconnected with the historical
Antony and Cleopatra, of whom Shakespeare had read in
Plutarch long before he decided to re-create them. Indeed he
had been brooding on the subject while writing *Macbeth*:

> 'under him
> My Genius is rebuk'd, as it is said
> Mark Antony's was by Cæsar,'

remarks Macbeth of Octavius, against whom the Soothsayer
advises Antony in the later tragedy:

> 'near him thy angel
> Becomes a fear, as being owerpower'd . . .
> thy spirit
> Is all afraid to govern thee near him . . .'

And there is a remarkable parallel in the two plays, a comparison between Macbeth's lament over Duncan and Cleopatra's outburst over Antony revealing the total difference in the emotion informing each work:

> Macbeth: Had I but died an hour before this chance
> I had lived a blessed time; for, from this instant,
> There's nothing serious in mortality.
> All is but toys; renown and grace is dead,
> The wine of life is drawn, and the mere lees
> Is left this vault to brag of.

> Cleopatra: O, see my women!
> The crown o' the earth doth melt. My lord!
> O, wither'd is the garland of the war!
> The soldier's pole is fallen; young boys and girls
> Are level now with men; the odds is gone,
> And there is nothing left remarkable
> Beneath the visiting moon.

Before writing *Antony and Cleopatra* it was vital to Shakespeare that he should be able to take a detached view of his period and of his own experiences; and after his illness this vision was granted to him. The fight was behind him; life was being renewed; and he could see it all now with the eyes of one who, having passed on, looks back from rising ground to the plain where he has struggled. The brilliance of *Antony and Cleopatra* comes from Shakespeare's superacute observation of the world he had lived in; its poetry from his private life.

Nothing in the history of his time had affected him like the fall of Essex, and he gives Antony a few of that misguided nobleman's qualities: his habit of challenging opponents to single combat in order to decide a campaign; his personal popularity amongst his followers—

> 'I thank you all;
> For doughty-handed are you, and have fought
> Not as you served the cause, but as't had been
> Each man's like mine;'

his folly, which overstrained the loyalty of friends—

> 'Sir, sir, thou art so leaky
> That we must leave thee to thy sinking, for
> Thy dearest quit thee.'

But Shakespeare put far more of himself than of Essex into Antony. He it was who had

> 'become the bellows and the fan
> To cool a gipsy's lust;'

who had been 'transformed into a strumpet's fool'; who had learnt from bitter experience that

> 'when we in our viciousness grow hard—
> O misery on't!—the wise gods seel our eyes;
> In our own filth drop our clear judgments; make us
> Adore our errors; laugh at's while we strut
> To our confusion;'

and who could now murmur

> 'Unarm, Eros; the long day's task is done,
> And we must sleep.'

Shakespeare understood, having keenly felt, the awful urge of lust, knew that it could weaken a man's hold on reality and ultimately ruin him. Antony loses the battle of Actium because Cleopatra turns tail and he cannot help following her:

> 'Egypt, thou knew'st too well
> My heart was to thy rudder tied by the strings,
> And thou shouldst tow me after; o'er my spirit
> Thy full supremacy thou knew'st, and that
> Thy beck might from the bidding of the gods
> Command me.'

The first person to perceive that Cleopatra is Shakespeare's portrait of his mistress was Georg Brandes, the Danish critic. Frank Harris took the hint and developed it, took a further hint from Thomas Tyler's book on the *Sonnets* and developed that. There can be no doubt that Cleopatra is a portrait from life and very little doubt that she is identical with the 'black'

mistress of the *Sonnets*. Shakespeare's women are not quite
so wonderful as people like to think them. Desdemona,
Hermoine, and Viola are creatures of pure poetry and have an
indescribable charm; Portia and Rosalind have the attraction of
zest; and something may be said for the others; yet none of
them except Mistress Quickly is on a level with his best male
characters, the reason being that he was forced to visualise
them as played by boys. But not even the fact that 'some
squeaking Cleopatra' would 'boy the greatness' of his mistress
could prevent him from giving life to one who had got into
his blood; and Cleopatra is his greatest female creation, by far
the most amazing female creation in literature.

In the *Sonnets* the poet addresses his mistress:

> 'Whence hast thou this becoming of things ill,
> That in the very refuse of thy deeds
> There is such strength and warrantise of skill,
> That, in my mind, thy worst all best exceeds?'

Antony admonishes Cleopatra in the same key:

> 'Fie, wrangling queen,
> Whom every thing becomes, to chide, to laugh,
> To weep; whose every passion fully strives
> To make itself, in thee, fair and admir'd!'

And Enobarbus echoes Antony:

> 'Age cannot wither her, nor custom stale
> Her infinite variety; other women cloy
> The appetites they feed, but she makes hungry
> Where most she satisfies: for vilest things
> Become themselves in her, that the holy priests
> Bless her when she is riggish.'

How Shakespeare and his mistress played at pretence, each
knowing that the other was lying, we are told in sonnet 138;
while Cleopatra emphasises this aspect of their relationship:

> 'good now, play one scene
> Of excellent dissembling, and let it look
> Like perfect honour.'

That they were for ever bickering is implied in the *Sonnets*, and Antony stresses it:

> 'Now, for the love of Love and her soft hours,
>   Let's not confound the time with conference harsh.'

The darkness of Cleopatra's complexion, though the original was a Greek, matches the descriptions of Shakespeare's mistress in the *Sonnets*; in fact the only difference between the two lies in the picture of a woman by a man enslaved by passion and of the same woman by the same man emancipated from passion. He could now see her objectively, and the portrait of Cleopatra, though ruthless, glows in the splendour of his imagination.

She is certainly, as Enobarbus calls her, 'a wonderful piece of work.' She knows exactly how to play on her lover's nerves; but her instinct teaches her the right moment to work on his passions:

> 'Eternity was in our lips and eyes,
>   Bliss in our brows' bent, none our parts so poor
>   But was a race of heaven.'

>   'Your honour calls you hence;
>   Therefore be deaf to my unpitied folly,
>   And all the gods go with you! Upon your sword
>   Sit laurel victory! and smooth success
>   Be strew'd before your feet!'

His own outbursts are more spontaneous:

>   'O thou day o' the world,
>   Chain mine arm'd neck; leap thou, attire and all,
>   Through proof of harness to my heart, and there
>   Ride on the pants triumphing!'

But hers are more superb:

>   'Lord of lords!
>   O infinite virtue! com'st thou smiling from
>   The world's great snare uncaught?'

During his absence in Rome she wishes to

> 'sleep out this great gap of time
> My Antony is away,'

and acts the eternal tragi-comedy of the lonely lover:

> 'O Charmian
> Where think'st thou he is now? Stands he, or sits he?
> Or does he walk? or is he on his horse?
> O happy horse, to bear the weight of Antony!
> Do bravely, horse! for wot'st thou whom thou mov'st?
> The demi-Atlas of this earth, the arm
> And burgonet of men. He's speaking now,
> Or murmuring, "Where's my serpent of old Nile?"
> For so he calls me: now I feed myself
> With most delicious poison.'

She tries to kill time and calls for music, changes her mind the next instant and suggests a game of billiards, changing it again a moment later, her lust prompting her to an entertainment that will imaginatively appease it:

> 'Give me mine angle; we'll to the river: there,
> My music playing far off, I will betray
> Tawny-finn'd fishes; my bended hook shall pierce
> Their slimy jaws, and as I draw them up,
> I'll think them every one an Antony,
> And say "Ah, ha! you're caught." '

A messenger arrives from Rome and her first words to him contain a lascivious image:

> 'Ram thou thy fruitful tidings in mine ears,
> That long time have been barren.'

There follow two scenes which are more vivid than anything could be in real life. The messenger tells Cleopatra that Antony has married again, and the news infects the speaker:

> 'Hadst thou Narcissus in thy face, to me
> Thou wouldst appear most ugly':

but it cannot wholly taint Antony:

> 'Let him for ever go—let him not—Charmian:
> Though he be painted one way like a Gorgon,
> The other way's a Mars.'

Later she learns that Antony's new wife is shorter than herself, low-voiced and round-faced; which qualities enable her to visualise her competitor as dwarfish, dull of tongue and foolish. After Antony's death she cries:

> 'It were for me
> To throw my sceptre at the injurious gods,
> To tell them that this world did equal theirs
> Till they had stolen our jewel.'

When she realises that Octavius intends to use her merely for his own glory she prepares to die:

> 'My resolution's plac'd, and I have nothing
> Of woman in me: now from head to foot
> I am marble-constant; now the fleeting moon
> No planet is of mine.'

And with her last speech she enters the paradise of poetry:

> 'Give me my robe, put on my crown; I have
> Immortal longings in me: now no more
> The juice of Egypt's grape shall moist this lip.
> Yare, yare, good Iras; quick. Methinks I hear
> Antony call; I see him rouse himself
> To praise my noble act; I hear him mock
> The luck of Cæsar, which the gods give men
> To excuse their after wrath. Husband, I come:
> Now to that name my courage prove my title!
> I am fire and air; my other elements
> I give to baser life.'

Shakespeare's final tributes to his mistress are paid by Charmian:

> 'Now boast thee, death, in thy possession lies
> A lass unparalleled';

and by Octavius:

> 'she looks like sleep,
> As she would catch another Antony
> In her strong toil of grace.'

This recalls Bertram's description of Diana in *All's Well That Ends Well*: 'Her infinite cunning, with her modern grace,' which proves that even when Shakespeare was not portraying his mistress he could not help describing her, for Antony calls Cleopatra 'cunning past man's thought.'

Incidentally, the little we know of Shakespeare's wife rather suggests that he lifted the curtain on his home life for an instant when Enobarbus says 'Octavia is of a holy, cold and still conversation.' Menas asks, 'Who would not have his wife so?' Enobarbus replies, 'Not he that himself is not so, which is Mark Antony.'

Enobarbus represents that side of Shakespeare's nature which is not in Antony. He is the poet's intelligence commenting on the poet's emotions. There was normally a cleavage between the two, which accounts for the over-stressed remorse of Enobarbus when he deserts Antony:

> 'I am alone the villain of the earth,
> And feel I am so most . . .
>   I will go seek
> Some ditch wherein to die; the foul'st best fits
> My latter part of life.'

Was there something on Shakespeare's conscience in connection with the Essex affair? Had he allowed his brain to get the better of his heart, his prudence of his loyalty? Had he played Peter? We can only wonder.

At least two other characters in *Antony and Cleopatra* were drawn from life. Shakespeare had followed with interest the career of Sir Walter Raleigh, and had realised that between Essex (Antony) and Cecil (Octavius) the great sailor's footing in the state was insecure. Raleigh's success in the Azores during the absence of Essex, under whom he was serving, had infuriated his superior, and Shakespeare makes use of the incident:

> 'Better to leave undone than by our deed
> Acquire too high a fame when him we serve's away.'

Raleigh's position in England roughly corresponded with Pompey's in the play. Both were being robbed of their rights by a full-blooded adventurer and a cold-blooded politician. Raleigh, like Pompey, was a great sea captain; and with each of them either self-distrust or a sense of honour undermined an ambition to achieve absolute power.

But Pompey is only a sketch; whereas Octavius Cæsar is a full-length likeness of Robert Cecil, the cool, far-seeing, diplomatic, cautious, calculating machine-man, who founded a House on the security of the State. Cecil knew that he could never work in harmony with Essex, and Octavius felt the same about himself and Antony:

> 'for 't cannot be
> We shall remain in friendship, our conditions
> So differing in their acts.'

Cecil's spies kept him fully informed of the doings of Essex, as those of Octavius did of Antony:

> 'I have eyes upon him,
> And his affairs come to me on the wind.'

Cecil was unadventurous and conciliatory, like Octavius:

> 'you shall see
> How hardly I was drawn into this war;
> How calm and gentle I proceeded still
> In all my writings.'

Both had infinite patience, cared little for personal feelings, and waited on Fate:

> 'Be you not troubl'd with the time, which drives
> O'er your content these strong necessities;
> But let determin'd things to destiny
> Hold unbewail'd their way.'

Lastly, Essex and Cecil are sketched miraculously in two short sentences during the carousal on Pompey's galley, 'Be a child o' the time,' says Antony. 'Possess it, I'll make answer,' retorts Octavius, who also reproves the revellers in Cecil's preoccupied vein:

'our graver business
Frowns at this levity.'

We do not know whether *Antony and Cleopatra* was ready for the Christmas season of 1607-8 at the Court, where the King's men were much in evidence, performing thirteen plays between 26th December and 7th February at £10 a time. It was an exceptionally severe winter. The Thames was frozen over; multitudes sported on it; fires blazed on it; shops appeared on it; no highway could compete with it. Two businesses suffered from the cold; those of the watermen and the players. In spite of the distribution of 'pans of coal' about the house, people were frozen out of the roofless Globe, and the owners decided to take a theatre that would be less subject to climatic extremes. Fortunately for them the children at the Blackfriars theatre annoyed the King in March, 1608, by representing him and his favourites on the stage 'in a very strange fashion.' James dissolved their company and the Blackfriars was taken over by the Globe people. The plague prevented the King's men from acting there until the end of 1609. From July, 1608, to November, 1609, they were in the provinces. We find them at Marlborough and Coventry in 1608, at Ipswich, Hythe and New Romney in 1609, and at Whitehall for the usual Christmas festivities of 1608-9, presenting twelve plays before the King, Queen and Princes Henry and Charles, and receiving £120 for their services, with a further £40 'by way of his Majesty's reward for their private practice in the time of infection.' After 1609 there was no serious recurrence of the plague until 1625, though just enough of it to keep them for a few weeks in the provinces each summer.

The Blackfriars had a roof, and as it was more central than the Globe, and on the fashionable side of the river, it gradually displaced the Southwark theatre as the company's head-quarters. The Burbages, Shakespeare, Heminge, Condell and others had shares in the new house, which became a very profitable concern, taking nearly twice as much money as the Globe, though the number of performances given in it during the winter months, about 150, was no greater than the number given at the Globe in the summer months. Shakespeare's holding in the Blackfriars when the King's men opened there was one-sixth, and never dropped below one-seventh, whereas his holding in the Globe varied from one-eighth to one-twelfth, which shows that his affairs were prospering. Clearly it was he who paid for the burial of his youngest brother Edmund in St. Saviour's, Southwark, on 31st December, 1607, because the fee was a considerable one, twenty shillings, equivalent to about £15 before the 1939 war. Nothing is known of Edmund except that he died at the age of twenty-seven, was an actor, and had an illegitimate son, who predeceased him. With his increase of fortune Shakespeare seems to have become a little too provident. In the summer of 1608 he sued a 'gentleman' of Stratford, John Addenbroke, for a debt of £6; he obtained a verdict the following February, but in June further proceedings were 'stayed,' so he may have thought better of it. This was not the first time that he had been forced to obtain his dues by legal process. A few years earlier he had supplied one Phillip Rogers with some malt and a loan, and had brought an action for recovery of the debt. Perhaps these business men had an idea that poets could easily be imposed upon. If so, this poet disabused them of the notion.

In September, 1608, Shakespeare's mother died. It is quite likely that her death was responsible for the softer touches in the relationship between mother and son in *Coriolanus*, which the poet was working on this year, but there is not a particle of evidence to suggest that Mary Arden remotely resembled Volumnia, who is taken straight from Plutarch. One cannot imagine Mrs. John Shakespeare coining the phrase 'peace with honour,' nor advising son William

> 'I would dissemble with my nature, where
> My fortunes and my friends at stake requir'd
> I should do so in honour';

though she was quite capable of loading him

> 'With precepts that would make invincible
> The heart that conn'd them.'

Shakespeare's wife Anne had as little in common with Coriolanus's wife Virgilia as his mother had with Volumnia, and it was his general knowledge of wives and mothers that enabled him to write this:

> *Menenius*:   Is he not wounded? he was wont to come home
> wounded.
> *Virgilia*:   O, no, no, no!
> *Volumnia*:   O, he is wounded! I thank the gods for 't.

Coriolanus has been quoted by democrats to prove that Shakespeare favoured democracy and by aristocrats to prove that he favoured aristocracy, and no doubt by dictators to prove that he favoured dictatorship. It must therefore be repeated that Shakespeare was an artist: he could see all sides of a question, and could feel strongly on any particular side for as long as one of his characters was taking it, after which he could feel equally strongly on the opposite side for as long as another of his characters was taking that. Anyone who studies *Coriolanus*, according to Hazlitt, 'may save himself the trouble of reading Burke's Reflections, or Paine's Rights of Man, or the Debates in both Houses of Parliament since the French Revolution or our own. The arguments for and against aristocracy or democracy, on the privileges of the few and the claims of the many, on liberty and slavery, power and the abuse of it, peace and war, are here very ably handled, with the spirit of a poet, and the acuteness of a philosopher.'[1] Shakespeare did not, of course, love the mob: but then no one does, not even the units who comprise it. He liked Tom, Dick or Harry; not Tom, Dick *and* Harry. His feelings in this respect remained the same all his life, from his creation of Jack Cade to his creation of Coriolanus. 'The mutable, rank-scented many' were obnoxious to him; the individuals among them were his fellow creatures. In *Lear* Cornwall's servants revolt against his cruelty; Timon's servants are the only decent people in the play; and the fickle multitude in *Coriolanus* is made up of citizens who often speak common sense when they speak separately. One of them tells the truth about the wealthy

---

[1] It may indeed be confidently said that if a young man, on setting forth in the world, were to read, mark, learn, and inwardly digest *Julius Caesar*, *Macbeth*, *King Lear*, *Timon of Athens* and *Coriolanus*, he would have sufficient knowledge of men and affairs to dispense with everything that the philosophers, the historians and his own observation of life could teach him.

classes of all ages: 'The leanness that afflicts us, the object of
our misery, is as an inventory to particularise their abundance.'
The same man also tells the truth about the majority of so-
called patriots: 'Though soft-conscienced men can be content
to say it was for his country, he did it to please his mother and
to be partly proud.' Another member of the labouring class
hits another truth when he says that in peace-time men hate
one another 'because they then less need one another.'

Perhaps the only people in the play to whom the dramatist
is not conspicuously fair are the tribunes, 'the herdsmen of
the beastly plebeians.' But in order to be fair to demagogues
one would have to be taken in by them; and Shakespeare, as an
honest man, obviously disliked the tribe; he never refers to
politicians but with contempt. In passing we may note that
Act 4 contains an astonishing prevision of the British political
scene just before September, 1939.

Shakespeare, however, did not write *Coriolanus* with the
object of ridiculing the 'common cry of curs' or the wolves
who led them. He wished to depict another human obsession:
that of pride. Coriolanus

> 'disdains the shadow
> Which he treads on at noon.'

His pride is such that he scorns the praise of others and cannot
remember the name of a man who has been kind to him. He
refuses to sue the people for their votes and insults them
instead, his highhanded manner receiving this comment from
an officer: 'Now, to seem to affect the malice and displeasure
of the people is as bad as that which he dislikes, to flatter them
for their love.' Though normally against any change in the
constitution, he would sweep away customs to which he
personally objects:

> 'What custom wills, in all things should we do't,
>   The dust in antique time would lie unswept,
>   And mountainous error be too highly heap'd,
>   For truth to o'er-peer.'

One of the tribunes admonishes him:

> 'You speak o' the people,
> As if you were a god to punish, not
> A man of their infirmity.'

Having antagonised the mob, he wants to fight them all single-handed, and Cominius reasons with him:

> ' 'tis odds against arithmetic,
> And manhood is called foolery, when it stands
> Against a falling fabric.'

But 'what his breast forges, that his tongue must vent,'[1] and he would rather

> 'Follow his enemy in a fiery gulf
> Than flatter him in a bower.'

His mother begs him to be reasonable, and in his promise to speak soft words there is a hint of the poet's dislike of what he had so often had to do:

> 'Away, my disposition, and possess me
> Some harlot's spirit!
>   . . . a beggar's tongue
> Make motion through my lips, and my arm'd knees,
> Who bow'd but in my stirrup, bend like his
> That hath receiv'd an alms!'

Unlike the desire for power, the lust of the body, and greed, which Shakespeare had already dealt with, pride is not a disintegrating passion. But because it excludes sympathy it provokes enmity. Coriolanus only just escapes being torn to pieces by the mob, and is eventually murdered at the instigation of his rival, whose vanity has been pricked by his pride:

> 'If you have writ your annals true, 'tis there,
> That, like an eagle in a dove-cote, I
> Fluttered your Volscians in Corioli:
> Alone I did it! Boy!'

---

[1] Of Troilus we are told that what he thinks he shows, of Benedick that 'what his hearts thinks his tongue speaks.' And as Troilus, Benedick and Coriolanus are wholly dissimilar in character, there is not the slightest doubt that Shakespeare is describing himself.

CHAPTER X

SUNSET

SHAKESPEARE'S reputation during his lifetime was at its peak in 1609, when the *Sonnets*, which until then had only been read by friends in manuscript, were given to the world, and even an unpopular play, *Troilus and Cressida*, found a publisher. The latter was issued with a preface, the writer of which was under the impression that it had not been seen on the stage, had not been 'sullied with the smoky breath of the multitude,' as he put it; an impression he was forced to revise, because the title-page was altered and the preface omitted in a later edition. Nevertheless his error earns our gratitude, for the preface tells us what Shakespeare's contemporaries thought of his works: 'that are so framed to the life that they serve for the most common commentaries of all the actions of our lives, showing such a dexterity and power of wit, that the most displeased with plays are pleased with his comedies.' It was in 1609, too, that Shakespeare's portrait was painted by Martin Droeshout, a Flemish artist, whose son was to make such a poor job of the engraving (from the portrait) which appeared in the Folio of 1623.

If fame and financial security could have brought peace to his soul, Shakespeare would have been a happy man in 1609. But his last plays do not convince us that he found peace of mind, much though he longed for it. In one of his earliest comedies he had written:

> 'All things that are,
> Are with more spirit chased than enjoy'd';

and at the very outset of his career he had realised that achievement does not bring happiness:

> 'What win I, if I gain the thing I seek?
> A dream, a breath, a froth of fleeting joy.
> Who buys a minute's mirth to wail a week?
> Or sells eternity to get a toy?

> For one sweet grape who will the vine destroy?
>   Or what fond beggar, but to touch the crown,
>   Would with the sceptre straight be strucken down?'

But it is in human nature to continue the struggle for what one knows to be unattainable, and Shakespeare's later works are so many attempts to make real all the perfect things in life that he had failed to find: purity, innocence, flawless love, charity, self-sacrifice, spirituality and ultimate happiness. These qualities, mostly figured in the youthful heroines, who are therefore more abstract than their predecessors, he surrounds with a crowd of characters who, typifying all the opposite qualities, resemble the more objectionable human beings he has met or known; and the pictorial effect is that of a dark room filled with demons through the window of which one can see an angel in the sunlight. Shakespeare, in fact, was not himself. The wonderful resuscitation of his strength and genius that had produced *Antony and Cleopatra* had not been maintained. *Coriolanus*, though enough to immortalise any other poet, was relatively feeble, entirely lacking the glow of his greatest works; and the plays that followed were a hotch-potch of his earlier ones, of old romances and nursery stories. 'He re-entered the kingdom of dreams,' says Hugh Kingsmill, 'which the child leaves for the world of reality and to which the old and exhausted return. Fairy-tales complete existence for the young, and replace it for the old.' Wicked uncles, wrathful fathers, bad stepmothers, fairy princes and princesses, loyal servants, comic vagabonds, clowns, good and evil spirits, hobgoblins, and all the other fabulous creatures from children's books jostle one another and play their pranks in the panto-mimic settings of Shakespeare's final period. He had lost his sense of reality, though it returned in occasional flashes, and except at moments his poetry no longer flows easily: it is jerky and involved, expressive of his mental struggle.

In *Cymbeline* (1609) there are traces of *Lear*, *Othello*, and *As You Like It*, to say nothing of Holinshed, Boccaccio, and a famous fairy-tale, *Snow-white*. The general effect of the play on two intelligent critics was not quite what the author had intended. Dr. Johnson noted: 'To remark the folly of the

fiction, the absurdity of the conduct, the confusion of the
names and manners of different times, and the impossibility
of the events in any system of life, were to waste criticism upon
unresisting imbecility, upon faults too evident for detection,
and too gross for aggravation.' Bernard Shaw went to the
Lyceum production of the play during the partridge-shooting
season of 1896, and wrote: 'I confess to a difficulty in feeling
civilised just at present. Flying from the country, where the
gentlemen of England are in an ecstasy of chicken-butchering,
I return to town to find the higher wits assembled at a play
three hundred years old, in which the sensation scene exhibits
a woman waking up to find her husband reposing gorily in her
arms with his head cut off.' The biographer is more easily
satisfied. First of all he notices the curious fact that Shakespeare
refers to James the First's new favourite, Robert Carr, in
terms too preicse to be mistaken:

> 'The king he takes the babe
> To his protection, calls him Posthumus Leonatus,
> Breeds him and makes him of his bed-chamber:
> Puts to him all the learnings that his time
> Could make him the receiver of: which he took,
> As we do air, fast as 'twas minister'd,
> And in 's spring became a harvest: lived in court—
> Which rare it is to do—most prais'd, most lov'd:
> A sample to the youngest, to the more mature
> A glass that feated them, and to the graver
> A child that guided dotards . . .'

Is it possible that the poet, in his present desire to picture
perfection, was able to idealise Carr? It is possible. He was
also able to extract some comfort from the fact that his mother's
family were gentlefolk:

Lady: Who's there that knocks?
Cloten: A gentleman.
Lady: No more?
Cloten: Yes, and a gentlewoman's son.
Lady: That's more
         Than some whose tailors are as dear as yours
         Can justly boast of.

A sidelight on Shakespeare's spiritual discomfort over his worldly success is furnished by another outbreak on the corrupting influence of money, a theme in *Timon*, though he never mentions gold without˙ repulsion, from *Romeo and Juliet*—

> 'There is thy gold, worse poison to men's souls,
>   Doing more murder in this loathsome world,
>   Than these poor compounds that thou mayst not sell—'

to *Cymbeline*:

> "All gold and silver rather turn to dirt!
>   As 'tis no better reckon'd, but of those
>   Who worship dirty gods.'

He particularly detests usury:

> 'I know you are more clement than vile men,
>   Who of their broken debtors take a third,
>   A sixth, a tenth, letting them thrive again
>   On their abatement.'

But his object now is to show that all's for the best in the worst of all possible worlds; so he introduces his son-in-law in the part of a wise humane doctor, a servant who is incorruptible, a gaoler who declares 'I would we were all of one mind, and one mind good,' a monarch who says 'Pardon's the word to all,' and a hero who lets off a villain in these terms:

> 'The power that I have on you is to spare you;
>   The malice towards you to forgive you: live,
>   And deal with others better.'

This is worse than *Measure for Measure*. Rulers, gaolers and even heroes do not entertain such sentiments in real life. Shakespeare's feet were no longer on the earth.

Fortunately for his fellow-shareholders in the Globe and Blackfriars, the divorce between his intelligence and his emotions did not affect the takings. Pageantry and masques were becoming extremely popular, and sentiment was displacing sense in the theatre, as it always does when society abandons itself to cynicism and corruption. Following their long absence on tour, the King's men opened at the Blackfriars in December, 1609, and were greatly in demand at Court, performing thirteen times at Whitehall 'before Christmas and in the time of the holidays, and afterwards,' for which they were paid £130. In April, 1610, the Globe started operations, and we know that *Othello* was revived during the season there. The company were on the road again in July, and we learn of their presence at Dover, Oxford, Shrewsbury, Stafford and Sudbury.

Between his touring dates Shakespeare managed to put in a fair amount of time at Stratford in 1610. This is proved by the domestic and rustic nature of his next comedy, *The Winter's Tale*, which is rich in the recollection of his youth, replete with present pain, and ripe with his wishes for the future. 'Past and to come seems best; things present, worst,' says the Archbishop in *Henry IV*, Part 2; and Shakespeare was now feeling the truth of this far more acutely than when he wrote it. Of the past he gives us two versions. The first is the imaginative picture which advancing age likes to paint of its idyllic youth:

> 'What we chang'd
> Was innocence for innocence; we knew not
> The doctrine of ill-doing, nor dream'd
> That any did.'

The second is the reality, which Shakespeare never wholly lost touch with in his humour: 'I would there were no age between ten and three-and-twenty, or that youth would sleep out the rest; for there is nothing in between but getting wenches with child, wronging the ancientry, stealing, fighting.' Of the present he gives us a Warwickshire sheep-shearing festival, and something else so startling that we can scarcely believe it was not a record of personal feeling. Leontes is altogether too vivid to be the mere outcome of observation. When Shakespeare had tried to depict jealousy in *Othello*, he had failed to be convincing, because the human element had been submerged by the main theme, a clash between good and evil. Emilia however had seen that people are jealous for no particular reason but because it is their disposition so to be; and Shakespeare makes up for his failure in the person of Leontes, a character so

horribly true to life that we must assume its autobiographical
nature, especially when we remember its creator's present
surrender to illusion, of which there is sufficient proof in *The
Winter's Tale*. It is noteworthy that the only time his sense of
reality fully functions for more than a few phrases together in
these last plays is in the portrayal of one whose sense of reality
is in abeyance.

Having asked his wife to entreat their guest Polixenes to
remain another week with them, Leontes is madly jealous
when she succeeds, muttering to himself:

> 'Too hot, too hot!
> To mingle friendship far is mingling bloods.
> I have tremor cordis on me: my heart dances;
> But not for joy; not joy.'

His imagination supplies the evidence for which there is no
basis in fact:

> 'And many a man there is, even at this present,
> Now, while I speak this, holds his wife by the arm,
> That little thinks she has been sluic'd in 's absence
> And his pond fished by his next neighbour, by
> Sir Smile, his neighbour . . .
>   be it concluded,
> No barricado for a belly; know't;
> It will let in and out the enemy
> With bag and baggage.'

The clipped and tortuous style of Shakespeare's last plays is
exactly right for the breathless babblings of Leontes:

> 'Ha' not you seen, Camillo—
> But that's past doubt, you have, or your eye-glass
> Is thicker than a cuckold's horn—or heard—
> For to a vision so apparent rumour
> Cannot be mute—or thought—for cogitation
> Resides not in that man that does not think—
> My wife is slippery? . . .
>   Is whispering nothing?
> Is leaning cheek to cheek? is meeting noses?
> Kissing with inside lip? stopping the career

Of laughter with a sigh?—a note infallible
Of breaking honesty—horsing foot on foot?
Skulking in corners? wishing clocks more swift?
Hours, minutes? noon, midnight? and all eyes
Blind with the pin and web but theirs, theirs only,
That would unseen be wicked? is this nothing?
Why, then the world and all that's in 't is nothing;
The covering sky is nothing; Bohemia nothing;
My wife is nothing; nor nothing have these nothings,
If this be nothing.'

Insanity, insomnia, and instability are his:

'I have drunk, and seen the spider.'

'Nor night nor day no rest: it is but weakness
To bear the matter thus; mere weakness.'

'I am a feather for each wind that blows.'

The lines ache with personal suffering; and we can hardly escape the conclusion that the domestic situation in the Davenant household is partly dramatised in the Leontes-Hermione-Polixenes relationship, Leontes having the moody temperament of Davenant, Hermione the charm and vivacity of Mrs. Davenant, while Shakespeare gave his own jealousy and suffering to the Oxford puritan. 'Methinks my favour here begins to warp,' says Polixenes, and there must have been many occasions when Shakespeare felt himself unpopular in the Davenant home. Perhaps, like Polixenes, he suddenly sensed that the atmosphere was becoming unhealthy, and for the sake of Mrs. Davenant as well as himself he cleared out. He was tired; anxious to retire, to settle down as a country gentleman; as to which he tries to reassure himself in this play that a writer may be every bit as much a gentleman as one who does not work for his living:

'As you are certainly a gentleman; thereto
Clerk-like experienced, which no less adorns
Our gentry than our parents' noble names,
In whose success we are gentle.'

He wants to forget the years of toil and passion, though a memory of the plucked eyebrows of his one-time mistress strays into the text:

> 'Your brows are blacker; yet black brows, they say,
> Become some women best, so that there be not
> Too much hair there, but in a semicircle,
> Or a half-moon made with a pen,'

He would like to spend his declining days between his library and his garden. He is anxious to prepare his plays for publication, betraying the wish in a phrase:

> 'How would he look, to see his work, so noble,
> Vilely bound up?'[1]

While his love of flowers is disclosed in Perdita's poetic catalogue, which contains lines of tear-provoking loveliness:

> 'daffodils,
> That come before the swallow dares, and take
> The winds of March with beauty.'

Living in the future, he prays above all things for a male heir. His daughter Susanna had disappointed him, giving him a granddaughter in 1608. His other daughter Judith, aged twenty-five in 1610, was still unmarried, and he probably idealised her in Perdita and Miranda. His parental hopes for Judith appear in his desire to be consulted about her choice of husband:

> 'The father, all whose joy is nothing else
> But fair posterity, should hold some counsel
> In such a business;'

in his longing to see her wedded:

> 'What might I have been,
> Might I a son and daughter now have looked on,
> Such goodly things as you!'

and in his wish she should not follow his example:

---

[1] Dr. Johnson's comment: 'Thinking of his own works his mind passed naturally to the Binder. I am glad that he has no hint at an Editor.'

> 'Your honour not o'erthrown by your desires,
>   I am a friend to them and you.'

As in *Cymbeline*, everyone is forgiven; the wicked become good, the jealous man ceases to be jealous, the nagging woman ceases to nag, the poor are made rich, the exile returns home, the lost are found, the dead come to life, and everyone lives happily ever after.

The Winter's Tale was no doubt in the repertoire of the King's men by Christmas, 1610, when they appeared fifteen times before the Court at Whitehall and were paid £30 over and above their usual £10 a performance because for six weeks anterior to Christmas 'infection' had prevented them from appearing at the theatres. The Globe was going strong again in April and May, 1611; we hear of a *Macbeth* revival and of *The Winter's Tale*, the character of Autolycus impressing one member of the audience so much that he noted 'Beware of trusting feigned beggars or fawning fellows,' the thought of which probably satisfied his conscience and closed his purse whenever a deserving case was brought to his notice thereafter.

> 'The aim of all is but to nurse the life
>   With honour, wealth and ease, in waning age,'

wrote Shakespeare at a discreditably early period of growth; and he now determined to enjoy his cash and gentlehood. In 1611 he retired to Stratford and wrote his valediction, which he called *The Tempest*. Its setting was suggested by a recent occurrence. On 2nd June, 1609, some five hundred folk left England for Virginia. During a storm at sea three of the nine ships got separated from the rest and after being nearly sunk ran ashore on the coast of Bermuda. The survivors built two pinnaces, sailed away, and in September, 1610, arrived home. Their tales of what had happened lost nothing in the telling. Two narratives were published; whilst a third, by the secretary of the Virginia Company, William Strachey, did not appear until 1625, because it gave a too realistic account of the condition of Virginia. Either Shakespeare's friendship with Southampton, who was treasurer to the Virginia Company, or his friendship with Thomas Russell, whose stepson Sir Dudley

Digges was a member of the Virginia Council, enabled him to read Strachey's manuscript report, some ideas and phrases from which he used in *The Tempest*. But he is caustic about these yarn-spinners:

> 'travellers ne'er did lie,
> Though fools at home condemn 'em:'

and the tropical details merely served his imagination, giving colour to such lyrics as

> 'Full fathom five thy father lies;
>   Of his bones are coral made;
> Those are pearls that were his eyes:
>   Nothing of him that doth fade,
>   But doth suffer a sea-change
> Into something rich and strange.'

He now frankly enters fairyland; not that of *A Midsummer Night's Dream*, where the faries are spirits, but that of autumnal retrospection, where the fairies are symbols. He is surveying his life, and among other things the play is an attempt by a prematurely old man to revenge the slights he has endured in his days of adversity:

> 'At this hour
> Lie at my mercy all mine enemies,'

says Prospero, who is a rather cumbersome edition of Shakespeare as a gentleman, and who must therefore, in the poet's present mood, forgive all his enemies after he has made them feel uncomfortable:

> 'they being penitent,
> The sole drift of my purpose doth extend
> Not a frown further:'

must even dismiss their iniquities from his thoughts:

> 'Let us not burden our remembrances with
> A heaviness that's gone.'

Looking back on his career, he recognises his achievement as
an artist, and lets us know what he thinks of it. His borrowings
from others have been improved upon:

> 'On their sustaining garments not a blemish,
>   But fresher than before.'

Ariel, the shaping spirit of his imagination, tells him how he
has been served:

> 'Remember I have done thee worthy service;
>   Told thee no lies, made thee no mistakings, serv'd
>   Without grudge or grumblings.'

He admits it:

>   'so, with good life
> And observation strange, my meaner ministers
> Their several kinds have done . . .
>   Spirits, which by mine art
> I have from their confines called to enact
> My present fancies.'

He is proud of his power:

>   'graves at my command
> Have wak'd their sleepers, oped, and let 'em forth
> By my so potent art.'

And he knows that he will be sorry when he can no longer
exercise it:

> 'Why, that's my dainty Ariel! I shall miss thee;
>   But yet thou shalt have freedom.'

The character of Caliban, which seems to have mystified
many ingenious critics, is as easily explained as that of Ariel.
He is simply Shakespeare's final picture of Man, with special
reference to the brute as he appeared in the audience of the
Globe theatre.

>   It was mine art,
> When I arriv'd and heard thee, that made gape
> The pine, and let thee out,'

says the author to the 'groundlings' he has emancipated from
the muck they had wallowed in before he came:

> 'I have used thee,
> Filth as thou art, with human care; and lodg'd thee
> In mine own cell, till thou didst seek to violate
> The honour of my child:'

in other words, he had given them what they liked until they
tried to drag him down to their own level.

> 'I pitied thee,
> Took pains to make thee speak, taught thee each hour
> One thing or other . . .
> I endow'd thy purposes
> With words that made them known. But thy vile race,
> Though thou didst learn, had that in 't which good natures
> Could not abide to be with.'

He concludes that his time has been wasted:

> 'A devil, a born devil, on whose nature
> Nurture can never stick; on whom my pains,
> Humanly taken, all, all lost, quite lost;
> And as with age his body uglier grows,
> So his mind cankers.'

The brute has of course been useful; his many-headed presence
had covered the theatre's running expenses:

> 'he does make our fire,
> Fetch in our wood, and serves in offices
> That profit us.'

For this reason Shakespeare had begun by playing down to the
creature's intelligence, and Caliban complains to Prospero:

> 'When thou camest first,
> Thou strokedst me, and madest much of me; wouldst
>   give me
> Water with berries in 't; and teach me how
> To name the bigger light, and how the less,
> That burn by day and night.'

In fact the cur admits that the poet's art is of such power that everyone submits to it. But the moment another charmer comes along, one who can give him the degrading stuff his soul craves for, he quickly deserts the master who sets him tasks and worships the man who can drug him. Nevertheless Shakespeare wants to be fair to the animal, who has momentary glimpses of beauty, when asleep:

> 'and then, in dreaming,
> The clouds methought would open, and show riches
> Ready to drop upon me; that, when I wak'd,
> I cried to dream again':

and so, on a note of hope, Man is dismissed, muttering as he goes:

> 'I'll be wise hereafter,
> And seek for grace.'

There are in *The Tempest*, as in all his works, phrases of scalp-tingling beauty; but Shakespeare is tired out, nervy, and shows that he is losing interest in life by occasional hits at the throne. 'What care these roarers for the name of king?' asks the Boatswain when the waves are dashing over the ship. 'They say there's but five upon this isle: we are three of them; if th'other two be brained like us, the state totters.' says Trinculo, and it sounds like the dramatist's personal opinion of King James's Privy Council. He is sick to death of people who have panaceas for this and that, and in a single phrase he gives us his view of utopians: 'Every man shift for all the rest, and let no man take care for himself.' Miranda's cry, 'O brave new world!' is in effect ironical. Prospero's prosiness reveals Shakespeare's weariness; and it is clear that he is very much on edge:

> 'Sir, I am vex'd;
> Bear with my weakness; my old brain is troubl'd:
> Be not disturb'd with my infirmity:
> If you be pleas'd, retire into my cell,
> And there repose: a turn or two I'll walk,
> To still my beating mind.'

A sense of the futility of life is creeping over him:

> 'We are such stuff
> As dreams are made on; and our little life
> Is rounded with a sleep.'

> 'I'll break my staff,
> Bury it certain fathoms in the earth,
> And deeper than did ever plummet sound
> I'll drown my book.'

In his retirement at Stratford

> 'Every third thought shall be my grave';

his strength is 'most faint,'

> 'And my ending is despair,
> Unless I be relieved by prayer,
> Which pierces so, that it assaults
> Mercy itself, and frees all faults.'

In the words of Polonius 'he is far gone.' This is not the same man who made Mistress Quickly say to the dying Falstaff when he called upon God: 'Now I, to comfort him, bid him a' should not think of God; I hoped there was no need to trouble himself with any such thoughts yet.'

The Tempest was performed before the King and Court on November 1st, 1611. Four days later *The Winter's Tale* was seen at Whitehall. Between October and the following April the King's men appeared twenty-two times, either at Whitehall or Greenwich, *Twelfth Night* being another of their contributions. Prince Henry, heir to the throne, Prince Charles, afterwards Charles I, and Princess Elizabeth, seemed to be as enthusiastic as the King over their performances, which on this occasion brought them in £166 13s. 4d. Following a successful season at Court, at the Blackfriars and the Globe, they left London for a while, and we find them at Winchester and New Romney in the spring of 1612.

By this time Shakespeare had settled permanently at Stratford, visiting London every year, which was perhaps why he contributed with a number of other Stratfordians to the charge of prosecuting a Bill in Parliament for the repair of the highways.

On May 11th, 1612, he gave evidence at the Westminster Court of Requests in a case brought by Stephen Bellott against his father-in-law, Christopher Mountjoy. It will be remembered that Mountjoy was a wig-maker with whom Shakespeare had lodged in 1604. He may have stayed there on subsequent occasions; but actors often change their diggings between one tour and another, and Shakespeare cannot have liked Mountjoy. The interesting thing about his evidence is that at the age of forty-eight, as we should have guessed from his breakdown after *Timon* and the marked decline in power after *Antony and Cleopatra*, his memory was failing him. The Huguenot, Mountjoy, described by the elders of the French church in London as of a debauched and licentious life, had promised to pay £60 on the marriage of his daughter Mary to his apprentice Bellott, to leave her a further £200 in his Will and to furnish her with certain household goods. He had not carried out his promise and disputed the claim when his son-in-law sued him. Evidence of the negotiations preceding the marriage was indispensable, and William Shakespeare, 'of Stratford-upon-Avon gentleman of the age of forty-eight years or thereabouts,' was called as a witness. He had known plaintiff and defendant for about ten years, he said. Bellott 'did well and honestly behave himself' as apprentice to Mountjoy, and though the latter had never said in Shakespeare's hearing 'that he had got any great profit and commodity' by Bellott's service, yet he, Shakespeare, considered Bellott 'a very good and industrious servant.' Further, Mountjoy had always borne 'great goodwill and affection' towards Bellott, and Shakespeare had heard both Mountjoy and his wife frequently praise Bellott as 'a very honest fellow.' Mountjoy had suggested the marriage between Bellott and his daughter Mary, while at Mrs. Mountjoy's entreaty Shakespeare had done his best to influence Bellott 'to effect the said marriage.' Although Shakespeare could remember that Mountjoy had promised a marriage-portion with Mary, he could not remember the actual sum named, nor when it was to be paid, nor whether a legacy of £200 had been agreed upon, nor what 'implements and necessaries of household stuff' were handed over; in spite of the fact that 'they had amongst themselves many conferences' concerning the marriage. Another witness, Daniel Nicholas, declared that Shakespeare had told him, presumably at the period of the negotiations, that £50 or thereabouts was the sum promised, together with some household stuff, and had added that if Mary did not marry Bellott her father had threatened 'she should never cost him a groat.' The case was still being heard on June 19th, but Shakespeare somehow got out of giving any further evidence. It may be doubted whether the Mountjoy household provided the right atmosphere for the man who was then writing *Othello*.

Though he had retired from the stage and penned his official farewell, his fellow shareholders would not leave him alone. King James's daughter, Elizabeth, aged sixteen, was about to be married to the Elector of Palatine, a week younger than herself, and great preparations were being made for the Christmas celebrations. The general rejoicings were somewhat marred by the sudden death in November of Prince Henry, the heir to the throne, who would certainly not have embroiled England in a Civil War as did brother Charles, but the performances by the King's men were not cancelled, six plays being given at Whitehall for the King's benefit, fourteen for that of the Princess, the Elector and Prince Charles, between Christmas, 1612, and the beginning of April, 1613, including *Henry IV*, Parts I and II, *Much Ado About Nothing*, *The Tempest*, *The Winter's Tale*, *Othello* and *Julius Cæsar*. The company duly received £153 6s. 8d. for their services, the remuneration for acting before the happy pair being apparently on a lower scale than that fixed for the entertainment of Majesty. The plays were not the poet's only participation in the events of the hour. The Earl of Rutland, who took part in the annual Accession Tilt at Whitehall, wished to parade an *impresa*, which Shakespeare designed and Burbage painted, each of them receiving forty-four shillings.

There is no mention of *Henry VIII* among the dramas presented at Court that season; but as it was done at the Globe in the spring of 1613 we may be sure that the royal nuptials called it forth. What happened, obviously, was that Burbage and the rest pestered Shakespeare for a big historical play, full of the pageantry then so popular, that would take the town by storm. The story of Henry VIII seemed just right for the purpose, because a lot of patriotic piffle about Queen Elizabeth and King James could be dragged in, the theme was a showy one, royal marriages were in the air, as they had been in Bluff King Hal's day, and there was enough material in Holinshed for Shakespeare to get his teeth into. As he could do what was required on his head, but as he had no intention of toiling all through another play unaided, Shakespeare agreed to patch up and pull together someone else's work and let it pass as his own for the sake of the box office. While on the job he became interested in Queen Katherine, and Dr. Johnson was unquestionably right when he said that 'the genius of Shakespeare comes in and goes out' with her. The play is a good pot-boiler and has never failed to boil the pot since it was written. Apart from Katherine we recognise our poet's hand in several places. He cannot forget Essex, aspects of whose character reappear in Buckingham's, as when

> 'he sweat extremely,
> And something spoke in choler, ill and hasty.'

Again Shakespeare pictures his former hero as 'the mirror of all courtesy,' and this time he speaks his mind on the subject of Francis Bacon's betrayal of Essex:

> 'This from a dying man receive as certain:
> Where you are liberal of your loves and counsels
> Be sure you be not loose; for those you make friends
> And give your hearts to, when they once perceive
> The least rub in your fortunes, fall away
> Like water from ye, never found again
> But where they mean to sink ye.'[1]

We are reminded of the poet's life-long love of music:

> 'In sweet music is such art,
> Killing care and grief of heart.'

[1] In order to improve his worldly prospects, Bacon had flattered Essex, had gained his confidence, had received his patronage, had become his friend. Then, in order to improve his worldly prospects, Bacon had acted as counsel for the prosecution at the trial of Essex.

But we are not reminded of his feelings towards Queen Elizabeth. Some other dramatist is responsible for the cheap prophecies that fall from the Lord Chamberlain (speaking of Anne Bullen):

> 'who knows yet
> But from this lady may proceed a gem
> To lighten all this isle?'

and from the Duke of Suffolk:

> 'I persuade me, from her
> Will fall some blessing to this land, which shall
> In it be memorised.'

While the nauseating nonsense spoken by Cranmer about Elizabeth, ending with

> 'A most unspotted lily shall she pass
> To the ground, and all the world shall mourn her':

and about King James:

> 'Wherever the bright sun of heaven shall shine,
> His honour and the greatness of his name
> Shall be, and make new nations . . .'

must have been improvised when Shakespeare was absent from rehearsals. We know from Davenant that the putative author produced the play.

Shakespeare was still making more money that he could spend, because in March, 1613, he bought the Gatehouse[1] near the Blackfriars theatre for £140, though he promptly mortgaged it for £60 to the vendor and leased it to a friend, John Robinson, a witness to his Will. Another friend, William Johnson, the host of the Mermaid tavern in Bread Street, was one of his trustees for the purchase. It was lucky for him that all his eggs were not in one basket, for on Tuesday, June 29th, 1613, the Globe Theatre was destroyed by fire during a performance of *Henry VIII*. The play was staged in a very spectacular manner;

---

[1]The site was near what is now the entrance to Ireland Yard from St. Andrew's Hill.

so much so that a visitor thought the magnificent costumes worn by the players would shortly bring 'greatness' into contempt. When King Hal arrived in disguise at Cardinal Wolsey's house he was received with a salvo of cannon. At the performance on June 29th, the paper of a blank cartridge ignited the thatch of the building, which at first only smoked, and the audience were too much thrilled by the show to notice the danger. But the fire 'kindled inwardly and ran around like a train, consuming within less than an hour the whole house to the very ground.' The theatre was packed and there were only two narrow exits, but the audience escaped, one man having his breeches set alight, 'that would perhaps have broiled him if he had not by the benefit of a provident wit put it out with bottle ale.' Forced into the provinces by this mishap, the company went to Folkestone, Oxford, Stafford, Shrewsbury and elsewhere; but as Shakespeare was no longer with them, having retired from business, their future tours do not interest us.

He returned home. Two of his brothers had recently died, Gilbert in February, 1612, aged forty-five, and his last surviving brother Richard in February, 1613, aged thirty-nine. His sister, Joan Hart, aged forty-four, was still at the old Henley Street house, with her husband and three sons. His daughter Susanna was close by with her husband Dr. Hall and their child Elizabeth. His other daughter, Judith, not yet married, was living with her father and mother at New Place; while many other relations and many friends resided in Stratford and the neighbourhood. 'Crabbed age and youth cannot live together,' he had once written, but he seems to have remained on affectionate terms with his daughters, nephews and grand-daughter. We may picture him in these last years as stoutish, nearly bald, heavy-footed, easily tired. Good company as ever when in good form, his wit did not flow so easily as of old and had a sharper sting in it. He was often moody and morose. Long spells of silence might be followed by brief periods of slightly hysterical hilarity. One day ill and weary, the next he would seem in perfect health, mount his horse and trot along the lanes to spend a few hours with some friend or other. The abnormal sensitiveness of his youth had become, with failing strength, an excessive touchiness. Anger might suddenly flare out for no apparent reason, and kindliness give way to resentment, but the charm was still there, more welcome than ever when it operated, like the sun in winter. So much can be gleaned from the reports that have come down to us, from his later writings, and from our general knowledge of the man.

In lighter moments he amused himself with doggerel and epitaphs on friends and acquaintances. An old usurer named John Combe, who left 'Master William Shakespeare' £5 in his Will, was rewarded by the legatee with the following:

> 'Ten in the hundred the devil allows,
> But Combe will have twelve, he swears and avows;
> If any one asks who lies in this tomb,
> Oho! quoth the devil, 'tis my John-a-Combe!'

Many people have wondered why the inscription on his own grave, written by himself, is so commonplace:

> 'Good Friend, for Jesus' sake forbear,
> To dig the dust enclosed here:
> Blest be the man that spares these stones,
> And curst be he that moves my bones.'

The reason is obvious. He had seen with disgust the church charnel-house, which was filled with skulls and bones that had been dug up in the vicinity and left there to moulder, higgledy-piggledy. He did not relish the idea of his bones joining the heap, and so expressed his wish in words that would convey his meaning to simple sextons, who might have misunderstood the instructions if delivered in the language of King Lear.

Shakespeare, it is pleasant to remember, took no part in municipal affairs on his retirement, leaving the tedious mechanism of existence to tedious people, of whom there were so many, all anxious to increase the tedium of life. Some of his leisure was occupied by the preparation of his plays for publication, but his uncertain health and the drudgery of such work were too much for him. He delayed and delayed and at

last abandoned the effort, leaving the job for his fellow players. [1]
It would be interesting to know whether he ever talked of his
works to his neighbours. Almost the only memorable line in
Titus Andronicus runs: 'For when no friends are by, men praise
themselves.' He does not appear to have given much attention
to his business affairs. We know from his friends that he was
upright and frank in all his dealings—'honest' and 'gentle'
are the two adjectives most frequently used to describe his
nature—and the lines in *Pericles*:

> 'I'll take thy word for faith, not ask thine oath:
> Who shuns not to break one will sure crack both'

reveal his opinion and practice. In the controversy that resulted
from the threat by William Combe, who had inherited some of
his uncle John's estate, to enclose the common fields of
Welcombe, Shakespeare took little part, though as a freeholder
and farmer of the tithes it closely concerned him. Combe
offered to indemnify him against any loss he would suffer from
the conversion of arable land into pasture, and he accepted the
offer on his own behalf and on that of his cousin Thomas
Greene, Town Clerk of Stratford. But he cannot have taken
either the threat of enclosure or the offer seriously, because
when Greene called upon him in London late in 1614 he did
not mention the offer, merely saying that he and his son-in-law,
Dr. Hall, believed that no enclosure would be attempted.
However, Combe meant business, and Greene, back at
Stratford, wrote to tell Shakespeare what was happening. A
free fight between Combe's men and several Stratfordians who
objected to the enclosure was followed by a petition to the
Lord Chief Justice, who ruled against Combe. It then became
certain that Combe would not rest until he could get the law
on his side; and as he was elected High Sheriff of the county in

---

[1] Nineteen of his plays were published separately before the Collected Edition
appeared, these separate issues being known as Quartos. Some were pirated,
some had clearly received his supervision. They were: *Henry VI*, Parts 2 and 3,
Love's Labour's Lost, *A Midsummer Night's Dream*, *Romeo and Juliet*, *The
Merchant of Venice*, *Henry IV*, Parts 1 and 2, *Henry V*, *The Merry Wives of
Windsor*, *Much Ado About Nothing*, *Titus Andronicus*, *Richard II*, *Richard III*,
Troilus and Cressida, *Pericles*, *King Lear*, *Hamlet* and *Othello*. The remaining
eighteen plays first appeared in the Collected Edition of 1623, known as the
Folio.

1615, Shakespeare woke up to the danger, declaring that he was 'not able to bear the enclosing of Welcombe,' giving his future support to the opposition, and helping the executors of a defunct leaseholder at Welcombe to get fair play.

This was not the only thing to cause him annoyance in his last years. In 1613 his daughter Susanna Hall was slandered by a young man named John Lane, a bit of a drunkard and a violent anti-puritan, who said that she 'had been naught with Rafe Smith at John Palmer's.' Susanna's husband, Dr. Hall, prosecuted Lane in the ecclesiastical court at Worcester, and he was duly excommunicated. The following year, on Saturday, July 9th, there was a tremendous fire at Stratford, the third in the poet's lifetime. Inside two hours fifty-four dwelling-houses were destroyed, together with other valuable property, and for a while it looked as if the entire town would be consumed: New Place escaped, but as a houseowner Shakespeare cannot have watched the conflagration solely with an eye to its artistic effect.

We do not know whether he was in London for the Christmas season of 1613-14, when his company played before the King and Prince Charles sixteen times between November and February; but he was certainly there for the season of 1614-15, when the King's men appeared before James I eight times only, Prince Charles now having his own troupe of players. The Globe had just been rebuilt, with tile over the stage and top gallery instead of thatch, its shape being octagonal not circular. The new theatre was reported to be 'the fairest that ever was in England'; but the Blackfriars had become the fashionable playhouse, an Italian visitor being much impressed by the audience of noblemen 'so finely arrayed that they looked like so many princes, and listening with such silence and respect. And many honourable and fair ladies come there with perfect freedom, and take their seats amongst the men without hesitation.' All the same Shakespeare's company, with nothing fresh from his pen, were steadily losing ground. In January, 1615, a correspondent at Court wrote that the plays given by the actors were 'such poor stuff that instead of delight they send the auditory away with discontent . . . of five new plays there is not one that pleases; and therefore they are driven to publish over their old, which stand them in best stead and bring them most profit.' The long decline of the British drama had begun: its sun had set: henceforth

> 'Truth may seem, but cannot be;
> Beauty brag, but 'tis not she;
> Truth and beauty buried be.'

Shakespeare said farewell to London, where he had been so happy and so wretched, in the spring of 1615, perhaps

> 'Bearing away the wound that nothing healeth,
> The scar that will, despite of cure, remain.'

His daughter Judith was about to be married to Thomas Quyney, the son of his old friend Richard, who had died in 1602 as a result of a blow on the head while carrying out his duties as Bailiff of Stratford. Thomas was a vintner, four years younger than Judith. The ceremony was arranged for the end of January, 1616, and Shakespeare prepared his Will, which he evidently intended to sign and seal after the wedding. For many years he had been a comparatively wealthy man, earning about £200 annually, equivalent in modern purchasing power to something like £3,000 a year. In the first draft of his Will he left the estate, except for a few bequests, to his two daughters and their husbands. The Halls were to have New Place. For some obscure reason Judith's wedding did not take place before the 28th January, on and after which marriages were inhibited until April 6th. Only by obtaining an expensive special licence could people be married between those dates. Thomas and Judith did not worry about the licence, their wedding taking place on February 10th. It was reported to the ecclesiastical authorities; the Quyneys were summoned to Worcester, ignored the order, were fined 7s., forced to pay the licence-fee, and excommunicated.

Shakespeare was annoyed by these irregular proceedings, his annoyance being increased by the fact that Thomas Quyney had broken his agreement to settle £100 in land on his wife and prospective children, a provision to that effect having been made in the poet's Will. March came, and Shakespeare took to his bed with a fever. There is something significant in the fact that his son-in-law Hall made no reference to the cause of his ailment in the thousand 'Observations' noted down in the doctor's case-book. We learn from other sources that Shakespeare, Drayton and Ben Jonson 'had a merry meeting, and it seems drank too hard, for Shakespeare died of a fever there contracted.' There is nothing improbable in the story. Michael Drayton often stayed at Clifford Chambers, close to Stratford, and Ben Jonson doubtless visited New Place on several occasions. The only qualification necessary is that, in normal times, a little wine went a long way with Shakespeare, and in his present state of health two glasses, which his hard drinking probably amounted to, were one too many for him. At any rate he was so ill that he sent to Warwick for his attorney, Francis Collins, and revised his Will, from which the name of Thomas Quyney was removed and that of Judith substituted. He made several additions of note, Richard Burbage, John Heminge and Henry Condell each receiving 26s. 8d. for a memorial ring; which suggests that between the first and second drafts of the Will he had asked Heminge and Condell to edit his plays for publication and had hinted that Burbage might help them. Another addition has caused controversy: 'Item, I give unto my wife my second-best bed with the furniture.' It was an interlineation, obviously put in after he had mentioned the contents of the Will to his wife, who then asked for this particular bed. The reason she did not otherwise appear in the Will was that by common law she was entitled to the Widow's Dower: a life-interest in one-third of her husband's heritable estates, except a relatively small portion that had been legally barred from dower. She also had the right to reside at New Place for the rest of her life.

Shakespeare died on April 23rd, 1616, aged exactly fifty-two. Two days later he was buried in the chancel of the parish church, a situation to which his property, not his poetry, entitled him.

A few years later a monument by Gerard Johnson was placed above the grave. Shakespeare's old companions must have seen the work in progress, because Johnson's workshop was near the Globe theatre, but the sculptor, perhaps to please the poet's relations, laid greater stress on the gentleman than on the genius. Little need be added about his relations. His widow died in August, 1623. She wished to be buried in his grave, but no one dared to risk the curse he had thoughtfully provided for his tombstone, and she was laid by his side. Susanna Hall died in 1649; Judith Quyney in 1662, her children having predeceased her. Susanna's daughter Elizabeth was married first to Thomas Nash in 1626. He died in 1647, and two years later she married John Barnard, lord of the manor of Abingdon, who was created a baronet at the Restoration in 1661. Lady Barnard, Shakespeare's granddaughter and last descendant, died in 1670.

The second most notable event in literary history occurred at London in the autumn of 1623, when the Collected Edition of Shakespeare's works, known as the Folio, was published. The editors were Heminge and Condell, who in their Epistle to the Readers implied that the poet had been preparing his works for the press: 'It had been a thing, we confess, worthy to have been wished, that the Author himself had lived to have set forth and overseen his own writings; but since it hath been ordained otherwise, and he by death departed from that right, we pray you do not envy his friends the office of their care and pain to have collected and published them. . . . His mind and hand went together: and what he thought, he uttered with that easiness, that we have scarce received from him a blot in his papers.' The Folio was dedicated to the Earls of Pembroke and Montgomery, who were told that the editors had 'done an office to the dead, without ambition either of self-profit or fame, only to keep the memory of so worthy a Friend and Fellow alive as was our Shakespeare.' Heminge and Condell also addressed the brother Earls in this fashion: 'Since your Lordships have been pleased to think these trifles something heretofore, and have prosecuted both them and their Author living with so much favour, we hope that . . . you will use the like indulgence toward them, you have done unto their Parent.' It would have surprised the Earls of Pembroke and Montgomery if, instead of this fulsome dedication, some Webster had informed them that their only chance of being remembered was to have their names printed in a book containing 'these trifles.' However, we must not be too hard on the players, for one fears that their 'Friend and Fellow' would have approved their servility; and Ben Jonson's Ode to the 'Sweet Swan of Avon,' printed in the Folio, helps us to forget it:

> 'Soul of the Age!
> The applause! delight! the wonder of our stage!
> My Shakespeare rise! . . .
> Triumph, my Britain, thou hast one to show,
> To whom all Scenes of Europe homage owe:
> He was not of an age, but for all time!'

Among the eighteen plays published for the first time in the Folio were *Antony and Cleopatra*, *Twelfth Night* and *Macbeth*, which, together with the two parts of *Henry IV* and *King Lear*, contain a richer humour, a more exquisite beauty, a deeper wisdom, a more intense passion, and a profounder understanding of human nature, than we can find elsewhere in the world's literature.

SHAKESPEARE'S
POETRY

Note: If I had collected all my favourite passages from Shakespeare's poetry, this anthology would have been at least three times its present length. Instead, I have mostly chosen my favourite lines from my favourite passages; and what follows is for me the quintessence of his poetry.

H.P.

POEMS

Venus and Adonis

Leading him prisoner in a red-rose chain . .

By this, poor Wat, far off upon a hill,
Stands on his hinder legs with listening ear,
To hearken if his foes pursue him still:
Anon their loud alarums he doth hear;
   And now his grief may be compared well
    To one sore sick that hears the passing-bell.

Then shalt thou see the dew-bedabbled wretch
Turn, and return, indenting with the way;
Each envious briar his weary legs doth scratch,
Each shadow makes him stop, each murmur stay . . .

Love comforteth like sunshine after rain . . .

Lo, here the gentle lark, weary of rest,
From his moist cabinet mounts up on high,
And wakes the morning, from whose silver breast
The sun ariseth in his majesty;
   Who doth the world so gloriously behold,
    That cedar-tops and hills seem burnish'd gold.

The Rape of Lucrece

Bearing away the wound that nothing healeth,
The scar that will, despite of cure, remain . . .

There might you see the labouring pioneer
Begrim'd with sweat and smeared all with dust;
And from the towers of Troy there would appear
The very eyes of men through loop-holes thrust,
Gazing upon the Greeks with little lust:
   Such sweet observance in this work was had
    That one might see those far-off eyes look sad.

Sonnets

Thou art thy mother's glass, and she in thee
Calls back the lovely April of her prime:
So thou through windows of thine age shalt see,
Despite of wrinkles, this thy golden time . . .

For never-resting time leads summer on
To hideous winter and confounds him there;
Sap check'd with frost and lusty leaves quite gone,
Beauty o'ersnow'd and bareness every where . . .

Now stand you on the top of happy hours . . .

And stretched metre of an antique song . . .

But thy eternal summer shall not fade . . .

The painful warrior famoused for fight,
After a thousand victories once foil'd,
Is from the book of honour razed quite,
And all the rest forgot for which he toil'd . . .

When, in disgrace with fortune and men's eyes,
I all alone beweep my outcast state,
And trouble heaven with my bootless cries,
And look upon myself, and curse my fate,
Wishing me like to one more rich in hope,
Featur'd like him, like him with friends possess'd,
Desiring this man's art and that man's scope,
With what I most enjoy contented least . . .

When to the sessions of sweet silent thought
I summon up remembrance of things past,
I sigh the lack of many a thing I sought,
And with old woes new wail my dear time's waste:
Then can I drown an eye, unus'd to flow,
For precious friends hid in death's dateless night,
And weep afresh love's long since cancell'd woe,
And moan the expense of many a vanish'd sight . . .

Full many a glorious morning have I seen
Flatter the mountain-tops with sovereign eye,
Kissing with golden face the meadows green,
Gilding pale streams with heavenly alchemy . . .

Like as the waves make towards the pebbled shore,
So do our minutes hasten to their end . . .

                . . . when his youthful morn
Hath travell'd on to age's steepy night,
And all those beauties whereof now he's king
Are vanishing or vanish'd out of sight . . .

When I have seen the hungry ocean gain
Advantage on the kingdom of the shore . . .

Since brass, nor stone, nor earth, nor boundless sea,
But sad mortality o'er-sways their power,
How with this rage shall beauty hold a plea
Whose action is no stronger than a flower? . . .

Tired with all these, for restful death I cry,
As, to behold desert a beggar born,
And needy nothing trimm'd in jollity,
And purest faith unhappily forsworn,
And gilded honour shamefully misplac'd,
And maiden virtue rudely strumpeted,
And right perfection wrongfully disgrac'd,
And strength by limping sway disabled,
And art made tongue-tied by authority,
And folly, doctor-like, controlling skill,
And simple truth miscall'd simplicity,
And captive good attending captain ill:
    Tired with all these, from these would I be gone,
    Save that, to die, I leave my love alone.

No longer mourn for me when I am dead
Than you shall hear the surly sullen bell
Give warning to the world that I am fled
From this vile world, with vilest worms to dwell . . .

That time of year thou mayst in me behold
When yellow leaves, or none, or few, do hang
Upon those boughs which shake against the cold,
Bare ruin'd choirs, where late the sweet birds sang.
In me thou see'st the twilight of such day
As after sunset fadeth in the west;
Which by and by black night doth take away,
Death's second self, that seals up all in rest . . .

Ah, do not, when my heart hath 'scaped this sorrow,
Come in the rearward of a conquer'd woe,
Give not a windy night a rainy morrow,
To linger out a purpos'd overthrow . . .

How like a winter hath my absence been
From thee, the pleasure of the fleeting year!
What freezings have I felt, what dark days seen!
What old December's bareness every where! . . .

From you have I been absent in the spring,
When proud-pied April, dress'd in all his trim,
Hath put a spirit of youth in every thing,
That heavy Saturn laugh'd and leap'd with him.
Yet nor the lay of birds, nor the sweet smell
Of different flowers in odour and in hue,
Could make me any summer's story tell,
Or from their proud lap pluck them where they grew:
Nor did I wonder at the lily's white,
Nor praise the deep vermilion in the rose . . .

Our love was new, and then but in the spring,
When I was wont to greet it with my lays;
As Philomel in summer's front doth sing,
And stops her pipe in growth of riper days:
Not that the summer is less pleasant now
Than when her mournful hymns did hush the night
But that wild music burthens every bough,
And sweets grown common lose their dear delight . . .

When in the chronicle of wasted time
I see descriptions of the fairest wights,
And beauty making beautiful old rhyme
In praise of ladies dead and lovely knights . . .

Alas, 'tis true I have gone here and there,
And made myself a motley to the view,
Gor'd mine own thoughts, sold cheap what is most dear,
Made old offences of affections new;
Most true it is that I have look'd on truth
Askance and strangely . . .

O, for my sake do you with fortune chide,
The guilty goddess of my harmful deeds,
That did not better for my life provide
Than public means which public manners breeds.
Thence comes it that my name receives a brand,
And almost thence my nature is subdu'd
To what it works in, like the dyer's hand:
Pity me then and wish I were renew'd . . .

Nor that full star that ushers in the even
Doth half that glory to the sober west,
As those two mourning eyes become thy face . . .

Lo, as a careful housewife runs to catch
One of her feather'd creatures broke away,
Sets down her babe, and makes all swift dispatch
In pursuit of the thing she would have stay;
Whilst her neglected child holds her in chase,
Cries to catch her whose busy care is bent
To follow that which flies before her face,
Not prizing her poor infant's discontent:
So runn'st thou after that which flies from thee,
Whilst I thy babe chase thee afar behind;
But if thou catch thy hope, turn back to me,
And play the mother's part, kiss me, be kind . . .

        O, how can Love's eye be true,
That is so vex'd with watching and with tears?

HISTORIES

Henry VI, Part 3

Come, make him stand upon this molehill here,
That raught at mountains with outstretched arms,
Yet parted but the shadow with his hand.

This battle fares like to a morning's war,
When dying clouds contend with growing light,
What time the shepherd, blowing of his nails,
Can neither call it perfect day nor night . . .
Here on this molehill will I sit me down.
To whom God will, there be the victory! . . .
 O God! methinks it were a happy life,
To be no better than a homely swain;
To sit upon a hill, as I do now,
To carve out dials quaintly, point by point,
Thereby to see the minutes how they run,
How many make the hour full complete;
How many hours bring about the day;
How many days will finish up the year;
How many years a mortal man may live.
When this is known, then to divide the times:
So many hours must I tend my flock;
So many hours must I take my rest;
So many hours must I contemplate;
So many hours must I sport myself;
So many days my ewes have been with young;
So many weeks ere the the poor fools will ean;
So many years ere I shall shear the fleece:
So minutes, hours, days, months, and years,
Pass'd over to the end they were created,
Would bring white hairs unto a quiet grave.
Ah, what a life were this! how sweet! how lovely!
Gives not the hawthorn-bush a sweeter shade
To shepherds looking on their silly sheep,
Than doth a rich embroider'd canopy
To kings that fear their subjects' treachery?
O, yes, it doth; a thousand-fold it doth:
And to conclude, the shepherd's homely curds,

His cold thin drink out of his leather bottle,
His wonted sleep under a fresh tree's shade,
All which secure and sweetly he enjoys,
Is far beyond a prince's delicates,
His viands sparkling in a golden cup,
His body couched in a curious bed,
When care, mistrust, and treason wait on him.

Richard III

   . . . girdling one another
Within their innocent alabaster arms:
Their lips were four red roses on a stalk,
Which in their summer beauty kiss'd each other.

Richard II

The language I have learn'd these forty years,
My native English, now I must forego:
And now my tongue's use is to me no more
Than an unstringed viol or a harp;
Or like a cunning instrument cas'd up,
Or, being open, put into his hands
That knows no touch to tune the harmony.

Banish'd this frail sepulchre of our flesh . . .

More are men's ends mark'd than their lives before:
The setting sun, and music at the close . . .

This royal throne of kings, this sceptr'd isle,
This earth of majesty, this seat of Mars,
This other Eden, demi-paradise;
This fortress built by Nature for herself
Against infection and the hand of war;
This happy breed of men, this little world,
This precious stone set in the silver sea,
Which serves it in the office of a wall,
Or as a moat defensive to a house,
Against the envy of less happier lands;

This blessed plot, this earth, this realm, this England . . .
This land of such dear souls, this dear dear land . . .

Our lands, our lives and all are Bolingbroke's,
And nothing can we call our own but death,
And that small model of the barren earth
Which serves as paste and cover to our bones.
For God's sake, let us sit upon the ground
And tell sad stories of the death of kings:
How some have been depos'd; some slain in war;
Some haunted by the ghosts they have depos'd;
Some poison'd by their wives; some sleeping kill'd;
All murder'd: for within the hollow crown
That rounds the mortal temples of a king
Keeps Death his court, and there the antic sits,
Scoffing his state and grinning at his pomp,
Allowing him a breath, a little scene,
To monarchize, be fear'd, and kill with looks,
Infusing him with self and vain conceit,
As if this flesh which walls about our life
Were brass impregnable; and humour'd thus
Comes at the last and with a little pin
Bores through his castle wall, and farewell king!
Cover your heads, and mock not flesh and blood
With solemn reverence, throw away respect,
Tradition, form, and ceremonious duty,
For you have but mistook me all this while:
I live with bread like you, feel want,
Taste grief, need friends: subjected thus,
How can you say to me, I am a king?

I'll give my jewels for a set of beads,
My gorgeous palace for a hermitage,
My gay apparel for an almsman's gown,
My figur'd goblets for a dish of wood,
My sceptre for a palmer's walking-staff,
My subjects for a pair of carved saints,
And my large kingdom for a little grave,
A little little grave, an obscure grave;
Or I'll be buried in the king's highway,
Some way of common trade, where subjects' feet
May hourly trample on their sovereign's head.

'Tis very true, my grief lies all within;
And these external manners of laments
Are merely shadows to the unseen grief,
That swells with silence in the tortur'd soul.

Think I am dead, and that even here thou takest,
As from my death-bed, thy last living leave.
In winter's tedious nights sit by the fire
With good old folks, and let them tell thee tales
Of woeful ages long ago betid;
And ere thou bid good-night, to quit their griefs,
Tell thou the lamentable tale of me,
And send the hearers weeping to their beds.

            . . .but whate'er I be,
Nor I nor any man that but man is
With nothing shall be pleased, till he be eased
With being nothing.

King John

There was not such a gracious creature born . . .
Grief fills the room up of my absent child,
Lies in his bed, walks up and down with me,
Puts on his pretty looks, repeats his words,
Remembers me of all his gracious parts,
Stuffs out his vacant garments with his form.

I am amazed, methinks, and lose my way
Among the thorns and dangers of this world.

This England never did, nor never shall,
Lie at the proud foot of a conqueror,
But when it first did help to wound itself.
Now these her princes are come home again,
Come the three corners of the world in arms,
And we shall shock them. Nought shall make us rue,
If England to itself do rest but true.

Henry IV, Part I

    . . . not an eye
But is a-weary of thy common sight,
Save mine, which hath desired to see thee more;
Which now doth that I would not have it do,
Make blind itself with foolish tenderness.

Henry IV, Part II

    O sleep, O gentle sleep,
Nature's soft nurse, how have I frighted thee,
That thou no more wilt weigh my eyelids down,
And steep my senses in forgetfulness? . . .
Wilt thou upon the high and giddy mast
Seal up the ship-boy's eyes, and rock his brains
In cradle of the rude imperious surge,
And in the visitation of the winds,
Who take the ruffian billows by the top,
Curling their monstrous heads, and hanging them
With deafening clamour in the slippery clouds,
That, with the hurly, death itself awakes?
Canst thou, O partial sleep, give they repose
To the wet sea-boy in an hour so rude,
And in the calmest and most stillest night,
With all appliances and means to boot,
Deny it to a king? Then, happy low, lie down!
Uneasy lies the head that wears a crown.

O God! that one might read the book of fate,
And see the revolution of the times
Make mountains level, and the continent,
Weary of solid firmness, melt itself
Into the sea! and, other times, to see
The beachy girdle of the ocean
Too wide for Neptune's hips; how chances mock,
And changes fill the cup of alteration
With divers liquors! O, if this were seen,
The happiest youth, viewing his progress through,
What perils past, what crosses to ensue,
Would shut the book, and sit him down and die.

O Westmoreland, thou art a summer bird,
Which ever in the haunch of winter sings
The lifting up of day.

Let there be no noise made, my gentle friends;
Unless some dull and favourable hand
Will whisper music to my weary spirit.

I stay too long by thee, I weary thee.

Only compound me with forgotten dust ...

Henry V

The singing masons building roofs of gold ...

We would not die in that man's company
That fears his fellowship to die with us.
This day is called the feast of Crispian:
He that outlives this day, and comes safe home,
Will stand a tip-toe when this day is nam'd,
And rouse him at the name of Crispian.
He that shall live this day, and see old age,
Will yearly on the vigil feast his neighbours,
And say, 'To-morrow is Saint Crispian':
Then will he strip his sleeve and show his scars,
And say 'These wounds I had on Crispin's day.'
Old men forget; yet all shall be forgot;
But he'll remember with advantages
What feats he did that day ...
This story shall the good man teach his son;
And Crispin Crispian shall ne'er go by,
From this day to the ending of the world,
But we in it shall be remembered;
We few, we happy few, we band of brothers ...
And gentlemen in England now a-bed
Shall think themselves accurs'd they were not here,
And hold their manhoods cheap whiles any speaks
That fought with us upon Saint Crispin's day.

Henry VIII

Orpheus with his lute made trees,
And the mountain tops that freeze,
  Bow themselves when he did sing;
To his music plants and flowers
Ever sprung, as sun and showers
  There had made a lasting spring.

Every thing that heard him play,
Even the billows of the sea,
  Hung their heads, and then lay by.
In sweet music is such art,
Killing care, and grief of heart,
  Fall asleep, or hearing die.

COMEDIES

The Taming of the Shrew

Come, madam wife, sit by my side,
And let the world slip: we shall ne'er be younger.

The Two Gentlemen of Verona

O, how this spring of love resembleth
The uncertain glory of an April day,
Which now shows all the beauty of the sun,
And by and by a cloud takes all away!

Didst thou but know the inly touch of love . . .

The current that with gentle murmur glides,
Thou know'st, being stopped, impatiently doth rage;
But when his fair course is not hindered,
He makes sweet music with the enamell'd stones,
Giving a gentle kiss to every sedge
He overtaketh in his pilgrimage;
And so by many winding nooks he strays,
With willing sport, to the wild ocean.
Then let me go, and hinder not my course:
I'll be as patient as a gentle stream,
And make a pastime of each weary step,
Till the last step have brought me to my love;
And there I'll rest, as after much turmoil
A blessed soul doth in Elysium.

Except I be by Silvia in the night,
There is no music in the nightingale.

O thou that dost inhabit in my breast,
Leave not the mansion so long tenantless . . .
Repair me with thy presence, Silvia.

Love's Labour's Lost

These earthly godfathers of heaven's lights,
That give a name to every fixed star,
Have no more profit of their shining nights
Than those that walk and wot not what they are.

For valour, is not Love a Hercules,
Still climbing trees in the Hesperides?
Subtle as Sphinx; as sweet and musical
As bright Apollo's lute, strung with his hair;
And when Love speaks, the voice of all the gods
Makes heaven drowsy with the harmony.

When icicles hang by the wall,
    And Dick the shepherd blows his nail,
And Tom bears logs into the hall,
    And milk comes frozen home in pail,
When blood is nipp'd and ways be foul,
Then nightly sings the staring owl,
            Tu-whit;
Tu-who, a merry note,
While greasy Joan doth keel the pot.

When all aloud the wind doth blow,
    And coughing drowns the parson's saw,
And birds sit brooding in the snow,
    And Marian's nose looks red and raw,
When roasted crabs hiss in the bowl,
Then nightly sings the staring owl,
            Tu-whit;
Tu-who, a merry note,
While greasy Joan doth keel the pot.

A Midsummer Night's Dream

For aye to be in shady cloister mew'd,
To live a barren sister all your life,
Chanting faint hymns to the cold fruitless moon.
Thrice blessed they that master so their blood,
To undergo such maiden pilgrimage;

But earthlier happy is the rose distill'd,
Than that which, withering on the virgin thorn,
Grows, lives, and dies in single blessedness.

Your eyes are lode-stars; and your tongue's sweet air
More tunable than lark to shepherd's ear,
When wheat is green, when hawthorn buds appear.

And in the wood, where often you and I
Upon faint primrose-beds were wont to lie . . .

And on old Hiems' thin and icy crown
An odorous chaplet of sweet summer buds ' . .

> You spotted snakes with double tongue,
>   Thorny hedgehogs, be not seen;
> Newts and blind-worms, do no wrong,
>   Come not near our fairy queen.

> Weaving spiders, come not here;
>   Hence, you long-legg'd spinners, hence!
> Beetles black, approach not near;
>   Worm nor snail, do no offence.

So doth the woodbine the sweet honeysuckle
Gently entwist; the female ivy so
Enrings the barky fingers of the elm

            A cry more tunable
Was never holla'd to, nor cheer'd with horn,
In Crete, in Sparta, nor in Thessaly.

The Merchant of Venice

Your mind is tossing on the ocean;
There, where your argosies with portly sail,
Like signiors and rich burghers on the flood,
Or, as it were, the pageants of the sea,
Do overpeer the petty traffickers,
That curtsy to them, do them reverence,
As they fly by them with their woven wings.

A day in April never came so sweet,
To show how costly summer was at hand.

How all the other passions fleet to air . . .
O love, be moderate; allay thy ecstasy;
In measure rain thy joy; scant this excess!
I feel too much thy blessing: make it less . . .

The moon shines bright: in such a night as this,
When the sweet wind did gently kiss the trees
And they did make no noise, in such a night
Troilus methinks mounted the Troyan walls,
And sigh'd his soul toward the Grecian tents,
Where Cressid lay that night . . .
                    In such a night
Stood Dido with a willow in her hand
Upon the wild sea banks, and waft her love
To come again to Carthage.

How sweet the moonlight sleeps upon this bank!
Here will we sit, and let the sounds of music
Creep in our ears: soft stillness and the night
Become the touches of sweet harmony.
Sit, Jessica. Look how the floor of heaven
Is thick inlaid with patines of bright gold:
There's not the smallest orb which thou behold'st
But in his motion like an angel sings,
Still quiring to the young-eyed cherubins;
Such harmony is in immortal souls;
But whilst this muddy vesture of decay
Doth grossly close it in, we cannot hear it.

That light we see is burning in my hall.
How far that little candle throws his beams!
So shines a good deed in a naughty world.

Much Ado About Nothing

How still the evening is,
As hush'd on purpose to grace harmony!

As You Like It

Sir, fare you well:
Hereafter, in a better world than this,
I shall desire more love and knowledge of you.

Happy is your Grace,
That can translate the stubbornness of fortune
Into so quiet and so sweet a style.

If thou remember'st not the slightest folly
That ever love did make thee run into,
Thou hast not loved:
Or if thou hast not sat as I do now,
Wearing thy hearer in thy mistress' praise,
Thou hast not loved:
Or if thou hast not broke from company
Abruptly, as my passion now makes me,
Thou hast not loved.

Under the greenwood tree
Who loves to lie with me,
And turn his merry note
Unto the sweet bird's throat,
Come hither, come hither, come hither:
Here shall he see
No enemy
But winter and rough weather.

But whate'er you are
That in this desert inaccessible,
Under the shade of melancholy boughs,
Lose and neglect the creeping hours of time;
If ever you have look'd on better days,
If ever been where bells have knoll'd to church,
If ever sat at any good man's feast,
If ever from your eyelids wip'd a tear
And know what 'tis to pity and be pitied,
Let gentleness my strong enforcement be.

Thou seest we are not all alone unhappy:
This wide and universal theatre
Presents more woeful pageants than the scene
Wherein we play in.

It was a lover and his lass,
    With a hey, and a ho, and a hey nonino,
That o'er the green corn-field did pass
    In the spring time, the only pretty ring time,
When birds do sing, hey ding a ding ding:
    Sweet lovers love the spring.

Between the acres of the rye,
    With a hey, and a ho, and a hey nonino,
These pretty country folks would lie,
    In spring time . . .

This carol they began that hour,
    With a hey, and a ho, and a hey nonino,
How that a life was but a flower
    In spring time . . .

And therefore take the present time,
    With a hey, and a ho, and a hey nonino,
For love is crowned with the prime
    In spring time . . .

Twelfth Night

If music be the food of love, play on;
Give me excess of it, that, surfeiting,
The appetite may sicken, and so die.
That strain again! it had a dying fall:
O, it came o'er my ear like the sweet sound,
That breathes upon a bank of violets,
Stealing and giving odour!

'Tis beauty truly blent, whose red and white
Nature's own sweet and cunning hand laid on.

If I did love you in my master's flame,
With such a suffering, such a deadly life,
In your denial I would find no sense;
I would not understand it.
                        Why, what would you?
Make me a willow cabin at your gate,
And call upon my soul within the house . . .

    O mistress mine, where are you roaming?
    O, stay and hear; your true love's coming,
       That can sing both high and low:
    Trip no further, pretty sweeting;
    Journeys end in lovers meeting
       Every wise man's son doth know.

    What is love? 'tis not hereafter;
    Present mirth hath present laughter;
       What's to come is still unsure:
    In delay there lies no plenty,
    Then come kiss me, sweet and twenty,
       Youth's a stuff will not endure.

Now, good Cesario, but that piece of song,
That old and antique song we heard last night:
Methought it did relieve my passion much . . .
Come hither, boy: if ever thou shalt love,
In the sweet pangs of it remember me;
For such as I am all true lovers are,
Unstaid and skittish in all motions else,
Save in the constant image of the creature
That is belov'd. How dost thou like this tune?
It gives a very echo to the seat
Where love is thron'd.

O, fellow, come, the song we had last night.
Mark it, Cesario, it is old and plain;
The spinsters and the knitters in the sun
And the free maids that weave their thread with bones
Do use to chant it: it is silly sooth,
And dallies with the innocence of love,
Like the old age.

Come away, come away, death,
   And in sad cypress let me be laid;
Fly away, fly away, breath;
   I am slain by a fair cruel maid.
My shroud of white, stuck all with yew,
     O, prepare it!
My part of death, no one so true
     Did share it.

Not a flower, not a flower sweet,
   On my black coffin let there be strown;
Not a friend, not a friend greet
   My poor corpse, where my bones shall be thrown:
A thousand thousand sighs to save,
     Lay me, O, where
Sad true lover never find my grave
     To weep there!

When that I was and a tiny little boy,
   With hey, ho, the wind and the rain,
A foolish thing was but a toy,
   For the rain it raineth every day . . .

A great while ago the world begun,
   With hey, ho, the wind and the rain,
But that's all one, our play is done,
   And we'll strive to please you every day.

Measure for Measure

Ay, but to die, and go we know not where;
To lie in cold obstruction and to rot;
This sensible warm motion to become
A kneaded clod; and the delighted spirit
To bathe in fiery floods, or to reside
In thrilling region of thick-ribbed ice;
To be imprison'd in the viewless winds,
And blown with restless violence round about
The pendent world; or to be worse than worst
Of those that lawless and incertain thought
Imagine howling:—'tis too horrible!

The weariest and most loathed worldly life
That age, ache, penury, and imprisonment
Can lay on nature is a paradise
To what we fear of death.

Take, O, take those lips away,
  That so sweetly were forsworn,
And those eyes; the break of day
  Lights that do mislead the morn:
But my kisses bring again, bring again;
Seals of love, but seal'd in vain, seal'd in vain.

Cymbeline

         What should we speak of
When we are old as you? when we shall hear
The rain and wind beat dark December, how
In this our pinching cave shall we discourse
The freezing hours away?

         With fairest flowers,
Whilst summer lasts, and I live here, Fidele,
I'll sweeten thy sad grave.

Fear no more the heat o' the sun,
  Nor the furious winter's rages;
Thou thy worldly task hast done,
  Home art gone and ta'en thy wages:
Golden lads and girls all must,
As chimney-sweepers, come to dust.

Fear no more the frown o' the great;
  Thou art past the tyrant's stroke;
Care no more to clothe and eat;
  To thee the reed is as the oak:
The sceptre, learning, physic, must
All follow this and come to dust.

Fear no more the lightning-flash,
  Nor the all-dreaded thunder-stone;
Fear not slander, censure rash;
  Thou hast finish'd joy and moan:
All lovers young, all lovers must
Consign to thee and come to dust.

The Winter's Tale

We were, fair queen,
Two lads that thought there was no more behind,
But such a day to-morrow as to-day,
And to be boy eternal.

. . .daffodils,
That come before the swallow dares, and take
The winds of March with beauty; violets dim,
But sweeter than the lids of Juno's eyes
Or Cytherea's breath; pale primroses,
That die unmarried, ere they can behold
Bright Phoebus in his strength . . .

Stars, stars,
And all eyes else dead coals!

I, an old turtle,
Will wing me to some wither'd bough and there
My mate, that's never to be found again,
Lament till I am lost.

The Tempest

In the dark backward and abysm of time.

Full fathom five thy father lies;
    Of his bones are coral made;
Those are pearls that were his eyes:
    Nothing of him that doth fade,
But doth suffer a sea-change
Into something rich and strange.

Be not afeard; the isle is full of noises,
Sounds and sweet airs, that give delight, and hurt not.
Sometimes a thousand twangling instruments
Will hum about mine ears; and sometime voices,
That, if I then had wak'd after long sleep,
Will make me sleep again; and then, in dreaming,
The clouds methought would open, and show riches
Ready to drop upon me, that, when I wak'd,
I cried to dream again.

The cloud-capp'd towers, the gorgeous palaces,
The solemn temples, the great globe itself,
Yea, all which it inherit, shall dissolve,
And, like this insubstantial pageant faded,
Leave not a rack behind. We are such stuff
As dreams are made on; and our little life
Is rounded with a sleep.

Let us not burthen our remembrances with
A heaviness that's gone.

Now I want
Spirits to enforce, art to enchant;
And my ending is despair,
Unless I be relieved by prayer,
Which pierces so, that it assaults
Mercy itself, and frees all faults.

TRAGEDIES

Titus Andronicus

The eagle suffers little birds to sing,
And is not careful what they mean thereby,
Knowing that with the shadow of his wing
He can at pleasure stint their melody.

Romeo and Juliet

Madam, an hour before the worshipp'd sun
Peer'd forth the golden window of the east,
A troubled mind drave me to walk abroad;
Where, underneath the grove of sycamore
That westward rooteth from the city's side,
So early walking did I see your son.

Lady, by yonder blessed moon I swear,
That tips with silver all these fruit tree tops—

This bud of love, by summer's ripening breath,
May prove a beauteous flower when next we meet.

How silver-sweet sound lovers' tongues by night,
Like softest music to attending ears!

　　　　　. . . but come what sorrow can,
It cannot countervail the exchange of joy
That one short minute gives me in her sight.

Here comes the lady. O, so light a foot
Will ne'er wear out the everlasting flint.

For thou wilt lie upon the wings of night
Whiter than new snow on a raven's back.

　　　　　. . . look, love, what envious streaks
Do lace the severing clouds in yonder east:
Night's candles are burnt out, and jocund day
Stands tiptoe on the misty mountain tops.

O God! I have an ill-divining soul:

Death lies on her like an untimely frost
Upon the sweetest flower of all the field.

My bosom's lord sits lightly in his throne . . .

O my love! my wife!
Death, that hath suck'd the honey of thy breath,
Hath had no power yet upon thy beauty:
Thou art not conquer'd; beauty's ensign yet
Is crimson in thy lips and in thy cheeks,
And death's pale flag is not advanced there.

I still will stay with thee,
And never from this palace of dim night
Depart again: here, here will I remain
With worms that are thy chamber-maids; O, here
Will I set up my everlasting rest,
And shake the yoke of inauspicious stars
From this world-wearied flesh.

Julius Cæsar.

Enjoy the honey-heavy dew of slumber.

O mighty Cæsar! does thou lie so low?
Are all thy conquests, glories, triumphs, spoils,
Shrunk to this little measure? Fare thee well . . .

Live a thousand years,
I shall not find myself so apt to die:
No place will please me so, no mean of death,
As here by Cæsar, and by you cut off,
The choice and master spirits of this age.

O, pardon me, thou bleeding piece of earth,
That I am meek and gentle with these butchers!
Thou art the ruins of the noblest man
That ever lived in the tide of times.

But yesterday the word of Cæsar might
Have stood against the world: now lies he there,
And none so poor to do him reverence.

You all do know this mantle: I remember
The first time ever Cæsar put it on;
'Twas on a summer's evening, in his tent,
That day he overcame the Nervii.

The deep of night is crept upon our talk,
And nature must obey necessity.

> But this same day
Must end that work the ides of March begun;
And whether we shall meet again I know not.
Therefore our everlasting farewell take.
For ever, and for ever, farewell, Cassius!
If we do meet again, why, we shall smile;
If not, why then this parting was well made.

> O, that a man might know
The end of this day's business ere it come!
But it sufficeth that the day will end,
And then the end is known.

Night hangs upon mine eyes; my bones would rest,
That have but labour'd to attain this hour.

Troilus and Cressida

I am giddy; expectation whirls me round.
The imaginary relish is so sweet
That it enchants my sense: what will it be
When that the watery palates taste indeed
Love's thrice repured nectar? death, I fear me,
Swounding destruction, or some joy too fine,
Too subtle-potent, tun'd too sharp in sweetness
For the capacity of my ruder powers:
I fear it much, and I do fear besides
That I shall lose distinction in my joys,
As doth a battle, when they charge on heaps
The enemy flying.

O Cressida, how often have I wished me thus!

O that I thought it could be in a woman—
As, if it can, I will presume in you—
To feed for aye her lamp and flames of love;
To keep her constancy in plight and youth,
Outliving beauty's outward, with a mind
That doth renew swifter than blood decays!
Or that persuasion could but thus convince me,
That my integrity and truth to you
Might be affronted with the match and weight
Of such a winnow'd purity in love;
How were I then uplifted! but, alas!
I am as true as truth's simplicity,
And simpler than the infancy of truth.

When time is old and hath forgot itself,
When waterdrops have worn the stones of Troy,
And blind oblivion swallow'd cities up . . .

Time hath, my lord, a wallet at his back
Wherein he puts alms for oblivion . . .

Hamlet

But look, the morn in russet mantle clad
Walks o'er the dew of yon high eastward hill.

How weary, stale, flat and unprofitable
Seem to me all the uses of this world!

The glow-worm shows the matin to be near,
And 'gins to pale his uneffectual fire.

　　　　　To die: to sleep,
No more; and by a sleep to say we end
The heart-ache, and the thousand natural shocks
That flesh is heir to; 'tis a consummation
Devoutly to be wish'd. To die, to sleep;
To sleep; perchance to dream; ay, there's the rub;
For in that sleep of death what dreams may come,
When we have shuffled off this mortal coil,
Must give us pause: there's the respect
That makes calamity of so long life:
For who would bear the whips and scorns of time,

The oppressor's wrong, the proud man's contumely,
The pangs of despis'd love, the law's delay,
The insolence of office, and the spurns
That patient merit of the unworthy takes,
When he himself might his quietus make
With a bare bodkin? who would fardels bear,
To grunt and sweat under a weary life,
But that the dread of something after death,
The undiscover'd country, from whose bourn
No traveller returns, puzzles the will,
And makes us rather bear those ills we have
Than fly to others that we know not of? . . .

O wretched state! O bosom black as death!
O limed soul, that struggling to be free
Art more engag'd!

A station like the herald Mercury
New-lighted on a heaven-kissing hill . . .

Thought and affliction, passion, hell itself,
She turns to favour and to prettiness.

There is a willow grows aslant a brook,
That shows his hoar leaves in the glassy stream . . .

      Lay her i' the earth:
And from her fair and unpolluted flesh
May violets spring!

But thou wouldst not think how ill all's here about my heart:
but it is no matter.

If thou didst ever hold me in thy heart,
Absent thee from felicity a while,
And in this harsh world draw thy breath in pain,
To tell my story.

Othello

It gives me wonder great as my content
To see you here before me. O my soul's joy!
     . . . If it were now to die,
'Twere now to be most happy; for I fear
My soul hath her content so absolute
That not another comfort like to this
Succeeds in unknown fate . . .
I cannot speak enough of this content;
It stops me here; it is too much of joy . . .

       O, now for ever
Farewell the tranquil mind! farewell content!
Farewell the plumed troop, and the big wars
That make ambition virtue! O, farewell,
Farewell the neighing steed and the shrill trump,
The spirit-stirring drum, the ear-piercing fife,
The royal banner, and all quality,
Pride, pomp, and circumstance of glorious war!

But there, where I have garner'd up my heart,
Where either I must live or bear no life,
The fountain from the which my current runs,
Or else dries up; to be discarded thence! . . .

       O thou weed,
Who art so lovely fair and smell'st so sweet
That the sense aches at thee: would thou hadst ne'er been born!

       Unkindness may do much;
And his unkindness may defeat my life,
But never taint my love.

       Yet I'll not shed her blood,
Nor scar that whiter skin of hers than snow,
And smooth as monumental alabaster . . .
Put out the light, and then put out the light:
If I quench thee, thou flaming minister,

I can again thy former light restore,
Should I repent me: but once put out thy light,
Thou cunning pattern of excelling nature,
I know not where is that Promethean heat
That can thy light relume. When I have pluck'd the rose,
I cannot give it vital growth again;
It must needs wither: I'll smell it on the tree . . .

        Nay, had she been true,
If heaven would make me such another world
Of one entire and perfect chrysolite,
I'ld not have sold her for it.

Here is my journey's end, here is my butt
And very sea-mark of my utmost sail.

        . . . then must you speak
Of one that lov'd not wisely, but too well;
Of one not easily jealous, but, being wrought,
Perplex'd in the extreme; of one whose hand,
Like the base Indian, threw a pearl away
Richer than all his tribe . . .

Macbeth

Methought I heard a voice cry 'Sleep no more!
Macbeth does murder sleep'—the innocent sleep;
Sleep that knits up the ravell'd sleave of care,
The death of each day's life, sore labour's bath,
Balm of hurt minds . . .

How is't with me, when every noise appals me?
What hands are here? ha! they pluck out mine eyes!
Will all great Neptune's ocean wash this blood
Clean from my hand? No; this my hand will rather
The multitudinous seas incarnadine,
Making the green one red.

Had I but died an hour before this chance,
I had lived a blessed time; for from this instant
There's nothing serious in mortality:
All is but toys: renown and grace is dead;
The wine of life is drawn, and the mere lees
Is left this vault to brag of.

              Fears and scruples shake us:
In the great hand of God I stand . . .

Upon my head they plac'd a fruitless crown,
And put a barren sceptre in my gripe . . .

But let the frame of things disjoint, both the worlds suffer,
Ere we will eat our meal in fear, and sleep
In the affliction of those terrible dreams
That shake us nightly: better be with the dead,
Whom we, to gain our peace, have sent to peace,
Than on the torture of the mind to lie
In restless ecstasy. Duncan is in his grave;
After life's fitful fever he sleeps well;
Treason has done his worst: nor steel, nor poison,
Malice domestic, foreign levy, nothing,
Can touch him further.

              Light thickens, and the crow
Makes wing to the rooky wood:
Good things of day begin to droop and drowse,
Whiles night's black agents to their preys do rouse.

The west yet glimmers with some streaks of day:
Now spurs the lated traveller apace
To gain the timely inn . . .

Then comes my fit again: I had else been perfect,
Whole as the marble, founded as the rock,
As broad and general as the casing air. . .

              Can such things be,
And overcome us like a summer's cloud,
Without our special wonder?

Poor bird! thou'ldst never fear the net nor lime,
The pitfall nor the gin.

Dispute it like a man.
                I shall do so;
But I must also feel it as a man:
I cannot but remember such things were,
That were most precious to me.

I have lived long enough: my way of life
Is fall'n into the sear, the yellow leaf,
And that which should accompany old age,
As honour, love, obedience, troops of friends,
I must not look to have; but, in their stead,
Curses, not loud but deep, mouth-honour, breath
Which the poor heart would fain deny, and dare not.

Canst thou not minister to a mind diseas'd,
Pluck from the memory a rooted sorrow,
Raze out the written troubles of the brain,
And with some sweet oblivious antidote
Cleanse the stuff'd bosom of that perilous stuff
Which weighs upon the heart?

She should have died hereafter;
There would have been a time for such a word.
To-morrow, and to-morrow, and to-morrow,
Creeps in this petty pace from day to day,
To the last syllable of recorded time;
And all our yesterdays have lighted fools
The way to dusty death. Out, out, brief candle!
Life's but a walking shadow, a poor player
That struts and frets his hour upon the stage,
And then is heard no more. It is a tale
Told by an idiot, full of sound and fury,
Signifying nothing.

King Lear

That sir which serves and seeks for gain,
    And follows but for form,
Will pack when it begins to rain,
    And leave thee in the storm.
But I will tarry; the fool will stay . . .

I prithee, daughter, do not make me mad:
I will not trouble thee, my child; farewell:
We'll no more meet, no more see one another . . .

You see me here, you gods, a poor old man,
As full of grief as age; wretched in both:
If it be you that stirs these daughters' hearts
Against their father, fool me not so much
To bear it tamely; touch me with noble anger,
And let not woman's weapons, water-drops,
Stain my man's cheeks! No, you unnatural hags,
I will have such revenges on you both
That all the world shall—I will do such things—
What they are, yet I know not, but they shall be
The terrors of the earth. You think I'll weep;
No, I'll not weep:
I have full cause of weeping; but this heart
Shall break into a hundred thousand flaws,
Or ere I'll weep. O fool, I shall go mad!

No, I will weep no more. In such a night
To shut me out! Pour on; I will endure.
In such a night as this! O Regan, Goneril!
Your kind old father, whose frank heart gave you all—
O, that way madness lies; let me shun that;
No more of that.

Poor naked wretches, wheresoe'er you are,
That bide the pelting of this pitiless storm,
How shall your houseless heads and unfed sides,
Your loop'd and window'd raggedness, defend you
From seasons such as these? O, I have ta'en
Too little care of this! Take physic, pomp;
Expose thyself to feel what wretches feel,
That thou mayst shake the superflux to them
And show the heavens more just.

                    . . . henceforth I'll bear
Affliction till it do cry out itself
'Enough, enough,' and die.

O ruin'd piece of nature! This great world
Shall so wear out to nought.

Were all the letters suns, I could not see.

Thou must be patient; we came crying hither:
Thou know'st, the first time that we smell the air,
We wawl and cry . . .
When we are born, we cry that we are come
To this great stage of fools . . .

Thou art a soul in bliss; but I am bound
Upon a wheel of fire, that mine own tears
Do scald like molten lead.

    O, look upon me, sir,
And hold your hands in benediction o'er me.
No, sir, you must not kneel.
    Pray, do not mock me:
I am a very foolish fond old man,
Fourscore and upward, not an hour more or less;
And, to deal plainly,
I fear I am not in my perfect mind.

No further, sir; a man may rot even here.
What, in ill thoughts again? Men must endure
Their going hence, even as their coming hither:
Ripeness is all: come on.
    And that's true too.

Shall we not see these daughters and these sisters?
No, no, no, no! Come, let's away to prison:
We two alone will sing like birds i' the cage:
When thou dost ask me blessing, I'll kneel down
And ask of thee forgiveness: so we'll live,
And pray, and sing, and tell old tales, and laugh
At gilded butterflies, and hear poor rogues
Talk of court news; and we'll talk with them too,
Who loses and who wins, who's in, who's out,
And take upon 's the mystery of things,
As if we were God's spies: and we'll wear out,
In a wall'd prison, packs and sects of great ones
That ebb and flow by the moon.

The wheel is come full circle: I am here.

    O, our lives' sweetness:
That we the pain of death would hourly die
Rather than die at once!

Is this the promis'd end?
Or image of that horror?
                Fall and cease.
This feather stirs; she lives. If it be so,
It is a chance which does redeem all sorrows
That ever I have felt . . .
A plague upon you, murderers, traitors all!
I might have saved her; now she's gone for ever!
Cordelia, Cordelia! stay a little. Ha!
What is't thou sayst? Her voice was ever soft,
Gentle and low, an excellent thing in woman.
I killed the slave that was a-hanging thee.

Vex not his ghost: O, let him pass! he hates him
That would upon the rack of this tough world
Stretch him out longer.

I have a journey, sir, shortly to go:
My master calls me, I must not say no.

Timon of Athens

Men shut their doors against a setting sun.

Timon will to the woods, where he shall find
The unkindest beast more kinder than mankind.

How came the noble Timon to this change?
As the moon does, by wanting light to give:
But then renew I could not, like the moon:
There were no suns to borrow of.

            . . . my long sickness
Of health and living now begins to mend,
And nothing brings me all things . . .

Timon hath made his everlasting mansion
Upon the beached verge of the salt flood . . .

            . . . yet rich conceit
Taught thee to make vast Neptune weep for aye
On thy low grave, on faults forgiven . . .

Pericles

Why should this change of thoughts,
The sad companion, dull-eyed melancholy,
Be my so us'd a guest as not an hour
In the day's glorious walk, or peaceful night,
The tomb where grief should sleep, can breed me quiet?

Antony and Cleopatra

Let Rome in Tiber melt, and the wide arch
Of the rang'd empire fall! Here is my space;
Kingdoms are clay: our dungy earth alike
Feeds beast as man; the nobleness of life
Is to do thus; when such a mutual pair
And such a twain can do't . . .

Eternity was in our lips and eyes . . .

I saw her once
Hop forty paces through the public street;
And having lost her breath, she spoke, and panted
That she did make defect perfection,
And, breathless, power breathe forth . . .
Age cannot wither her, nor custom stale
Her infinite variety . . .

That time—O times!—
I laugh'd him out of patience, and that night
I laugh'd him into patience; and next morn,
Ere the ninth hour, I drunk him to his bed:
Then put my tires and mantles on him, whilst
I wore his sword Philippan.

Be you not troubled with the time, which drives
O'er your content these strong necessities;
But let determin'd things to destiny
Hold unbewail'd their way.

I am so lated in the world that I
Have lost my way forever.

Lord of lords!
O infinite virtue, com'st thou smiling from
The world's great snare uncaught?

O sovereign mistress of true melancholy,
The poisonous damp of night disponge upon me,
That life, a very rebel to my will,
May hang no longer on me: throw my heart
Against the flint and hardness of my fault . . .
And finish all foul thoughts. O Antony,
Nobler than my revolt is infamous,
Forgive me in thine own particular,
But let the world rank me in register
A master-leaver and a fugitive.

O sun, thy uprise shall I see no more . . .

Unarm, Eros; the long day's task is done,
And we must sleep.

I will o'ertake thee, Cleopatra, and
Weep for my pardon. So it must be, for now
All length is torture . . .

I am dying, Egypt, dying; only
I here importune death awhile, until
Of many thousand kisses the poor last
I lay upon thy lips.

My lord!
O' wither'd is the garland of the war . . .
And there is nothing left remarkable
Beneath the visiting moon.

. . . is it sin
To rush into the secret house of death . . . ?

A rarer spirit never
Did steer humanity: but you, gods, will give us
Some faults to make us men.

. . . it is great
To do that thing that ends all other deeds;
Which shackles accidents and bolts up change;
Which sleeps, and never palates more the dung,
The beggar's nurse and Cæsar's.

My resolution's plac'd, and I have nothing
Of woman in me: now from head to foot
I am marble-constant; now the fleeting moon
No planet is of mine.

Give me my robe, put on my crown; I have
Immortal longings in me . . .
                        Husband, I come:
Now to that name my courage prove my title!
I am fire and air; my other elements
I give to baser life . . .

Now boast thee, death, in thy possession lies
A lass unparallel'd.

            . . . she looks like sleep,
As she would catch another Antony
In her strong toil of grace.

INDEX

Accession Tilt, 1612, 182

Addenbroke, John, 163

Ainley, Henry, 11

Alexander, Sir George, 12

All's Well That Ends Well, 113, 160

Anne, Queen of England (Anne of Denmark), 138, 162

Antony and Cleopatra, 101, 147, 153-4, 160, 162, 168, 181, 192, 230-2

Arden, Edward, 24

—— Mary, *see* Shakespeare, Mary

Armada, Spanish, 25, 34, 70

Armin, Robert, 85, 119

As You Like It, 84-6, 88, 119, 120, 168, 211

Asher, Rev. Felix, 16

Astrophel and Stella, 34

Aubrey, John, 139

Bacon, Sir Francis, 105, 118, 183

Bancroft, Archbishop of Canterbury, 118

Bardolfe, George, 27-8

Barnard, Lady, *see* Hall, Elizabeth

—— Sir John, Bart., 191

Barnfield, Richard, 35

Barrie, Sir James, 88

Barrymore, John, 11

Bax, Clifford, (*Frontispiece*)

Beaumont, Francis, 148

Bedford Theatre, 12

Bellott, Stephen, 120-1, 181-2

Benson, Sir Frank R., 9, 11, 12

Berkeley, Baron, 33, 36

Betterton, Thomas, 139

Bible, The, 10, 20-1

Biron, Marshal, 50

'Black-eyed Mistress', 38-9, 53, 63, 66

Blackfriars Theatre, 105-6, 162-6, 170-1, 180, 184, 188

Blount, Sir Christopher, 103

Boccaccio, Giovanni, 113, 168

Bodleian Library, 21

Boswell, James, 120

Brandes, Georg, 155

Brend, Sir Thomas, 80

Brissot, Jean, 100

British Drama, 189

British Empire Shakespeare Society, The, 12

Burbage, Cuthbert, 79, 80, 102, 162

—— James, 30, 79, 162

—— Richard, 30, 39, 57, 79, 80, 102, 119, 125, 130, 162, 182, 190

Burghley, Lord, 93

Burke, Edmund, 164

Bushell, Edward, 103

Butler, Samuel, 139

Cade, Jack, 41-2

Caesar, Julius, 21, 85, 97-9

Capone, Al, 46

Carr, Robert, 146, 169

Castile, Constable of, 127

Catesby, Robert, 131-2

Catholic League, 50

Cecil, Sir Robert, *see* Salisbury, Lord

Certaine Sonnets, 35

Chambers, E. K., 18

Chapel Royal Choristers Company, 105, 107

HAMISH HAMILTON PAPERBACKS

'Among the most collectable of paperback imprints . . .'
Christopher Hudson, *The Standard*

All books in the Hamish Hamilton Paperback Series are available at
your local bookshop or can be ordered by post. A full list of titles and an
order form can be found at the end of this book.

LORD RANDOLPH CHURCHILL

Robert Rhodes James

Lord Randolph Churchill was at once a dazzling and pathetic figure whose mercurial character greatly enlivened the political scene of the 1880s, yet brought about his own downfall. In this outstanding biography Robert Rhodes James brings to life not only the man but also the colourful politics of the period.

'It is a splendid work and will, I am sure, meet with lasting success.' Sir Winston Churchill

'The book is very good indeed in giving the picture of the man. Lord Randolph Churchill returns to life with all his charm, wit, and irresponsibility.' A. J. P. Taylor, *Observer*

BISMARCK
THE MAN AND THE STATESMAN

A. J. P. Taylor

In this outstanding biography, A. J. P. Taylor discusses not only Bismarck's political ideas and achievements but also his strange complicated character. It is a fascinating essay on the psychology as well as the political understanding of a man who remains to this day a subject of controversy.

'Rich, learned, profound and yet highly readable . . . Mr Taylor has written many good books. This is the best.' Hugh Trevor-Roper, *Sunday Times*

TWO FLAMBOYANT FATHERS

Nicolette Devas

'A marvellous account of growing up in the artistic Bohemia of the 1920s with friends and mentors including the still-roaring Augustus John and the young Dylan Thomas, who was to marry her sister Caitlin. Candid, touching and engrossing: one of the finest autobiographies of our time.' Philip Oakes

THE SECRET ORCHARD OF ROGER ACKERLEY

Diana Petre

A letter opened on his death revealed that Roger Ackerley had had a mistress for many years and that she had borne him three daughters. Diana Petre's memoir describes her father's 'secret orchard', the secretive and isolated world in which she grew up, and attempts to solve the mysteries that surrounded her beautiful and fascinating mother, Muriel Perry.

'Mrs Petre has unfolded her story with skill and candour, and entirely without self-pity. In short, this is a very exceptional and indeed moving book.' John Morris, *Sunday Times*

HUGH WALPOLE

Rupert Hart-Davis

'Rupert Hart-Davis's book is a remarkable feat of understanding and restraint. . . . He shows us the man himself, and the spectacle is delightful.' Edwin Muir

'Fully to appreciate how remarkable an achievement is Mr Hart-Davis's biography of Hugh Walpole, it is necessary to read the book. No summarised comment can convey the complexity of the task accomplished or the narrative skill, restraint and self-effacement with which it has been carried through.' Michael Sadleir

'The most entertaining book about a writer of our time.' Terence de Vere White, *Irish Times*

THE LIFE OF ARTHUR RANSOME

Hugh Brogan

For a man who longed for a quiet existence, Arthur Ransome had an extraordinarily adventurous life comprising two stormy marriages, a melodramatic libel suit, and a ringside view of the Russian Revolution. In this absorbing book, Hugh Brogan writes with sympathy and affection of the author of some of the best loved books for children.

'The wonder is, from Mr Brogan's enthralling account, that Ransome ever got down to writing *Swallows and Amazons* at all.' A. N. Wilson, *Sunday Telegraph*

MARY BERENSON:
A Self Portrait from Her Letters and Diaries

eds. Barbara Strachey & Jayne Samuels

This superbly edited book of extracts from Mary Berenson's letters and diaries provides an absorbing picture of her extraordinarily complex relationship with Bernard Berenson, and of their life and work together in Italy.

'Mary . . . writes with a startling, unsettling, often hilarious candour which makes it hard to put the book down.' Hilary Spurling, *Observer*

A DURABLE FIRE:
The Letters of Duff and Diana Cooper, 1913–1950

ed. Artemis Cooper

For long periods before and after their marriage in 1919 Duff and Diana Cooper were apart, but they wrote to each other constantly, witty, gossipy letters that have been admirably edited by their granddaughter to form this delightful collection.

'It is rare to find a correspondence duo in which both sides are of equivalent verve and strength . . . a unique, inside account of a charmed circle whose members governed England between the wars.' Anthony Curtis, *Financial Times*

MEMOIRS OF AN AESTHETE

Harold Acton

In this outstanding memoir, deservedly regarded as a classic, Harold Acton writes a witty and vivid account of the first thirty-five years of his life from his boyhood among the international colony of dilettanti in Florence before the First World War, to his maturity when he discovered his spiritual home in Peking before the old Chinese culture was destroyed by Chairman Mao.

'He is a connoisseur of language. . . . His prose scintillates. It reminds one of Beerbohm and Waugh.' Patrick Skene Catling

'A truly magical memoir.' Linda O'Callaghan, *Sunday Telegraph*

NANCY MITFORD
A Memoir

Harold Acton

Nancy Mitford never completed an autobiography. Fortunately she was a voluminous letter writer and had a genius for friendship and laughter. In this delightful memoir, Sir Harold Acton has been able to show us, largely in her own words, almost every aspect of her personality, and her immense courage during the years of her final painful illness.

'Sir Harold Acton has memoralised a very gifted writer, and a unique personality, with affection, skill and truth.' Anthony Powell, *Daily Telegraph*

'The main lesson I derived from Sir Harold's stylish and loving evocation of Nancy Mitford's personality, is that she gave just as much pleasure to her circle of friends and relations as she gave to her readers.' Antonia Fraser, *Evening Standard*

THE SECRET ORCHARD OF ROGER ACKERLEY	Diana Petre	£4.95 ☐
ALBERT, PRINCE CONSORT	Robert Rhodes James	£4.95 ☐
LORD RANDOLPH CHURCHILL	Robert Rhodes James	£6.95 ☐
MARY BERENSON eds. Barbara Strachey and Jayne Samuels		£4.95 ☐
BISMARCK	A. J. P. Taylor	£5.95 ☐
THE YEARS WITH ROSS*	James Thurber	£4.95 ☐
THE DRAGON EMPRESS	Marina Warner	£4.95 ☐
QUEEN VICTORIA	Cecil Woodham-Smith	£5.95 ☐

All titles 198 × 126mm, and all contain 8 pages of black and white illustrations except for those marked*.

All books in the Hamish Hamilton Paperback Series are available at your local bookshop, or can be ordered direct from Media Services. Just tick the titles you want in the list above and fill in the form below.

Name_____

Address_____

_____

Write to Media Services, PO Box 151, Camberley, Surrey GU15 3BE.

Please enclose cheque or postal order made out to Media Services for the cover price plus postage:

UK: 55p for the first book, 24p for each additional book to a maximum of £1.75.

OVERSEAS: £1.05 for the first book, 35p for each additional book to a maximum of £2.80.

Hamish Hamilton Ltd reserve the right to show new retail prices on covers which may differ from those previously advertised in the text or elsewhere, and to increase postal rates in accordance with the PO.